DEAD MEN

DEAD MEN

Richard Pierce

THE OVERLOOK PRESS
NEW YORK, NY

This edition first published in hardcover in the United States in 2012 by
The Overlook Press, Peter Mayer Publishers, Inc.
141 Wooster Street
New York, NY 10012
www.overlookpress.com
For bulk and special sales, please contact sales@overlookny.com

First published in Great Britain in 2012 by Gerald Duckworth & Co.

Cataloging-in-Publication Data is available from the Library of Congress

Typeset by Ray Davies
Manufactured in the United States of America
1 3 5 7 9 10 8 6 4 2

ISBN 978-1-59020-868-7

Chapter 1

Wright spotted it first. A small rise in the featureless land-scape. His eyes ached against the relentless white. No shad-ows on a dull day. A cairn off to the right of their route. He waved the rest of the party to a stop. Eleven men in search of their missing leader and his four companions.

The snow crunched under Wright's frozen boots. As he approached it, the hummock seemed to grow. He walked around it, recognised the sharp shape of a tent under the soft outline of winter's drift snow. He stood still, uncertain now what to do. But he was sure of what he had found. He started back to the others. He would have to tell them.

Atkinson, now expedition leader, and Cherry-Garrard approached him.

'What is it?' Atkinson asked.

'It's the tent,' Wright said.

'Are you sure?'

'Yes.'

'How?'

'I just know.'

'It could be one of last year's cairns,' Cherry said. 'There must be three or four of them about here.' He looked around. 'It's directly on the old route.'

'There's a bamboo pole sticking out of the top of it,' Wright said. 'It *is* the tent.'

The three men walked across to the mound, out of the wind. They brushed the snow from the top of the silent shape. Green canvas surfaced.

'The ventilator flap. Dammit,' Atkinson grunted.

'The door should be directly below,' Cherry said.

They dug with their mittened hands until they reached the tent's outer funnel.

'Who?' Atkinson asked.

'I,' Cherry said, standing tall.

Cherry and Wright crawled into the tunnel. Unable to see, they crawled out backwards.

'It's too dark,' Cherry said.

'We're going to have to dig it out,' Atkinson said. He looked across to where the other men were waiting with their sledges and mules. 'They ought to make camp where they are. Doesn't seem right to set up any closer, if this is Captain Scott's tent.'

'Who else's?' Wright asked.

Atkinson shrugged. 'No one's.'

By now the other men had approached, almost on tiptoes. They huddled together in front of Atkinson, shovels in hand. He spoke with difficulty.

'We think this is the Owner's tent, but it's too dark inside to see anything. I'd like you ... and I know this isn't easy ... I'd like you to dig it out. Build a wall around it to keep the wind away.'

He looked at them. They were all tired, unshaven and shaken.

'Once we've cleared a lot of the snow, I'll go in. Then I'll call each one of you by name so you can come in and confirm what I have seen. Understood?'

They nodded in unison. By now some of them were crying. Their tears froze to their faces. Not one spoke. They began their work, created a circle of evenness around the tent.

Atkinson crawled in again. Half-light in there now, a frigid gloom. He saw only indistinct shapes and instinctively reached out. The canvas rustled. He needed more light. Slowly, it came. Three outlines of death. Two closed sleeping bags and one fearsome face.

He would never get used to the nightmares, never forget

the green light inside the tent, and their yellow, frost-bitten faces. He opened the two sleeping bags to reveal the bodies of Wilson and Bowers. They had slept themselves into death calmly, from what he could see, but the weather had carved mutilation into their faces.

Scott had thrown his sleeping bag wide open at the moment of death, or so it seemed. His face was distorted by a grimace of pain and fear, the skin glassy and scarred across his starved cheeks. Like the other two, he was frozen solid. They had lain here, under the snow, through the blackness of winter, in cold so fierce that boiling water would freeze when thrown in the air.

Atkinson did not try to close Scott's eyes; the eyelids would have shattered. He shook his head, tried to remember these three friends in life, but could not. When they hadn't returned at the end of the Antarctic summer the previous April, he knew they hadn't survived, of course, but he hadn't expected this, not to find them here, perfectly preserved in their last moment, and only two of them at peace.

Wilson reclined against a tent pole, a smile on his face, as if he had nodded off in the middle of a conversation. Bowers seemed fast asleep, exhausted from his efforts, comfortable in his repute as the expedition's hardest worker. Scott's arms were spread wide, touching the bags of the two men, one either side of him, as if he were trying to find a connection to them, or trying to grasp, in that final instant, their faith in a life after death.

As a naval surgeon, Atkinson was used to death, blood and gore, but he could not bring himself to closely examine the dead men. He would have to stay with them, he knew that, because he would have to search the tent, to find any notes they had made, any scientific evidence they had gathered on their journey. For now, however, he could not, and would not, move their bodies.

One by one he called the men in, asked them to confirm to him – and to their diaries if they were keeping one – that the three they had found were indeed Scott, Wilson and Bowers. Each man answered in the affirmative. Some of them made the sign of the cross, others merely buried their faces in their hands and sobbed the hurt of hard men into their frozen gloves.

Cherry was the last of them to crawl into the tent. He shuddered. 'Only eleven miles from safety,' he whispered to Atkinson. 'Only eleven miles from One Ton. It's my fault. I should have saved them.'

'You don't know when they got here, Cherry,' Atkinson answered. 'Who knows when they got here? It could have been weeks after you were at One Ton, a month even.'

'You're right. Of course you're right.'

They sat in silence for some minutes and cast their eyes about the shifting tent.

'How spotless it is,' Atkinson remarked.

'He always kept a very tidy tent, did the Owner,' Cherry whispered. 'That's why I hated sharing his tent. It made me feel inferior. As if I wasn't fit to be with him. I couldn't keep the same order.'

'I'm sure that's not what he thought.'

'Perhaps not. But I did.'

'Nevertheless ...'

'Nevertheless it was a disappointment to me that I couldn't go on to the Pole with him. They must have got there, mustn't they?'

'I don't know. I'll have to read his sledging diaries.'

'They must be in the wallet, under his shoulders.' Cherry gestured at the body.

Atkinson nodded.

'And those papers next to him?'

'Letters, probably. I haven't looked yet. I needed confirmation from you first that my senses weren't deceiving me.'

'How sad they were not, and that we didn't find them only sleeping.'

'Yes.'

'I've seen enough,' Cherry said, shifting uncomfortably in his partly thawed clothes. 'The men could do with some help.'

'Make sure you keep everything so we can decide later what to take and what to leave.'

'I will.'

Cherry moved slowly away, out through the inner opening. Atkinson heard him pull closed the outer flap. He sighed, braced himself. 'It has to be done,' he muttered, and moved to Scott's side.

He picked the letters up from the floor cloth. They were neatly folded and sealed – addressed, even. There was one to Wilson's mother. The paper felt brittle, like a communion wafer. The next was to Bowers' mother. More – to J.M. Barrie; to Sir Edgar Speyer, who gave money; to two vice-admirals; to Kinsey, his agent in New Zealand. Atkinson wondered how Scott had summoned the energy to write all these.

By Scott's head was some tobacco and some tea, and a lamp made of a tin with a wick fashioned from the lining of a boot. And some more letters, to those he held dearest – his mother, and Kathleen, his wife.

The wallet was secured by a strap to Scott's body, just as he had carried it with him in life. Atkinson gently tried to unloop the leather tie from the dead man's shoulders, moving it gingerly, half an inch after half an inch. He couldn't bear, though, to look into that face, that screaming face, nor into those open eyes, never to sleep again. In the end, the strap would not come loose. He would have to force it, would have to move Scott's arm to free the valuable words.

The men outside were ripped from their silent work by the crack of a pistol shot. It came from inside the tent. They rushed to the entrance. Cherry and Wright crashed through the flap, expecting the worst. It had been a dreadful winter, and the hope of spring had been broken.

Atkinson, on the floor cloth, clutched the wallet. 'I had to,' he sobbed, 'I had no choice ... it had to be done. I ... I ...'

Scott's arm, at a strange angle, pointed south.

'I had to break it, had to. Nothing else I could do.'

'We thought ...' Cherry said. 'The sound frightened us. We –'

'It's done now,' Wright said calmly. 'It's done. There was no other way.' He put his arm around Atkinson, briefly, awkwardly, and motioned Cherry outside.

Atkinson sat down, facing away from the bodies. He opened the wallet. There were three journals in there. He took them out, replaced them with the letters he had gathered. Now he turned the books over in his hands, and glanced at the flyleaf of each one. He knew Scott wrote on only one side of the paper until the end of a book was reached, then would reverse it and continue on the blank sides.

On the flyleaf of the second notebook, Scott had noted the ages of the final polar party. *Self 43, Wilson 39, Evans (P.O.) 37, Oates 32, Bowers 28. Average 36.* The first entry was for 22 December 1911, the last day Atkinson had seen Scott alive, the date Atkinson, Cherry, Wright and Keohane had turned back towards home, 450 miles from the Pole. And 500 miles back to the base at Cape Evans.

Atkinson opened the third notebook. Inside the front cover, scrawled faintly: *Diary can be read by finder to ensure recovery of Records &c., but Diary should be sent to my widow.* On the first page: *Send this diary to my wife.* There was a line through that last word, replaced by *widow* and signed.

What had happened to Oates and Evans? Atkinson stood up for a moment, moved his arms as briskly as he could. The cold seeped through his layers of clothes, and his hands numb out of their gloves, removed so that he could turn the pages of Scott's last testament.

Sitting down again, he read through the journal as quickly as he could. They had reached the Pole – after Amundsen. Evans had died at the foot of the Beardmore Glacier, Oates closer to home. Atkinson decided there and then to seek out the body of Oates, fallen less than thirty miles further south. He continued until the writing stopped. A final scrawl: *For God's sake look after our people.* Atkinson shivered and drew a deep breath, then flipped over a few more pages. And there – more writing, smaller, even more scrawled, tightly squeezed into what space there was: *Message to the public. The causes of the disaster are not due to faulty organisation, but to misfortunes in all risks which had to be undertaken.* That was enough for now. He put the diaries back into their bag, next to the letters, and crawled out of the tent.

By now the men had uncovered the polar party's sledge. On it lay the detritus of the polar journey and pounds of rocks they had gathered, probably on their trip back to this place. To end here … Atkinson shook his head again. Dreadful, dreadful. How alone and afraid they must have been. He dared not think further. He called the men to his side.

'We can't take them with us,' he said, simply. 'We must bury them here.' He paused, his thoughts confused. How? 'We should empty the tent of everything except the men and their sleeping bags. Everything else we keep.'

He crawled back into the tent, this time with Cherry. They moved all the gear to the entrance and passed it through to Wright outside. A flag, Wilson's diary, Bowers' diary, a mess of papers. Socks, finnesko boots, watches, spare clothing. They worked until the tent was empty of all they could move, all they wanted to move, until there was just an empty tent and three empty bodies.

The last things they took out were the bamboo sticks that held up the tent from inside. The men and the guy ropes still held it from the outside. All was done now, finished. It was all over. Cherry and Atkinson slowly crawled from the canvas tomb. Atkinson nodded at the men. The tent was lowered over the bodies. Then they shovelled snow to cover it – until no shred of green was to be seen.

They stood in a circle around the new mound of snow.

'They did reach the Pole,' Atkinson said. 'But they were not the first. Unfortunately.'

He held up his hands to stop the questions he guessed would come. He took out the final diary and read to them those parts they needed, wanted, to know, and then the final part of the 'message to the public', his voice failing by now.

'*We took risks ... we knew we took them ... things ... things have come out against us, and therefore ... we ... we have no cause for complaint, but ... bow to the will of Providence, determined still to ... do our best ... to the last.*' He blinked away the icicles. '*Had we lived, I should have had a tale to tell ... of ... of the hardihood, endurance, and courage ... of my companions.*' He looked around. '*For God's sake, look after our people.*'

He took the book they had identified as Wilson's bible, read aloud the burial service from Corinthians. He said prayers for the families, and for his still-living men. All bowed their heads and held the silence in the wind for some minutes. There was no need for more words.

The cairn-building began. Snow stone after snow stone piled up over where they had found their friends. They did not stop until the cairn was the height of two men. Tryggve Gran, the Norwegian, climbed to the top and fixed his skis there in the form of a cross. 'I'll wear the Owner's back to Cape Evans,' he said when he had descended. 'They must complete their journey.'

They built two smaller cairns, one on either side of the tomb, to support two sledges raised on end, the guardians of the dead. They left a note, signed by eleven crying men, put it in a metal tin, and nailed it to one of the sledges. At midnight, the clouds broke, and the low sun covered the camp in a cold light of gold. They would head south tomorrow to look for Oates.

They never found him.

Chapter 2

I spot her as soon as I get into the train. She leans against the door when it closes. There's nowhere else to go, and she can't be bothered to find somewhere to sit, doesn't seem the kind of woman who wants to be offered a seat. She's got boots on that make her legs appear really thin. I try not to make it too obvious that I'm staring at her. She gets a book out of her pocket, but I can't make out its cover. She's too far away from me, and I don't dare move closer. When I'm not expecting her to, she raises her eyes and scowls at me. How pale she is, how perfect. I hadn't realised how lonely I am. I turn away.

My stop approaches too soon. I'll have to walk past her to get out. As the train slows, I try to move across the carriage without catching her eye again. I'm halfway out when she collapses. There's nothing I can do but catch her. Her book drops out of her hands, her eyes closed. I stumble out with her in my arms, kick her book onto the platform. Everyone else just stares or pushes past me. No one bothers to help. Bloody London.

I drop down onto one of the benches by the wall and catch my breath. What now? I check her pulse. It seems OK, if a little shallow. Her face is so drawn, her teeth clenched, her lips tight and thin. Hell, I've got a real, warm, beautiful woman in my arms for the first time in ages and she's unconscious, and I don't know what to do. When the train's gone and the platform empty, I get up, turn, and lower her miniscule weight onto the bench.

Why am I doing this? I do give some of my time to charities, to help people who can't help themselves. And it's my duty to pick up this scrap of a girl in trouble. I can't just walk away. That's too easy. I did it once, a long time ago, and I've regretted it ever since. And I suppose part of me is thinking I might at last have found someone who'll want to depend on me, who will see me as a strong man. Because, despite everything I do, my life lacks that.

The platform's filling up again when her eyes flicker open and she tries to sit up. She puts her hands into her jacket pockets, and pulls them out again, empty.

'Where's my book?' she says. 'I need my book.'

I get down on my knees in front of her, retrieve it from under the bench, get up again, and hand it to her.

'What's that all about?' I say. '*The Worst Journey in the World*?'

'The Antarctic.'

'Oh.'

'I've got notes in it.' She seems calmer now, stuffs the dog-eared book back into her jacket, and tries to get up.

'Take it easy,' I say.

'I need to get to the Royal Geographical Society,' she says.

'You sure that's a good idea?'

'I don't have a choice.'

'Have you fainted before?'

'Coupla times. I just don't eat enough.' She scowls at me. She's a scary, skinny thing.

'You should get yourself checked out,' I say. 'And you need some food.' I'll get her up to the fresh air and then she can sort herself out. 'Come on.' I get up, throw my bag over my back and hold out my arm to her.

She grabs hold of it and pulls herself up.

'OK?' I say.

She nods, links arms with me, and doesn't let go as we walk along the tunnel towards the exit. In the lift up to the street, she leans against me, dizzy again. Her short, blonde hair smells of lemons, and she's trembling. She pulls away when we walk out into the fresh, cold November air. It's too much, and she trips. I catch her by her small hand. It's freezing cold. I let go as soon as I can. Touch talks, and I don't want her to know what I'm thinking.

'What now?' I say. 'You really need something to eat.'

'Can't be bothered.'

'Look, I'm sorry, and I don't even know you, but you're being stupid.'

She shakes her head. 'You don't understand. I've got to be there. It's important.'

I scratch my head. Why am I getting involved? I've sorted her out, haven't I? She'll be fine. I've got a meeting in an hour. But I can't forget that child in my head, that beggar child in Rome I walked past, now years ago, too weak even to ask for help. An hour later, on the way back, all I saw was a patch of blood on the pavement. My fault, to see that and walk away.

'It won't take a minute,' I say. 'You can get something over there.'

We walk across to the shop without talking. I watch her through the shop window, how narrow she is, how her clothes cling to her, how beautiful she is.

'Why did you keep eyeing me up on the Tube?' she says, her mouth full, when she comes out of the shop.

I blush. 'I wasn't really,' I say. 'I just like watching people.'

'That makes two of us, then.'

My blush fades. 'You seem OK now. I should get on.'

She throws the sandwich box violently into the bin. 'Tell you what,' she says. 'Why don't you come with me?'

'Why would I want to do that?'

'Because I'm asking you. It seems a shame to just let you go now that coincidence made us meet.'

My heart quickens. 'I've got a meeting in an hour.' I feel regret as I speak.

'Cancel it,' she says. 'Skive. You don't look like a man who does a lot of skiving.'

'But ...'

'Live a little.' She laughs.

I text to cancel my meeting. 'There,' I say. 'And, by the way, I'm Adam.'

'I'm Birdie.'

'Interesting name.'

'I'll explain it to you sometime.'

'There may not be another time.' I specialise in afterthoughts.

'Who knows?'

I can't make out if she's being patronising or flirtatious, so I say nothing and tag along, making sure, all the time, that she's not about to fall over again. On the Tube, I make her sit down. There's no seat for me, so I have to stand half a carriage away from her. But I don't play my usual game of counting how many fanciable women there are, and watch her instead, her stillness. I feel a confusing degree of tenderness for someone I've only just met. She fascinates me, draws me to her.

'D'you know anything at all about the Antarctic?' she says when we surface in South Ken.

'Just what I learned at school. Amundsen beat Scott to the South Pole. Amundsen got back. Scott didn't. Oh, and it's bloody cold out there, and dark most of the time.'

'Great summary. Go to the top of the class.' She shakes her head.

We carry on walking.

'You do know the Natural History Museum, though?' she says.

''Course. Been there. Dinosaurs and all that.'

'But what's it got to do with my book?'

'Should I care?'

She stops. I hadn't noticed she's out of breath. She has to crane her neck to look me in the face, smiles for the first time. I smile back at her brown eyes. 'The guy who wrote it, Apsley Cherry-Garrard, spent six weeks walking through the

17

pitch-black Antarctic winter to Cape Crozier, just to get three penguin eggs, and bring them back here.'

'The point being?'

'One of the blokes with him was Henry Bowers, also known as Birdie.'

'You've got a man's name?'

'Let me finish. Bowers died with Scott.'

'You're related to him, then?'

She smiles, despite herself, I think. 'No, he didn't have any kids as far as anyone knows. He still lived with his mum when he went on Scott's expedition.'

'So why the name?'

'My parents were obsessed with the Antarctic, and Dad reckoned he might find out he was the son of Bowers' love child, so they christened me Henrietta Birdie Bowers.'

'And you're mad about him?'

'I admire him, but he didn't live long enough to leave anything lasting behind.'

'That's sad.'

'It is a bit.' She gets the book out of her pocket. 'But Cherry meant this to be a memorial to him.'

'So why are you so keen to get to the RGS?'

'I've persuaded them to show me some stuff from the Scott expedition.'

'And it had to be today?'

She nods. 'The thing is, there's a mystery about the Pole journey no one's solved.'

'And that's why you're in a state.'

'I've been obsessing about it since Dad died.'

'Oh. Sorry.'

'That's done.' She wipes whatever pain she feels away with an impatient arm and starts walking again. 'Scott, Bowers and Wilson died eleven miles from the next food depot, and they were stuck there for ten days because of a blizzard, according to what Scott wrote.'

'What's odd about that?' I say.

'It's been scientifically proven that Antarctic blizzards only last three to four days.'

'Without a doubt?' This is interesting.

'Without a doubt. That's why I want to find out what really happened.'

'You think Scott was lying?'

She shrugs. 'Not necessarily. Delusions of a dying man, maybe.'

'Hasn't anyone else tried?'

'Lots of people, but no one's come up with anything that makes sense.'

'So why this sudden urgency?'

'It's nearly a hundred years since it happened. Time we knew the truth.'

'Does it matter?'

'It does to me. And I've never been near any of the gear they had with them,' she says. 'We're here. Want to come in with me?'

'I'd love to, but I don't want to intrude.'

'You won't. I need some support for once.'

'Then I will.' I willingly give in.

Inside, there's an unreal hush. She walks up to the reception desk, transforms herself into someone much taller, much more determined than the sick, grieving woman who fell into my arms and walked here with me.

'Miss Bowers here to see Leo McAllister,' she says to the woman behind the desk.

'I'll let him know you're here. Take a seat, please.'

We retreat to the high glass windows and watch the traffic.

'What are you expecting to see?' I say.

'Just a few things. Stuff from the expedition's spread out all over the world. Some here, lots more at the Scott Polar Research Institute in Cambridge, some in the Canterbury Museum in New Zealand. And the royals have got a stash of it, too, so we'll never get our hands on that.'

19

When Leo McAllister arrives, she introduces me as her assistant. He's tall and spare, and looks old. I follow the two of them along a maze of corridors and doors.

'I've laid most of our artefacts out on the table,' Leo says. 'As you know, you'll have to wear these cotton gloves to make sure there's no damage.'

'Sure,' she says.

The three of us pull on our gloves.

'I'll just explain what these are,' Leo says.

What I see looks insignificant. There are just a few ancient containers, a couple of sorry-looking cotton bags, and a stack of discoloured magazines.

Leo picks up one of these things after another, tells us where it was found, and what he thinks is significant about it. He only takes ten minutes, but what he says leaves me shell-shocked. I hadn't anticipated the rawness of history.

'I'll be back in an hour,' he says. 'Is that enough time for you?'

'Yes, thank you very much,' Birdie says. Does she always change like this, from surly to polite, from weak to strong, from panicked to calm?

He closes the door behind him, and we don't speak for a moment. The room shrinks. She takes a deep breath, steadies herself on one of the chairs, then finally picks up a metal matchbox holder, rusty, tinged with the brown flecks of time. Leo told us it was found next to Scott's body. The dead live on in their traces. She hands it to me. Its lightness catches me by surprise, and I almost drop it. I put it on the table and open it. There are still matches in here, unused ones. I count them out onto the table. Eighty-eight of them.

'Why didn't they use them all?' I say into her brittle silence.

'They ran out of fuel. They spent those ten days in that tent without any fuel. That's why they died. They couldn't even make themselves a cup of tea.' She shivers.

I put the matches back into the box. They'll never be used.

'Are you all right?' I say.

She doesn't answer, moves along the table to the provision bags that were found in the tent. She caresses them with her gloved fingers, looks around, and quickly pulls off one of the gloves, runs the back of her bare hand across the bags two or three times.

'What are you doing?' I whisper.

'I just needed to touch, feel, to get close to them. To something more organic than metal.' There's strain in her voice. Her tiny body trembles with it. I want to reach out, but I can't, I just can't. To have caught her fainting body that short hour ago is less of an intimacy than to put my arms around her now, although that's what I want to do – to wipe her face dry, to make her smile again.

She laughs tearily, pulls her gloves back on. She picks the bag up again, weighs it in the palm of her hand, sniffs at its ochre stains. 'Curry powder. You know ...' She takes a deep breath. 'Scott blamed himself for getting frostbite in his feet because, one evening, he accidentally mixed some of this with his food and it gave him the trots, weakened him.' She wipes her nose with the back of her hand.

'Does any of this get you any closer to finding out what happened?' I say. 'All this pain?'

She shakes her head. 'But it makes me closer to them. It's real after all the books and notes. This is an addiction it's impossible to cure.'

How many books has she read, how many notes has her father left her? Does she believe anything beyond what he told her? Maybe she's just dealing with her grief this way. Mourning for Bowers is mourning for her father. Maybe carrying his name has burdened her with another kind of grief and guilt, too, the kind we feel when the past drifts off beyond recollection and memory into anecdote and dream.

She drifts off along the table again, reaching out with her

long fingers. She's as lonely as me, isn't she, surrounded by her father's notes and books, and nothing but hopes and mysteries? She's lost in a world of trying to find something that may not exist. Maybe that's all she wants from her life, to dig over the remnants of passed time.

'What if there really was a ten-day blizzard? What if you're just kidding yourself about finding a new answer?'

'Impossible.' She glares at me. 'You think I'm a fool, don't you?'

'I didn't –'

'What? You didn't what?' The anger forces her muscles into sharp, defined patterns. Her legs, her arms, her stomach just visible above the waistband, her entire body, confront me with their taut challenge. I ward her off with open palms before she gets close enough to touch.

'Sorry. I didn't mean to hurt, or offend, whatever it is I did. It all just seems –'

'Stupid?' She raises her voice even more.

'Shhh. No, not that. Just somehow unreal. Dangerous for you, to your sanity.'

'You don't know me very well.' She turns away, looks towards the window at the end of this long grey room. 'You don't know me at all.' She stops moving, stands entirely still. 'And I don't know you. Sorry.'

We put on our coats, and retrace our steps to the reception where we shake hands again with Leo. It's over.

'Good luck,' he says.

And then we're out into the dampness of an English winter once again.

Chapter 3

She wraps herself into her short coat, buries her face between the lapels, and walks swiftly back towards the Natural History Museum. To me, she's an enigma: reckless, short-tempered, weak and beautiful all at once. I have to lengthen my stride to keep up with her. We reach the corner of two streets, have to pause, wait for the lights.

'Why didn't you bother looking at the magazines?' I say.

She shrugs. 'Dunno. Not to destroy my illusions? Because it's irrelevant? Because it *is* irrelevant.'

'Sorry,' I mumble.

'What for?' Her breath tumbles from her mouth in a veil of fog.

'You wouldn't be talking about your illusions if I hadn't spouted that load of crap in there.'

'Oh, but I would. I wake up every day asking myself if this is the right thing to do.'

'Is there nowhere else you can get more info?'

'Of course there is,' she says. 'That's why today was only the start.'

'So where is there?'

'Scott Polar in Cambridge, like I said. But ...'

'But?'

'But there's a six-month waiting list to get into their archives.'

'Can't you get in there more quickly?' Why am I getting impatient now, about that?

'No. Dad and I applied five months ago, so there's not

that much longer to wait. I go in a couple of weeks. It should've been Dad and me.' She sniffs.

'Is that why you came here today?' I have to ignore her sadness.

'Partly,' she nods. 'There are other reasons, too.'

'Like? You talk in riddles sometimes.'

'That comes from living alone.' She smiles, and her eyes light up for the first time since we met.

'I live on my own and I don't talk in riddles.'

'Maybe you don't spend enough time with your books trying to solve a puzzle that's been with you all your life.'

'Oh, no.' I shake my head. 'I have plenty of puzzles to keep me occupied. It's just that they're computer puzzles, and boring, mostly.'

'So who are you, actually?' she asks. 'I don't even know your surname.'

'Caird, my surname's Caird.'

'You're joking.' Her voice rises.

'Why would I be joking?'

The lights change to green. People push past us, in between us. She stands still, a rock in the deluge. 'Because it's too much of a coincidence.'

'Too much of a coincidence for what?'

She pulls a face. 'Stop interrupting.'

'Sorry.'

'You're serious, aren't you? You don't know anything about that name.'

'It's a bog-standard Scottish name. What's there to know?'

'Caird has Antarctic connections.'

'Go on.'

'When Shackleton got marooned in the Antarctic, he sailed to South Georgia in a tiny lifeboat, the *James Caird*.'

'I've heard of Shackleton, but I didn't know that.'

'I don't suppose that many people do know.'

'He's nothing to do with Scott, though?'

'He was on an expedition with Scott in 1901, and he did get to within ninety miles of the Pole in 1909, but no, not really. The *Caird* thing happened in 1916. But it's weird, anyway, you being called Caird.'

'Listen –'

'Look –'

We speak at the same time.

'After you,' I say.

'No, you started first.'

'I was wondering.'

'So was I,' she says.

'What?'

'There's a café in the NHM. Fancy a coffee?'

'Should you be drinking coffee after that fainting fit?'

'I guess not. I'll have a hot chocolate.'

'All right. I'll buy.'

She grunts, turns on her heels, and we walk up the long, slow rise of the drive that leads to the museum's main entrance. She's got multiple personalities, I think.

'Maybe we can get a look at those penguin eggs.'

'I don't think so,' she says. 'After all that, Cherry-Garrard had a problem even getting a receipt for them. They're probably lost again.'

So she's a cynic as well. Weird how much you can get to know about a person in the space of a couple of hours, and still not understand them. Some people marry and never get to know each other. Maybe that's why I've been a bachelor for so long. Because I don't want that to happen to me, to wake up one morning to find I've been living with a stranger for most of my life.

We sit down with our hot chocolates. The air is full of many languages. There's an old German on my right, talking quickly to two teenage girls who must be his daughters. There are two old dears to my left, talking about their mad friend and cathedrals and bridges and summer. Behind me, a trio of young women, tourists, all with their maps out, jabber away in what sounds like Spanish. And behind Birdie, there's nothing, no one, just a wall of red brick, a warm, dark frame around her light hair.

'You're staring again,' she says.

'Am I? Sorry. Just the contrast ... the wall and your hair and ... skin.'

She raises a blonde eyebrow. I blush. Push my glasses back up my nose.

'How sweet. An artist.' She stares at me, right at me, into my eyes, won't look away. 'I'm joking.'

'Anyway ...' I cough. And stutter. 'You were going to tell me about your other reasons for going to the RGS today.'

She looks down at her cup, breathes deeply. Once. Twice. Takes a sip. Her lips on the porcelain. My gaze on her lips. That voice in my head telling me not to be so stupid.

'It's ninety-six years since their bodies were found. Today.' She doesn't look up. 'That's why I had to go. Why it had to be today. It made the connection even stronger.' Now she raises her head. 'Can you understand that?'

'Sort of.'

I do understand her rage and her tears. Although I'm only just starting to feel connected to them or their reason. Should I tell her it's my birthday today? I don't think that's such a good idea.

She shakes her head.

'What?' I say.

'I really can't believe that you were never interested in Scott or Shackleton,' she says.

'I was never much of a one for history. I always thought it was better to look forward, not backwards. I didn't want to lumber my brain with useless half-truths. And with Scott, and most of the other things they wanted to teach us at school, there was too much Empire, so much propaganda. It's all done and dusted, finished. How can you glorify failure? It doesn't change anything. It hasn't changed the world we live in.'

'That's not really true. They made huge scientific advances.'

'They didn't invent the computer, did they?'

'That's silly,' she says. 'That's not what I meant.'

'What, then?'

'What they achieved for that time was amazing. They put their hut up in ten days. They anchored it into the permafrost. They measured wind speed, temperature, snowfall every two hours. They were hard as nails, really. Courageous.'

'Look, I understand what you mean. I just don't think it's relevant in this day and age. Not when there are millions of starving kids in Africa.'

'And why do you think those kids are starving? Don't you think it might have something to do with people not caring, because this age is one where no one gives a toss about anything anymore? Don't you think that if all people had respect for others, the world would be a much better place?'

'Yes, but –'

'And don't you think that to remember people who've died with courage and integrity might actually encourage those alive now to live with some respect, some dignity, some endeavour?' Her cheeks have gone very red, their pale skin aflame with that anger of hers which seems to appear from nowhere. The conversations around us stop. She flashes a big smile around the room, changes into another one of her many selves. The buzz starts again. People lose interest. They're all happy to be smiled at.

'Who are you?' I ask. 'Really?'

'Google me,' she says, and rummages in her coat. 'And here's a card.'

'What?' I look at the card. An abstract splash of colour, a number and a stencil: *Storm Moon*. 'What's this?'

'Go away. Read some books about what I've told you. See if you don't become addicted. If you can't see the mystery, if you don't see how someone wouldn't want to let go of finding out what really happened to those men, then don't call me. If you end up wanting to find out more, ring me.'

'Are you serious?'

'Why shouldn't I be?'

'You hardly know me.'

'So? I haven't asked you to marry me.'

I half wish she would. I want to wrap her into warm sheets and kiss her face, want to watch her scamper across the wooden floor of my house dressed in my baggy jumpers and shirts, kicking pillows off the bed with her naked feet. I want her to put those strong hands on my face and kiss me. I'm a fool.

'I don't have your energy,' I say, and try to pull myself together. 'Nor your faith.'

'You may have. Some day.'

She grabs her coat and runs for the door. I rush out after her. She's disappeared into the crowd. I make for the main entrance, head outside into the cold wind. No. She's gone. There's no point looking for her.

I'll have to do as she said and read books about the Antarctic, about Scott and his expedition, about the real Birdie Bowers – Henry. And what if they don't move me? What if I don't feel the way she does? Do I still call her? Probably not. Why make life complicated? But it became complicated the moment I decided to stand in the same carriage as her, and when all those following moments, those little shards of time, joined together into this fragile coincidence. Today, on my birthday, something's changed. I've changed. And won't ever be the same again. But for now, all I'm left with is her card and the lemony scent of her perfume.

Chapter 4

Suddenly, I'm a drifter, a vagrant between emotions. I'm lost without her. For a few hours I had some kind of focus, to take my mind off how repetitive my life's become; how, despite what I said about history, I've started looking back more than ever, because I can't imagine anything to look forward to. But she's gone before I have a chance to do anything about it, before I'm brave enough.

Computers may have a soul, but they can't replace flesh and bone, nor real voices and warmth. And it's computers I spend all my time with. It's no surprise I'm lonely. I'm serially, seriously, monogamous. The last real girlfriend I had left me over three years ago. Too much gloom, she said, too much analysis of what, why, how. Too much talk, she said, and not enough action.

It's too easy to fall in love, especially for someone like me who might fall for anyone who's nice to me. It's a vicious circle, that women start to like me because they feel I'm needy, and then, when they find out I really am needy, that I'm an emotional retard, they decide enough's enough, that I'm getting too serious, that I'm a control freak. So I'd stopped even thinking about finding someone, was resigned to becoming an archetypal old bachelor, until today.

I really want to find out who she is, what she does, track down what Storm Moon means. I could always catch the train home, try to Google her on my flaky mobile connection, but after that I wouldn't know what to do with an early afternoon back in my tiny Suffolk village. Solve more computer puzzles? Staying in London would be a real pain, although it would mean I could rearrange that meeting

I cancelled. Not cheap, though, hotels. And my address book isn't exactly overflowing with people I could cadge a bed from for the night.

There's always John. He's almost as sad as me, although he's been married for nearly twenty years. He's at work from five in the morning, and gets home at about half past three every afternoon. And then he drinks. Unless he's in training for some marathon or something similarly beyond my capabilities or inclination. And he's got broadband. And lets me use it. And there's a pub just a couple of minutes' walk away from his front door.

So I text him.

'U gonna b at home in a couple of hours?'

I keep my phone in my hand. I wonder how long it'll take him to text me back.

'Home now. Cldn't b arsd 2 work slow.'

'On way. C u in 1 hr.'

'Beers r in fridge.'

Nice to have some friends, even if they don't know when it's your birthday.

An hour later I'm in his warm living room, a can of beer on the table in front of me. He's got some weird modern music on, as usual. We don't speak much, to begin with, as usual. And his wife's out until much later, as usual.

'So, what's up?' he says, on his second can since I got here.

'Not much.'

'Been a while.'

'Always is.'

'Mm.' He drinks some more, thinks his usual thoughts. 'Where d'you want to eat, then?' he says.

'What's easiest?'

'Pub. They've got a new cook. French. Good stuff. Cheap.'

That's the way he always talks. It's like he hates using too many words. He uses just one where one will do.

30

'Could do with a pint, anyway.' He says that all the time, as well.

It's only once we're at the pub, pints in front of us on the table, waiting for food, that he starts talking properly.

'Tell me, then,' he says. 'Something's happened today. What's her name?'

'Birdie. I think.' I take a sip of my Guinness. 'And she's gorgeous.'

'You need your head testing.'

'Why?'

'Because you're too old for this crap.' He looks at me laughing. 'You always do this. It comes up to your birthday. You start feeling old. You decide to fall in love. They don't give a damn. You take almost a year to recover from the blow. Then it starts all over again.'

'So you do know when my birthday is?'

'Yeah. 'Course. Just don't really care. Bit like you.'

So I ignore the banter for a bit. I tell him everything that's happened today. He stops laughing after a while. He just listens and drinks his beer. Then he gets us another. The food always takes a long time in here, no matter who's cooking it.

'And you don't know where she lives?'

I shake my head. 'Look.' I get the card out of my pocket. 'It's not even what she said she was called.'

'You're an idiot. Storm Moon. How dickish is that?'

The food arrives. The waitress is quite nice.

'Oh, give over,' he says.

'Sorry.'

'Why don't you just phone her?'

'The waitress? I haven't got her number.'

'You know what I mean.'

'She sort of forbade me to. Until I decide if I'm getting obsessed with the Antarctic '

'Well, are you?'

'Too soon to decide.'

'Let's Google her when we get back.'

'D'you think we'll find anything?'

'Would she have told you to Google her otherwise?'

'I don't know.'

When we've finished eating, we play the usual obligatory five frames of pool and drink a couple more beers. And then we're off. I smoke on the way back. I've been smoking incessantly, between pints and talk and loneliness, for most of my life.

He's already made up the sofa bed in the spare room that's also his office. He's good like that. We climb over it to get to his computer, nightcap in hand, of course. Even though I configured this machine for him, it takes ages to start up. What the hell does he do to these things? I can't be arsed to fix it now. I'll do that in the morning.

And so I start searching for her. *Henrietta Bowers*, I type into Google's advanced search. It comes up with all sorts of weird stuff, and then some interesting stuff. *Henrietta Bowers Duterte, an African American woman who was the first female undertaker in Philadelphia, and also an Underground Station Master who helped slaves by hiding them in caskets.* That's not her. I include *London* in the search. It might reduce the hits I get, but I still get nothing useful. Just references to old dowagers and people like that who died well over a hundred years ago. That figures, I suppose. It is an old-fashioned name.

So I look for *Storm Moon* instead. The search comes up with lots of information about paganism and Wicca. She didn't look like a pagan to me. And then a definition on Wikipedia – *the moon which occurs in March during shifting weather patterns in the Northern hemisphere; also called moon of winds, moon of the snow-blind.* Now that's interesting; there's a connection there, isn't there?

At the bottom of the page, it says *See Also*, and under that there are a couple of links – *Storm Moon (disambiguation)*, and *Storm Moon, graffiti artist and painter*. I click on it. The page loads, littered with other links in a narrow column on the left. The rest is almost blank.

Storm Moon is a pseudonymous graffiti artist and painter, now best known for her abstract renditions of E. A. Wilson's Antarctic sketches. Her graffiti art appeared first in London in the late 1990s, leading many to believe she was English. It consisted mainly of a black or white moon above black or white ice cliffs, normally subtitled with subversive or questioning slogans, such as 'no one looks for the lost any more', or 'if governments don't listen, why should the people?' Her first oil with an Antarctic theme was auctioned in New York in 2001, and sold for over half a million pounds. Since then, her work has been shown and sold at many venues around the world. She is reputed to attend her showings without revealing her identity. Occasional graffiti pieces are still found, although it is uncertain how recent they are. This Storm Moon article is a stub.

'That sound like her?' John says over my shoulder.

'No,' I say. 'It can't be her. She didn't look like she had two pennies to rub together.'

'Must've been having you on then, mate.'

'Maybe not. It explains the Antarctic link.' I point at the screen.

'I guess,' he says, but doesn't sound convinced. He slurps the last beer out of the can. 'Another?'

'Oh, go on, then. Just one more. Might as well celebrate properly.'

While he's in the kitchen, I search for images of Henrietta Bowers. None that come up look like her; they're all of the worthy helper of slaves. And when I search for images of Storm Moon, I just get those abstract paintings and the street art. So I Google the blogs. Nothing again but supposition.

Some bloggers reckon she must be an old crow if she never shows her face.

'What you doing now?' he asks.

'Just trying different places. There must be more about her somewhere.'

'D'you care? You just fancy her.'

'No. It's more than that.'

'It always is. Just bloody phone her.'

'I can't.'

'You're not telling me you're going to stick to that cockeyed promise.'

'Yes. It'll do me good to do a bit of reading from bits of paper for a change.'

'You're a mad bastard.'

'I know. That's why you like me so much.'

He splutters on his beer. 'Oh yeah. Forgot that bit.' He laughs. 'Come on. Turn the damn machine off and let's listen to some music.'

'Yeah. I'll fix it in the morning.'

'What – is there something wrong with it?'

'Dickhead.' I thump him.

The next morning, I'm a bit thick-headed. I'm not used to drinking so much beer. John, and his wife, have already left by the time I get up. I have a quick juice, a quick shower, and a quick smoke on the balcony. Then I fix his machine, like I always do.

I get to my rearranged meeting without anyone fainting on me this time. The suits tell me what they need. I tell the suits what I need. We talk round and round the same thing for hours. Then we agree that they'll be in touch with me, and I'll be in touch with them. Bloody waste of time. That's how they make their money. And I suppose that's how I make mine.

Released from the claws of the accountants, I wander into the Waterstones by Trafalgar Square. The one with the café on the first floor. I browse the Travel and Exploration section. Ah. Lots of books on Antarctica. Which to choose? In the end I buy six, including the book Birdie had with her. I make sure I get Scott's diaries and Amundsen's account of his trip, too. It wouldn't do to be one-sided.

There's a table free in the café, so I plonk all my gear down there, get a coffee, and start reading. It's harrowing, some of this stuff. It really is. I can't imagine what it must have been like. Of course, being male, I straightaway look for the parts where people die. And, anyway, they are the bits that Birdie's interested in. They're the mystery – if there is indeed a mystery.

Three large coffees and two Danish pastries later, I'm convinced. Convinced I'm not pretending to be hooked just for the sake of a girl, but hooked because of the race between Amundsen and Scott, the two nations, the idea of spending years in an icy place to reach another point on the ice that someone else says is important. It's either very foolish or very brave. But isn't every point on the globe a pole of sorts?

Birdie's card marks the page in Scott's diaries where there's a photo of his last entry. Even a cynic like me finds it difficult to read *It seems a pity but I do not think I can write more* without feeling for the man. What is it like to die that way? I pick up the card, stare at the colours and the name. I take out my phone, key in the number and wait. It rings nine times. I count, because I always count. I usually hang up if no one's answered after ten rings.

'Hello?' Her voice sounds different.

'It's Adam.'

'Who's Adam?'

'We met yesterday.'

'Oh, it's you. Hello, Mr Caird.'

Could I sense a smile?

'Hello, Birdie.'

'I thought I told you to wait a while to decide if you were interested in the fate of my namesake.'

'I've just read bits of six books and I've already decided.'

'Interesting.' There's an intervening hiss. 'I wonder what you're really interested in.'

You, you, you, I want to shout down the phone.

'Waterstones is a very cool place to read books, you know.'

'I don't doubt that. But what do you expect me to do now that you've called me?'

'Erm ... I hadn't actually thought about that.'

'Maybe you should.' She hangs up.

I'm puzzled. I'm sweating as well. Ridiculous. Maybe I am doing the wrong thing, maybe she is just taking the mick, and I shouldn't be falling in love with someone who appears to be much younger than me. Maybe it's The Change. But no. I know what I feel. I want this. I call her again.

'Hello, Adam.'

'Hello, Birdie.'

'Have you started stalking me now?'

'What?'

'Have you got time now?' she asks.

'Yes.'

'Meet me at Manor House Tube in about an hour?'

'You sure?'

'I'm sure.'

She hangs up again. I'm sweating even more now.

Manor House is up in north London, on one corner of Finsbury Park. It's ages since I've been up here. I used to hang out round this place a long time ago. But I got tired of London. It was too loud, too noisy, too dirty. A girl I was going to marry left me. Riots and dead policemen. All too real, I guess. Too much out of my control.

Damn, which exit does she want me to take? I opt for the one that comes up on the corner of Seven Sisters Road. But I can't see her. Mind you, I don't suppose she'd be standing there waiting for me. She'll probably make me wait. I lean against the wall and light a cigarette. I can't remember the last time I was this nervous.

Just as I'm beginning to lose hope, I feel an arm round my waist.

'Adam.'

'Birdie.'

'Come with me.'

She doesn't let go, and we walk down the hill as if we've always been friends.

Chapter 5

'It's not far,' she says.

'Good. I'm too old for walking.'

She doesn't reply, just keeps walking. She drags me along, almost. Not that I'm reluctant. I can't help noticing she's wearing even less than yesterday, not that it should matter. But to a man, it always matters.

And then we're here. She lets us into the nondescript, whitewashed house. She doesn't stop, walks straight through to the kitchen and opens the back door. Except it's not the door to a garden. It leads into a glass tunnel that takes us across the grass into a red-brick building. We step into a huge space. It must have been a factory at some point.

Even on this dark November day, the light is bright in here. White walls hung with huge canvases. Some are covered in angry lines, some in broad, bold strokes. Others are barely marked, just the occasional interruption of white by black or bright colour. And, in between the monumental ones, small pictures break the pattern with their miniscule details, their chatter of pencils and brushes.

'This is where I live,' she says. She spreads her arms out wide and turns in two circles. 'Not in there.' She points back down the tunnel. 'Like it?'

'You are *that* Storm Moon, then. What can I say?'

'Not a lot, I guess.'

'Where?'

'Just drop your stuff anywhere. We need to talk.'

I do as I'm told. I put down my bag and coat where I'm standing. She's already moved off into one of the spaces leading off the hall. I follow. She's in control. I just can't work out why. Except that I suppose I'd do anything she asked me to. It's ridiculous to be enthralled by someone so young and tiny and unpredictable.

This room is nothing less than a library. Shelves and books stretch up to the ceiling, all round the windows and above. There's even one of those classic push-along ladders. Old books and new litter the shelves, spines whole, spines broken, leather, paper, cardboard. The scent of paper fills the room. I feel a sense of excitement. And, dancing in front of the shelves, is that blonde elf, exuberant, commanding, dangerous.

'You'll read all these, then?' she says. 'So I can be sure you're committed? So I know I can trust you?'

'Committed?'

'You said you were, when you called me. You said you were convinced that this mystery should be solved, that you were addicted. Didn't you? Didn't you?' She stomps up to me, stares at me, her breath hot.

'Well, yes, but –'

'No buts. Yes or no?' she shouts. I need to know. You're no use to me if you're not really up for this.'

'Calm down.' I move towards her, but she's too quick for me. 'Explain this properly.'

She sprints out into the hall again. 'You explain it,' she shouts. 'You tell me what all this is about. You said you knew. You said it. Prove it.'

I give up trying to chase her. I stand there, with my hands on my hips. Does she have any medication she ought to be taking? This craziness might be a bit much, even for me. The thought crashes out of my head as she rushes from one picture to the other, nose up to one, then leaning back from another, skidding and sliding, and her shoes screeching on the wooden floor. And her clothes are so tight I can see every muscle move, bend and flex.

'You asked me if the mystery interested me,' I say as

calmly as I can. Because she takes my breath away. 'And it does. From what I've read so far.'

'You mean you weren't up all night wondering about it?' She races past me, out of reach.

'I Googled you last night. And went to see a friend.'

'What's her name? What's her name? Don't care. Not listening.'

'It's a he. And I talked about you.'

'About me? Not about Henry and the others? Or about those ten days?'

Why's she not breathless yet? How can she keep racing and talking? How can she be running rings around a man who's so much older than her, mentally and physically?

'I don't want you to talk about me. I don't want anyone to talk about me. I'm not important. This is what's important. And those days. Nothing else matters. It musn't matter. Promise you won't tell anyone you know who I am.' She flails at me, drapes her arms round my shoulders. She's going to faint. 'Help me, Adam. Please help me.'

'What can I do when you behave like this?'

She pushes me away. 'I'm not mad,' she barks. 'Just this. Me.'

'Are you serious about me reading all those books?'

'You need to know what you're letting yourself in for.'

'Reading a load of books, obviously. But you've already read them.'

'You forget one thing,' she calls across from the largest canvas in the room.

'What's that?'

'Getting there,' she whispers. 'Getting there.'

'What?'

The last echo of our exchange passes away down the tunnel. We both stand still. I don't speak. What does she mean? I didn't say I wanted to go out there, to that cold place. People die out there. I don't want to die. Hell, look where my idiotic attraction to younger women has got me.

She's probably a psychopath. How many blokes have fallen for this and never got away? This place is big enough to hide any number of bodies.

'We need to go out there to solve this. We need to find Scott's tent.'

'What? How are you going to find it after almost a hundred years? Don't you think others have had the same idea?'

'Probably. But most people think the bodies have been crushed by the weight of the snow. That the tent has moved so far with the ice flow it would be impossible to find.'

'Well then.'

'But I don't believe them.'

'You *are* mad. How would you hope to find it?'

'That's where you come in.'

'What?'

'Oh, stop all the whats, computer genius.'

'Hey, hang on.' I hold up my palms. 'I said nothing about being a genius. I just fix machines and networks and mess about with puzzles, like I said.'

'You're obviously modest.'

'So you don't want me for my body?'

'Is that what you thought?' She laughs. She's laughing at me.

'I think I should leave.'

'Not so fast.' She stands in front of my gear. Her mouth is hard, aggressive. Hands on hips. I can't take my eyes off her pierced navel. 'Why are you men all so bloody one-dimensional? Is that all you think about? Getting into someone's knickers? Pathetic.'

'I can't deny that ... that I find you very attractive. But ...'

'Oh, but it goes deeper than that, does it? I bet you say that to all the girls. Because that sure is what all the boys say to me. And none of them mean it.'

'Guilty as charged,' is all I can say. 'I'm not going to argue with you. But I can walk away from here. Because I'd never try to take advantage.'

'D'you even think I'd let you?' she screams. 'You patronising bastard.'

'I didn't mean it like that.' My mouth is dry. 'Look, can't we just have a cup of tea or something and talk about this like normal people?'

I'm hoping she might switch to her more reasonable self if I keep myself calm, that she might actually talk to me rationally. Even though I know I'm a patronising you-know-what. But I didn't intend that. I just wanted to avoid saying stuff to her that other men obviously already have. Because I want her to love me. But I don't think she will. I'm an idiot.

'OK ... OK.'

Ten banality-filled minutes later we're sitting at the table in the library opposite each other, the teapot and milk between us. I stir my tea slowly and try to choose my words with care.

'Look, Birdie, just let me talk for five minutes without interrupting. Please.'

She nods. Sips her tea.

'What happened yesterday was a coincidence. Today isn't. Yesterday, you ran away. I didn't know what to do. I Googled you. Found out that you paint. That no one knows who you are. I bought some books to learn more about what you call a mystery. Phoned you. Sooner than we'd agreed, I admit. But I wanted to see you again. And the books dragged me in, got me interested. And all the time I had a picture of you in my head.'

I take the spoon out of my tea. I look at the swirling surface. Another whirlpool.

'I never imagined ... you and me, you know. I wouldn't presume. And I never thought about going there. I'm too set in my ways. I don't do adventures. I'm a stick-in-the-mud, a bit lost, and lazy. I couldn't hack it. I haven't got your will or your talent. I'd be a burden. And I hate the cold. There. I've probably said too much.'

The tea doesn't make my mouth less dry. I'm sweating heavily. It's over before it's even started. I'm demented and misguided.

She takes a deep breath. She smiles and starts to reach out across the table, but stops herself.

'You're a very sweet man,' she says, at last. 'Have I hurt you? Because you thought I only wanted you for your computers? Because you thought you couldn't have me?' There's an edge in her voice. 'I'm tired of men pretending to fall in love with me. Or even really falling in love with me because I'm blonde, because I'm thin, because I paint, because I've got money.'

'I ...'

'Let me talk now, without you interrupting. Fair's fair.' She puts her hands flat on the table, brushes away an imaginary mark on the shiny leather. 'You know I'm grateful to you for yesterday. The fainting's never happened in public before. And you know how important Henry and the others are to me. I can't be distracted by transcendent emotions. I can't give myself to this cause and to someone at the same time. But your kindness showed me that you're an honest man, that you don't hide behind your words. You only say what you mean. I need someone I can trust. Someone who's my equal. Who doesn't want me because of the money, the reputation. Someone who'll help me when I'm in trouble.'

'You think you can rely on me?'

'Yes.'

'I'd be scared of letting you down.'

'Don't be, and you won't.' She looks up from her hands. 'You know, when Scott sent Cherry back to the base, Cherry asked him if it was because he'd let Scott down. And Scott said – no, no, no. And I could never imagine you disappointing me.'

Her words move me. It's ridiculous, to become this involved so soon, to disappear into a crevasse of emotions, to fall too steeply, too deeply, and here, in this part of

43

London I swore I'd avoid forever, because I thought I'd always associate it with the pain I'd felt then. But I can't change what happened. And what's more, I can't change me. I never could and never will. When I fall in love, I fall heavily. And this time it's different, I swear it is. This time it's right.

'So, what now?'

'I'm not going to promise to change, because I can't. I try not to control myself, because then I couldn't paint. I want things. I can be faithless. And I'm mean.'

'I'll live with that. As long as I can defend myself.'

'Then there's one thing you should see before you decide if you're really with me on this.'

A short time later, we're in the British Library near King's Cross station, in a darkened room so dimly lit I almost fall over my own feet. She grabs my hand and leads me through the muted voices and whispers, past illuminated bibles and Shakespeare folios, past Beatles and Mozart scores, to a solitary glass box, to an anonymous, temperature-controlled container.

'This is what they've done to it,' she whispers, her voice a dying cry of betrayal.

I screw up my eyes, look into the case. One slab of text on a white card. I read the heavy black print.

DIARY OF CAPTAIN R. F. SCOTT, 29 MARCH 1912

Scott and his party set out for the South Pole on 1 November 1911. They arrived on 17 January 1912, only to discover that the Norwegian Roald Amundsen had been there one month earlier. The return journey was dogged by misfortune as temperatures fell to below −40 degrees. Evans suffered concussion in a fall and died on 17 February. Frostbite became a serious threat; Oates was the worst affected and on 17 March he sacrificed himself in the hope that without him the others would make swifter progress. However, on 20

March a blizzard descended making it impossible to complete the journey to the next depot only 11 miles away. The bodies of Scott, Wilson and Bowers were found in their tent the following spring. The diary is open at Scott's final entry, dated 29 March 1912. Add Ms 51035, ff. 38v-39

I look up at the diary. I can scarcely read the pencilled scrawl, because of the dimness of the light.

we shall stick it out
to the end but we
are getting weaker of
course and the end
cannot be far.
It seems a pity but
I do not think I can •
write more.
R Scott
Last Entry
For God's sake look
after our people

The diary is permanently pinned open at this page with straps of transparent plastic, like it's on the rack. I can't understand why it's kept here, rigid, and untouchable.

'Can't we steal it?' I whisper back to her. Our hands are still touching, on the edge of the case.

'No. That wouldn't be right, or fair. I want to see if I can borrow it at some point. But first I need to go to SPRI. And then out there.'

I know it doesn't do to ascribe human qualities to something as inanimate as a little black book. But it has his last words in it. It breathed through his struggles with him, and it survived his death. It saw the bright Antarctic sun. But in here, dusk is permanent. These are words in limbo, words that only add to Birdie's mystery, that make the pull of the unknown more intense, written in a strong hand, calling out. I want to know how and why this man and those with him really died.

'So, what do we do now?' I say.

'We go to see a doctor.'

Chapter 6

Fog. Nothing but fog. Amundsen and his men left Framheim, their home on the Antarctic, without looking back. There was nothing to see. The fog masked the hard edges of the land, the Pole now a far distance away, up across that barrier of ice. They had no wish to return. It was done. Slowly, the *Fram* pushed her way through the icebergs towards the open sea. It was the end of January 1912.

'Tasmania, still?' Nilsen asked Amundsen.

'Yes,' said Amundsen.

'It's further than New Zealand.'

'I don't care. I don't want us to finish our journey where the English started from.'

'They may yet beat us with the news.'

'I know. Even though we beat them to the Pole. That's why I want to land where no one knows us. I'll send my telegrams from Hobart. Get us there quickly.'

Nilsen shrugged and turned his eyes back to the bow. Amundsen was the boss, the governor. What he said must be done. The *Fram*, no longer heavily laden, was nothing more than an upturned walnut shell built to drift through ice. She was not for a sailing race. Nilsen prayed for a favourable wind.

The kind wind never came. The seas were restless. The cold did not ease. A week later they were still surrounded by the ice, an unhappy ship in dangerous waters, and a divided crew. Silence, not songs, filled the vessel. Where was victory now? Jagged tempers. And Amundsen, invisible, alone in his cabin, refining his first message, his story of triumph.

Gradually, too gradually, the endless daylight of the

Antarctic summer shrank into the gentler rhythm of night and day. They left the cold behind and moved into coolness. Then the air grew milder, and after four weeks, they reached the heat. It did nothing to soothe their tempers. Many of the men took their meals separately. They couldn't look each other in the eye.

'Land ahoy!'

March 1912 had just begun.

'At last.' Amundsen threw down the book he had been reading and went on deck. The faint outline of islands shimmered indistinctly in the distance.

'Tasmania?' he asked no one in particular.

'Yes,' Oscar Wisting said. 'We should be there in a couple of days.'

'No sooner?'

'Depends on the weather, you know that.'

'We need to get there quickly. We've spent too long on this damn ocean. The world must know of our achievement, must have proof we got there before the English.'

'Where do you think they are now?'

'Who cares? As long as they're safe. We were there before them. That's all anyone need know.'

'Shouldn't we have left that spare fuel at the Pole? We didn't need it in the end.'

'Maybe. Maybe not.' Irritation in his voice. 'It's not important now. Getting to land is.'

'A few more days, skipper; just a few more days.'

'I pray it is so.'

That night, the heat brought a hurricane. It swept the small ship back out to sea. Next morning, there was no land in sight. Another hope was defeated, and more time wasted. Amundsen started planning his next voyage. He would go north this time.

And so it went for days, the explorer trying, with steam and sail, to beat the elements. Nature, never appeased, relented for some hours, until land was in sight, and then the storms rose again to drive him away from his wish.

Amundsen, fiercer than ever, more silent than ever, grew more impatient, more desperate, a fire burning in the heat of the Southern hemisphere. The Pole would not be conquered until the world knew about it, until King Haakon knew Amundsen and his men had planted that red, white and blue flag into the foot of the Earth. No one need know more than that.

The sixth day of March dawned, the sixth day of waiting for land to be within reach. And then the storm came again. It blew them along Tasmania's coast, past Hobart, like a dried-out leaf in the wind of drought, tore sails, splintered a mast.

'Will this never stop?' Amundsen screamed at the mirror. 'I want my reward. My soul for my reward. My life, even.'

Silence. No wind. No smack of water against wood. No swell of sea or sky. Amundsen rushed to the bridge.

'Full steam ahead. Now,' he shouted. 'I won't be stopped this time.'

Five hours later, they dropped anchor off the coast. Finally.

At noon, a boat drew up to the *Fram*'s side. The local doctor's boat. The pilot and his customs officials scrambled up the rope ladder. Amundsen was waiting for them, his face fresh from shaving.

'Any news of the English?' he snapped.

'No, sir,' the pilot answered.

'Good. Let's go.' He grabbed his briefcase, danced down the ladder, and jumped into the boat. He glared at the other boats beginning to gather. 'Get rid of them,' he shouted up at Wisting. 'Don't let them on board.' He pointed at the men with notepads. 'Go away.'

An hour later, Amundsen unlocked the door of a room in the Hotel Orient. He threw his case onto the bed, ripped off his tie, and sat down in front of the desk. He wrote, in code, a note addressed to his king, a note to his patron, Axel Heiberg and, finally, a note with instructions to his brother Leon.

He dressed as an ordinary sailor and wandered, unrecognised, to Hobart's telegraph office, from where he had the coded messages sent. To avoid questions, he paid in coins, gave the exact change, muttered his thanks in broken English. He longed to be amongst his fellow countrymen again, to speak a proper language.

Back at the hotel, Amundsen lay down on his bed and closed his eyes. What now? Would he ever meet Scott? Would they ever become friends and laugh about their Antarctic race? He hoped so, and regretted having refused to meet the man in Oslo before the race had begun. He had been afraid to share their common goal, had kept his desires secret. Would it have been better to share the glory? He doubted it. He wouldn't have wanted to. At last, after five weeks of wakefulness, sleep grabbed him and wrapped him in its warm comfort, forgiveness even.

In Norway, Leon Amundsen decoded the message. *Pole reached, fourteenth to eighteenth December last year. All is well.* The world was theirs. At last.

Fog, nothing but fog.

When the flying boat took off from Tromsø late that June afternoon in 1928, the sun was shining weakly into the cockpit. Warmth and blurred shadows. For once, Amundsen smiled. He was going out into the wilds again, to rescue an enemy from the cold of the Arctic ice floes. He would own the world again.

Motionless in his seat, he watched the land drop away from them as the plane lifted away from the fjord. There were five others with him. He was confident they would succeed in rescuing the marooned Italian, Nobile, from the ice where his airship had crashed. What could stop them? Just like nothing had been able to stop his victory at the Pole.

His smile faded. Scott had won, ultimately, he reflected.

By dying and leaving behind all those fine words in journals the world had devoured, writing about himself and his courageous companions, every English gentleman would be proud of him. Scott had won by not coming back, by being a better writer than he, the explorer. The irony of it. Nothing mattered any more, nothing had ever mattered. All achievement was empty, all glory vain. Life had no meaning.

Amundsen bit back a sigh. How dearly he would have liked to smoke now they were at last up here in the air, away from all that threatened him. But he had left his broken lighter with his chemist friend in Tromsø, telling him he no longer needed it. What had possessed him to do that? His mood darkened. He couldn't speak with the four Frenchmen flying the plane. Nor could he speak with the one other Norwegian on board. There was nothing left to say. And he would not share his secrets.

Then the fog came. The sun just went out. No longer could they see where they were going, and their instruments weren't telling them. The drone of the engines fluttered. The plane shifted. They tried to settle it back into a pattern but couldn't. The turbulence increased. Gossamer demons smashed at the windshield. The noise of the buffeting was louder than the engines. They stuttered again, stalled, stopped.

'Hold on,' shouted Dietrichson.

'Try to start them again,' called Amundsen. 'Pull her up, pull her up.'

'I can't.'

'Let me try.' Amundsen was on his feet now, the old man with the need to be in control, always in control. He should never have trusted these people, should never have agreed to fly out in this wooden thing they all knew wouldn't survive a crash into the biting Arctic seas. He pushed Guilbaud out of the way, cared not that the man couldn't understand a word he was saying. He snatched at the instrument panel. Nothing. No response. He pulled at the joystick. Nothing, again. He turned to the others and shrugged.

'We will have to swim,' he said in English, and laughed. No one laughed with him.

They all survived the crash. All came through the sudden cacophony of noise in a sea of silence. There were no screams. The plane was in pieces, and they clung to those pieces they could grab hold of. The fog reached down into the water, the sun somewhere behind it, so close to the longest day. It was never dark here at this time of the year, but cold, so cold.

They scrambled up out of the sea, shivering by now. They tried to fashion one of the plane's floats into a life raft, but their freezing hands were useless. Their strength ebbing, they huddled together on the slippery surface of fragmented wood, but nothing would bring them warmth. One by one, they stopped breathing, slumped forward, and slid towards the remorseless sea. He could not hold them all. He had to let go, until only he and Dietrichson were left.

'No ... no hope,' Dietrichson stammered.

'Always hope, always,' Amundsen said quietly.

Dietrichson didn't answer. He fell onto his back, slowly. Amundsen closed the dead man's eyes, as gently as his shivers would allow. He wrapped himself into his wet clothes and lay down. There was no point fighting now. Is this what Scott had felt in his last moments? He looked up into the nothingness of the fog. All he could do was wait for his night to come. All he could hope for was freedom from pain.

Pictures rushed across his vision. His ships. His men. The white plains of the south. The desolation. The black tent they had pitched. The bright red of his flag. He stopped shivering. Scott stepped into his dying dream. Maybe they could be friends now. Amundsen raised his hand in welcome.

Chapter 7

So here I am in hospital, on an exercise bike, with a clip on my nose and a tube in my mouth. I'm puffing and panting, and some young bloke's checking my pulse every minute or so. My chest is sore. They shaved some of the hair off so the electrodes don't come loose. In front of me, a screen shows my heartbeat. This is ridiculous. And all because of her. This is what a man in love will do. Even if it's unrequited.

It's four weeks since we met. I've spent a lot of time at her place in those four weeks, reading those books in her library. Trying to sort out audits with accountants. Cooking for her in a kitchen I don't think she's ever used. Meeting a load of uninteresting people as part of my work. Meeting a load of people who wouldn't know passion if it snuck up on them and hit them in the face.

But I've not got any closer to her in that time. There's a distance between us that's difficult to explain, difficult to quantify. She's out in front of her canvases when I'm reading, and when I'm cooking. One minute she's all sweetness and light, the next minute she's hyper. And the next she moves so slowly it's difficult to understand how she has the energy to paint or to be obsessed. She jumps from one extreme to the other without transition, without warning.

I never stay there overnight. I sleep at John's place during the week, not always drinking too much and, strangely, not always talking about her. But when we do, he warns me. He tells me I'm being a fool, that I'm getting myself in too deep and trusting too much in someone I know little about.

Yet I go back to her every day. Sometimes it's early in the

morning, if I've got no meetings. Sometimes it's in the afternoon, and sometimes late in the evening, just for an hour, just to inhale her scent, to be somewhere close to her, just to be there. Because I'm addicted to her, to her tempers, to her obsession. But I don't have the will or the courage to bring things to a head. I'm content just to let it drift, to see where it might lead. I'm a tree bending with the wind.

Scott's diary has left a deep impression on me. I still think we should try to steal it, but she tells me it's not important. It's more important to get all these tests out of the way, she says. Why? Because that's what'll get us down to the Ice, as she's taken to calling it. Because she's applied to the New Zealand government to go down there. They run some programme called Artists to Antarctica that's meant to encourage people to create Antarctic art, that's supposed to raise awareness of Antarctica everywhere.

'What's the point?' I say.

'What do you mean what's the point?' she answers. 'Isn't it obvious? The more art we create about it, the more people will understand about the place and its history.'

'And?'

'So the more people understand, the more they'll be interested.'

'In going there?' I say.

'No, in understanding. I don't want more people to go down there.'

And so it goes on, until she convinces me that it'll be fine. Or at least until she thinks she's convinced me. I still don't like the idea of flying down there. Oh yes. She persuades me to go down there, too. The things love makes us do.

'What do you mean, you've got a place for me, too?' I say. 'That easy, is it?'

'Not really. But I applied for an assistant to go with me in the first place.'

'But who were you going to take?'

'I hadn't worked it out. I knew someone would turn up.'

'But why?'

'No way that I can do all this on my own. There had to be someone else.'

'So I could've been anyone, then, could I?'

'Well ... yes ... sort of.' She blushes. 'But I'm glad it's you.'

That's the first explicit sign of any kind of affection. Actually, there's not been much since. The past few weeks we've been filling in all sorts of obscure forms for the folks in New Zealand, and we've spent Lord knows how much each on these health checks. And even then it's not certain we'll get accepted onto the programme. It's all like shooting in the dark – with blanks.

We arranged to meet here this morning. I got here early, as usual. I'm early for everything. I stood outside the hospital chain-smoking, and, when there were only five minutes to go till our appointments, I texted her to let her know I was already here. Her text back simply told me to 'chill'. Great. Anyway, they'd put aside a room for us where we could leave our stuff. They'd arranged consecutive appointments for us. First to the doc for a general chat, then eye tests, then blood tests, then the cardiac tests. And then back to the doc, still just in shorts and T-shirt, to discuss the results of the bloods – which included a test for HIV. What's the point of that? Who the hell are you going to give HIV to when you're freezing to death? You're not exactly going to be feeling frisky, are you?

The doctor makes himself comfortable in his old chair and adjusts his tweed jacket. He tells me he moved here when he was twenty, over forty years ago, from Iraq. He'd always wanted to go back to his family, but couldn't. The troubles, you see – like your Ireland, just worse. I nod. What a dreadful life, to be in exile for forty years. I warm to him. I like the rhythm of his voice, the scratchy singsong of his language. He looks weary and sad. Anything else is irrelevant for the half-hour he talks to me.

And at the end of that little oasis of time in the middle of the rushing, he tells me that I'm fine. Not in bad shape for a man who smokes too much and drinks too much.

'Everything in moderation,' he says, as he shakes my hand. A good firm handshake, too. He smiles at me. 'Always in moderation.'

'I'll try,' I say, and hate lying to him. 'Thank you.'

Birdie's waiting for me, back in the windowless cubicle they gave us. She hasn't changed back into street clothes yet. It's the most naked I've ever seen her, but it's not very naked. And most of her is hidden by the Formica-topped table she's sitting behind. She doesn't stop reading when I open the door.

'And?' she asks me. 'What did he say?'

'He said I'm fine.'

'Nothing else?'

'Nope.'

'Same here.' She looks up. 'But he took a long time to say it.'

'He's homesick. And sad. And lonely.'

'Oh well.'

'You're heartless.'

'Just practical. I don't want to get sidetracked.' She loses some of her beauty now. Her face hardens, and the warmth goes out of her eyes, replaced by a cold fire. I'm appalled that she doesn't care. Is this what she's really like deep down? A hardness of soul that's unattractive, repulsive, even. But I'm soft, too soft. So I let it pass and just burble on regardless.

'And now what?'

'We send the forms to New Zealand, along with the reports they're printing off out there. And then we wait.'

'How long for?'

'Who knows? Does it matter?'

'Well, yes, sort of. What do I tell the people I work with?'

'Don't tell them. It's none of their business. Anyway, nothing's going to happen for a while yet.'

'I've got to plan this.'

She throws the papers onto the table and jumps up. She grabs me by my shirt and shakes me. 'Why are you so up yourself?' she shouts. 'Can't you just relax and enjoy yourself? What is it with you?'

She pushes me up against the examination couch in the corner of the room. She's damn strong for her size. I can feel her heat against me. I feel myself reacting to her. She rubs up against me. No, I mustn't. This is base. It's not what I intended, not here, not now. I grab her by her shoulders, hold her at arm's length, and slow my breathing.

'What the hell are you playing at?' I shout back at her. 'I thought you didn't want any distractions. Thought you only had time for this obsession of yours. And now this.'

She tries to wriggle out of my grasp, but I'm stronger than her this time.

'Sorry.' She's turned back into her scolded girl alter ego. 'I don't know why I did that. You just annoy me sometimes. I wanted to shake you up a bit.'

'That's not fair. You know I care for you. You've known all along. One day you're telling me blokes are just after one thing, and then you try it on. It doesn't make sense.'

She says nothing. She's not even looking at me.

'Listen, Birdie, I'm too old for this. If I'm going to be with someone now, it's got to be lasting, not just a quick fling type thing. I can't do that anymore.'

'Fine,' she says. 'Let's go.'

She gathers her clothes and disappears into the toilet. I just pull my stuff on over my shorts and shirt, and leave before she comes out again. I've had enough of this. She's too confusing, too hurtful, too dangerous.

Christmas comes and goes. I spend it alone, like I have the last three. I actually enjoy being on my own. It makes me feel free. I can choose to do what I want when I want. I have Christmas lunch at the pub in the village. It's not the best meal in the world, but it does me. And then I go for a long walk over the fields. Crisp sunshine follows me, and my shadow has sharp edges. I'm actually quite happy for once.

The months pass. Birdie doesn't get in touch with me. I don't try to call her. It's over as suddenly as it began. I don't care about the money I spent at the hospital. At least I know I'm as healthy as can be expected. Do I care about not seeing her? Difficult to say. Do I regret not taking her up on the offer of her body? No, not in the least. Sex for its own sake is all very well, but not with someone you think you're in love with. The moment I set eyes on her, I knew it would have to be forever, or not at all, not just a quickie in a consultation room in a hospital in London.

So life resumes its comfortable monotony. And there is a comfort in routine. It protects you from yourself. It numbs you to the pain of others around you. It's warm and familiar, like a pair of old socks. It doesn't surprise you, and it leaves you time to waste time. It is a joy. There's just one thing, though. It has no colour.

Of course I don't forget her. I love her, don't I? And I've been bitten by her bug. I carry on buying books about Antarctica. I read them. I read *The Worst Journey in the World* twice, three times, fascinated by Cherry and his deep friendship with Bowers and Wilson, his profound grief at losing them, his desperate wish to immortalise them. It makes me cry over and over again. I read pro-Scott books. I even read Roland Huntford's anti-Scott books. I read pro-Amundsen books, anti-Amundsen books. Books that obviously know what they're talking about. Books that obviously don't have a clue. And then I sleep. I sleep a lot. I'm waiting for spring. Because I hate the winter. I hate being cold and tired. But I like sitting by the fire on grey and miserable days, because I always hope tomorrow will be brighter. And that maybe someday my life will have a meaning.

I've started reading *Worst Journey* for the fourth time. Today has been truly rotten. I had to go down to London and back in a day. Four hours on the train for two one-hour meetings, meetings that achieved nothing. But I did make time to go to the British Library to have a look at the diary again. Does that mean I'm obsessed? I can't judge. It's just something to do. Or that's what I tell myself.

The fire's just got going. The evening is a gloom of cold and tiredness. The light from the flames colours Cherry's book a pale yellow. The words make their own shapes in my mind. I lose myself in a different world again. I dance to the tune of an explorer's voice.

I answer my phone without looking at the number on the display.

'Yes?'

'Adam?'

'Birdie?'

'We got our places.'

'What?'

'We got our places.'

'Are you mad?' I can't believe this. 'How can you call me after three months as if nothing had happened? It's all done and dusted. All finished.'

'I thought you'd be over it by now.'

'You're mad.'

'And I'm outside your front door.'

I get up, walk through the house, and open the front door. There she is, with her big coat and her boots, her phone in one hand and a bottle of champagne in the other. She smiles. I can't not let her in. She hands me the bottle.

'A peace offering,' she says. 'I'm sorry for being an arsehole. I get carried away sometimes.'

'I know,' I say. And let her kiss me. She doesn't just smell of lemons. She tastes of them, too.

Chapter 8

'I went to Scott Polar,' she says over breakfast.

'Find anything new?'

'I got hold of Henry's diary. It was exciting.' She glows. 'I wish I could've shared it with Dad.'

'Didn't he ever think of going to SPRI himself before you were old enough?'

'Oh, but he did go, ages ago. It's not the same, though, reading his notes. I wanted to hold that diary myself, turn the pages, sniff it.' She sighs. 'But even so, it was a bit disappointing.'

'Why?'

'It's just a load of loose pages, not notebooks, not like Scott's. I think Dad got more excited than me.' She shrugs. 'It's like Henry's got more charisma in other people's stories than in his own.'

'He wasn't a writer.'

'I guess not.'

'Where are your dad's notes, by the way?'

'At the house. I just didn't get round to showing them to you.'

'You mean you couldn't bring yourself to share them, really, don't you?'

'I suppose so.' The glow turns into a blush.

'It's all right, you know.' I reach across the table, flatten my fingers on the cool, smooth wood. 'Nothing wrong with having feelings.'

'It's weak,' she says. 'And mean sometimes. I don't want to inflict what I feel on people, despite how I seem.' She plays with her spoon. 'And now you think I don't trust you.'

'Rubbish. I can understand why you'd want to keep your dad's things to yourself. They're a part of you. They're the bond between him and you. Simple, really.'

I get up to put the dirty dishes into the dishwasher. It's bright outside.

'Anyway, what did Henry's pages smell of?'

'Museum. Nothing more exciting than that. Unfortunately.'

'Anything else?' I sit down again, strangely at home in this odd kind of domestic bliss.

'I saw that letter of Wilson's everyone keeps going on about. The one with Henry's note on the back.'

'The one Huntford thinks proves he was the last one to die?'

'Yes. Although I don't think it proves anything.'

'Neither do other people. Huntford doesn't actually mention it in his book. Just surmises on who was the last to go, with nothing to support it.'

'No. And, anyway, I'm not really that interested in who died last. What I want to find out is why they were stuck in the same place for ten days. The blizzard explanation just doesn't cut it for me.'

'Come on then,' I say. 'Explain to me exactly what you think did happen.'

'I don't know.'

'You must have some idea.'

'I told you when we met. If we find the tent and the bodies, we'll be closer to finding an answer.'

'But how are you going to find the tent?' I ask. I hold my hands up to stop her interrupting. 'And if, by some fluke, you do find it, how are you going to uncover it?' She's bursting to answer, but I hold my hands up again. 'And have you got a permit from the authorities to get anywhere close to where you think it might be?'

'I don't need one.'

'What?'

'There's no Antarctic government. Theoretically anyone with enough cash can just go out there and do what they want.' She looks round the kitchen. 'Within reason, I suppose.'

'Yes, but you're there courtesy of the New Zealand government. They're bound to put restrictions on you.'

'I'll cross that bridge when I come to it.'

I shake my head. 'You're unbelievable. You're going to lie to them, aren't you?'

'Maybe,' she shrugs. 'But, listen … finding the tent. That's where you come in.'

'What?'

'I've got hold of some numbers on how quickly people reckon the ice moves, has moved, since 1912. I've also managed to get hold of all the weather records that exist.'

'OK.'

'So we've got the numbers. We've got the 1912 positions of One Ton depot and of where they died, so couldn't you write a program to work out where the tent would be now?'

'Someone must have done that, surely.' I don't tell her I've started working on it already, just to keep myself busy. And I've done research into temperatures, ice flow, all that lovely science.

'Not that I know of.'

'It must be relatively easy to do.'

'That's what I thought.'

'But there are a lot of imponderables, too.'

'Like what?' she says.

'OK. How do you know there haven't been any massive freeze-and-thaw cycles in the time when nothing was recorded? They'd affect the flow of the ice. And the snowfall. The tent could've dropped down into the ice during a thaw, and then have been frozen into blue ice during the winter. And if parts of the tent froze or thawed at a different rate, the whole thing, including the bodies, could have been ripped apart.'

62

'Yuk.' She pretends to throw up.

'Very funny,' I say. 'But it screws up your idea.'

'Not really. It just means everything's possible. And, anyway, I don't think that would have happened. The tent's too small an area for bits of it to freeze at different speed.'

'Is it?'

'It doesn't matter, Adam. We're still going.'

'I love your certainty.'

'So do I.'

'OK, OK. Assuming I can write the program you want, assuming the tent is found –'

'We will find it.'

'Assuming you get to where my program says you should go.'

'*We* should go ...'

'Whatever. Taking all that as read, how are you going to shift twenty or thirty metres of compacted snow?'

'It won't necessarily need shifting.'

'Eh?'

'It might not need to be shifted,' she says.

'Why?' She's in dreamland again, I think.

'If we're going to use ground-penetrating radar to find it, any pictures we take of it might tell us everything we need to know.'

'How d'you work that out?'

'I didn't. I'm just guessing.'

'That's not very scientific, is it?'

'I'm not a scientist. I'm a painter.'

'That doesn't mean anything.'

'Look, Adam, it's not important. I can feel we're going to find what we need to find.'

She stares at me. That stare challenges me. She gets up and walks round behind my chair. I don't move. She puts her arms round me, burying me in her warmth. Kisses the top of my head.

'About last night,' she whispers.

'I'm sorry.'

'You shouldn't be.'

'Shouldn't I? It was just that I couldn't –'

'You could,' she says. 'You could. You just didn't want to.' She hugs me again. 'In a good way, though.' There's doubt in her voice, for once.

'What?'

'You did the right thing. I can't promise to love you forever, I can't even promise to love you. But you didn't make me feel bad. And you wouldn't, never would be able to. You made me feel good instead. It's like ...'

'Like?'

'Like I'm more than just a thing. Men I've known, they've just treated me like a toy, something to have, to play with, to own for themselves.'

'You're not exactly backward in coming forward. And don't take this the wrong way, but they'd probably say the same.'

'I'd never thought of that.' She laughs. 'It's more difficult than you think. When I paint, when I'm in that mood where nothing can stop me, I can't control my tempers. They're automatic, instinctive. But love isn't an instinct. Not for me, anyway. It scares me. I don't mind losing control, but I'm afraid of hurt and blame and the regret they bring.'

I unhook her arms from my shoulders. I stand and turn, put my arms around her. She buries her face in my shirt. She's trembling. She's a frightened little child. Does my strength of affection frighten her? Right now, I'd do anything for her, anything, just not that. It's not what she needs. It's not what I need. I hold her as tightly as I can. We stand like that for what seems like a lifetime.

'I *will* come with you,' I finally say. 'And this time I mean it. I was wrong to walk out on you like that. It was unkind. I'm sorry.'

'I'm the one who should be sorry,' she says. 'It's me who was unkind and thoughtless. But I can only think in one dimension sometimes. Not like in my pictures. My mind can go off in any direction there. That's when I'm free. Things make sense in them. Nothing makes sense out here. It's all too confusing and complicated. Too real and dangerous. And in my pictures there's silence. Total and utter silence. Nothing to disturb me. Nothing can hurt me.'

'Shhh ... shhh.' I stroke her face with the palm of my hand. 'There's nothing here to hurt you either.'

'I know that. I know.' She looks up at me, tears rolling down her face.

'You're safe here,' I say. 'You always will be.'

'But I can't love you back like that, not so totally.'

'That's not important now.' Although I wish she could. 'There's time. To be here for you is enough. That's all you need from me right now, nothing else.'

I can't help thinking she's going to forget what she's said and snap back at me any minute. That she'll forget the tears and the need for comfort, and bite back at me with that insane Birdie grin and sharpened voice. But she doesn't. She just nods and hugs me back, and doesn't let go. Until she pushes me away.

We go for a long walk under a sun that promises spring. We talk about everything and nothing, about the trip, about the scent of the wind, about the huge skies of Suffolk and their cathedrals of clouds. We laugh and shout, run around like children. We hold hands. We walk apart. We watch birds wheel and drift in the blue shards of sky. We say nothing, and walk without words. That's enough.

Back home, we sit on the bench in my tiny back garden. I ask her, 'Why can't you always be this relaxed?'

'Because the weather's not always this nice. I know I was born in November, but I hate the winter here. It's too damp.'

'I know what you mean.'

I breathe in. It's good when it's like this.

'Listen, Adam ...' Her voice wavers slightly.

'I'm listening.'

'There's just one more thing ...'

'Yes?'

'About this trip.'

'Spit it out.'

'It's not quite what I made it out to be.'

'What?'

'That artists' programme ... well, it's only for artists from New Zealand. I sort of used it as a ruse to persuade you to come with me.'

'What does that mean, exactly?' I'm not really surprised. She's capable of anything.

'It means I persuaded people over there to let us make the trip. I mean, the medicals were still necessary, but it's not like we're on an official project or anything like that.'

'Does that change anything?'

'Not really-ish.' She screws up her face and makes strange little hand movements. Tries to suppress a grin. Not very successfully.

'You're funny,' I say. I reach out to her and lace my fingers with hers.

Darkness comes again too soon.

Chapter 9

All they found of Oates were his sleeping bag and his boots, cut open down to the ankle to make room for his swollen, frozen, gangrenous feet – to carry his disintegrating body. Until the snow had taken him. Enveloped him in its white mercy. At last.

The searchers had marched thirteen miles in two days. Exhausted by the cold, the journey, and their grief, they managed only a few more miles before Atkinson decided to turn back. There was no point searching for a dead man, no point walking on. They had been lucky enough to find the Owner's tent. This was the furthest they would come this time. In any case, they had to get back to the hut at Cape Evans. There was another party of men, hopefully still alive, to look for, lost in the north. And the ship would be back soon, the *Terra Nova*, to take them home. None of them wanted to spend a third winter on this cruel continent, however foreign home might be when they finally got there.

So they built a cairn for Oates where they had come to a standstill, roughly where the diary had told them he had walked out of the tent to his death. They put a cross on the cairn and wrote another elegy to another fallen comrade. *Hereabouts died a very gallant gentleman* … Atkinson and Cherry signed the note, then tied it to the cross against the rapacious wind. The men bowed their heads. They turned northwards into the gale and walked away. Another hard march to come.

With nothing to hold them, they forced themselves over those thirteen miles in one day, and set up camp within sight of the grave cairn. Cherry tried to draw it in his notebook, but his hands were too cold in the blizzard. He retreated to the tent he shared with Wright. They had to rest if they wanted to survive. The tent chores were finally done three hours later. Men slowed down in the cold. Once wrapped in their bags, they tried to sleep.

'Did you hear that?' Wright asked Cherry.

'I thought it was your breath freezing,' Cherry answered.

'And I thought it yours.'

They didn't move. Instead, they held their breath.

'Gone,' Cherry said.

It began again, a low whisper. It was not from the wind, nor from any movement of the tent's cloth. A wave of mumbled sounds arose, shapes of jumbled words, not quite clear enough to make out, a rising, falling murmur, a gentle flow.

'Whatever it is,' Cherry said, 'it doesn't sound frightening or afraid.'

'It feels contented and calm.'

'I hope they are at peace now. I dearly hope so.'

'I'm sure they are, my friend. I'm sure they are.'

'Should we get up and see where it's coming from?'

'I don't think there would be any point,' Wright said. 'We wouldn't be able to locate it, even if it did exist.'

'But it would be so wonderful to see them.'

'I fear we would become them if we ventured out now.'

'Maybe that would be best.'

'And what of our futures?'

'I believe you were meant to write their story, not bury it with them.'

'Will they still talk to me at home?'

'What do you think?'

'I would rather stay here with the sound of their voices.'

'And who will tell their story then?'

'There are many of you who could.' Cherry started to undo his sleeping bag.

'No, Cherry, for the love of God, don't go out there.' Wright put his hand on his friend's shoulder. Held him back.

'I won't be long.'

'You wouldn't last long either, even though it's spring.'

'But –'

'Listen, Cherry, you need to tell your story, too. You're the only one left alive who walked to Cape Crozier in the dark.'

'I suppose I need to deliver those eggs, too,' Cherry said. 'I'd forgotten about them.'

'You see, there is a reason for you to go home. You have to.'

'But I shall never come back here, and I shall miss them. This place no longer seems so woeful with their voices in the air.'

'They've stopped now.' Wright sighed. Tried not to show his relief. 'We can sleep again.'

'I hope you're right. I don't think I shall ever sleep well again.'

Wright said nothing.

'You know, I have heard those voices before,' Cherry went on.

'Oh?' Wright murmured.

'When I was at One Ton with Dimitri, for the entire six days. As soon as we got there, I started to listen. It was like a song, yes, like a song of home and remembrance, and celebration. And we were only eleven miles from them.' He swallowed hard. 'It came to us on the wind. From the south. It swirled and rose and dipped, and the words were as unintelligible as they are now. It was the wind, the voices were the wind. They were the blizzard. And I don't mean I mistook the wind for voices. They literally were the wind. The blizzard was a blizzard of voices. The song of all songs.'

And still Wright said nothing.

'I should have followed them there and then, should have gone on, past One Ton, past here. I should have met them as they walked in.'

'You had orders not to.'

69

'The orders were unclear. The instructions were not to overwork the dogs in case Scott needed to make another attempt on the Pole. They didn't mention the possibility of using them for a rescue. I should have ignored the orders.'

'I don't believe you would have come back. You would have been here with them for us to find. You could not have saved them, I am sure.'

'What a strange thing to say.'

'But you feel the same, Cherry, don't you? You've said so already. And it is not just because you think the voices are theirs. It's so difficult to pull yourself, ourselves, away from them, from this. Like the Song of the Sirens. There must have been something. You heard those voices when Bill Wilson and Birdie and the Owner were still alive.'

'I suppose I did. I hadn't thought of that ... So I can stop blaming myself?'

'I don't think you ever had reason to blame yourself.'

'But then who are the Sirens?'

'I wish we knew.'

'The dead will tell us.'

'We cannot afford to listen to the dead.'

'Perhaps they will listen to us,' Cherry said. He closed his sleeping bag again. Wrapped himself into its damp half-warmth.

'I don't think we will ever find out what happened here,' Wright said. 'And maybe it is for the best.'

'Perhaps.'

Cherry said nothing more. Wright forced himself to stay awake until he was sure his friend was asleep. That he, too, should feel the pull of those unexplained sounds surprised him. Perhaps science didn't have all the answers, after all. Perhaps it never would, never could.

The next morning, the two men didn't mention their conversation to the others. They didn't talk about it to each other either. When their eyes did meet, they shrugged quietly, smiled. Wright hoped that they would not need to talk of it again. He didn't think he would have the strength to pull Cherry back from the abyss again, was afraid he would not be able to resist, either. It was so tempting just to lie in the cold and listen, and drift and fall asleep. He was glad Atkinson was driving them as hard as he could, in his hurry to get back to the hut, relieved when Atkinson asked him to lead the caravan. He had to concentrate so hard on steering straight through the blinding snow towards the drifting horizon it was impossible for him to think of anything else. But then another blizzard caught them and stopped them in their tracks.

'Have you heard them again?' Cherry asked when they were alone in the tent, the wind raging outside.

'I think I may have.'

'So have I. But I keep repeating to myself what you said.'

'Thank you.'

'You have nothing to thank me for. You saved me, not I you.'

'I fear for us, Cherry, all of us. If we don't get back, if we miss the ship, who will know then that the Pole was conquered by us, too?'

'Does it matter?'

'What if Amundsen didn't get back to his base? What if he died, too? Then all our efforts will have been in vain.'

'But we have the letter to his king he left at the Pole for Scott to find.'

'How fortunate Gran discovered it in that boot we were going to throw away.'

'How uncharitable of Amundsen to make Scott his messenger boy.'

'Do you think he did it out of spite?'

'I can't be sure.'

'I don't think he did. That would have been an unkindness beyond any human.'

'Perhaps.'

'Let's make sure we get home,' Wright said.

71

'We will. I am sure of that now. Thank you again.'

'The best way to thank anyone is to write that book.'

'What shall I call it?'

'I don't think that will matter. As long as you tell the truth.'

Two weeks after discovering the bodies of the polar party, Atkinson and his men finally returned to Cape Evans. The lost men from the north had returned by then, too, black-faced after a winter spent in a cave rancid with the smoke of seal blubber. They would not need to be found now. That evening was full of exuberant storytelling and relief. But some of the bunks were empty. And each lull in the celebration was full of the words of the dead.

Cherry searched out the rolls of film they had found with Bowers' body. As he walked past the crowded wardroom table he remembered how they had celebrated Scott's birthday around that table over a year ago. Pennants had livened the space then, and warmth had flooded the hut. That was a different age, free of grief.

At the far end of the hut, Cherry locked himself into Ponting's darkroom. Ponting, the expedition's photographer, had sailed back to England with the ship before the winter had come, before anyone had known for certain that the polar party had perished. But he had left the equipment Cherry needed now.

Some time later, Cherry had developed the film. There were so many things to take in. Bowers had left an almost perfect record of their courage, their success, and their failure. On the bright snow Amundsen's tent loomed, a threatening shadow. In one of the pictures, Wilson was by the entrance of that black tent, tentatively staring into it, as if afraid to enter. And the other three, Scott, Evans and Oates, heads bowed, waiting, not wanting to go any closer to that ... that thing, the first glimpse of which had told them they had lost the race. The sun added to the desolation of that place, fading shadows blurred.

Another picture showed the five of them, all standing, looking beyond the camera, leaning on ski sticks hung with sledging flags. Bowers, penguin-footed on the right, the smallest in stature, the hardest in body; Wilson, bow-legged and looking strong and hopeful, on the left. In between them, Scott, haggard and hunched into the cold; Evans, face almost hidden by his headgear, beard burgeoning; and Oates, arms down, in a posture of quiet resignation.

And yet, thought Cherry, they looked fairly fit. Their clothes were not iced up. They should have made it back. Even across 900 miles of ice and snow, and wind and cold, they should have made it back. He reached out and touched the photographs. Tried to stop himself from crying. They had become his friends, especially Bowers and Wilson. They had given sense to his life, stopped him from drifting. They had accepted him, had praised him, turned him into a better man. And now he was alone again. He wiped the tears from his stinging eyes and took three deep breaths, thankful that the darkroom was soundproof.

Cherry took the pile of photographs, opened the door, and slowly walked to the table. The conversation stopped.

'Here they are,' he said. 'They look so well.'

None of them spoke as the pictures went round the table, each man studying the faces with care and affection. The occasional grunt, the odd sniff, a murmured expression. This was their wake. This was the memorial hour. They would not forget.

'And now?' Cherry asked as the pictures came back to him.

'Now we work on science, and prepare for a third winter here,' Atkinson said.

Chapter 10

She's all edges, although she's wrapped in one of my jumpers and tracksuit bottoms. Edges that wake me. She talks in her sleep, shouts names I know nothing about. She writhes, screams, and kicks angrily. Then she's calm and gentle. Until I begin to fall asleep again. And then the cycle starts over again. I'll be black and blue by morning.

Not that I can really sleep, anyway. This could be the first big adventure of my life. How do you go through so many years without any excitement, or anything significant to remember? It's depressing. I lie in the dark and try to fathom my insignificance, my loss, and my failures. Does any of it make sense, any of what is now past and lost? How many men look back on their life at some point or another, only to realise it's been wasted? Such disappointment. And what then? What can we do to repair our old weaknesses?

I look at her shadow. Is she my redemption? That's silly. She doesn't even love me. She's just here because she feels like it, not because some overriding emotion compelled her to be. What is it with love that always makes us believe in something higher, makes us think there's some noble purpose, some greater meaning? Why do we think love or religion can save us? What if there's nothing out there, no salvation, no gods, nothing but emptiness? Our eyes close, as they all will. Our hearts stop, as they all will. Finished. How could love change that? How could faith? No, there's nothing. That's all there is to it.

So why does it have to be forever, Birdie and me? Is it just my age? Or is it me hoping she'll fall in love with me? Why am I filled with feelings that make me respect her? Even that's a first for me. I can't get it out of my head that this all started with a stupid coincidence, a quirk of timing and nature, that our lives could have totally passed each other by. We'd never have known. It wouldn't have mattered. Life would have plodded its standard course towards my demise. Who'll remember me, anyway?

'D'you know you snore?' She's leaning on her side, those eyes right by mine, those lips parted, warm breath from her on my face, her hair fuzzy, not spiked anymore, the grey light of morning behind her.

'What?'

'You don't sleep very lightly, do you?'

'What do you mean? I hardly slept. You kept me awake with your shouting and cursing and endless moving around.'

'I can't have done. You were asleep every time I woke up.'

'You're weird.'

'So are you.'

'I'm normal and boring.'

'No, you're not.' She reaches out and strokes my hair, for some odd reason. 'I've got to go.' She jumps out of bed.

'It's Sunday.'

'So?'

'What's there to do on a Sunday?'

'Enough.'

She starts to get dressed. I turn away.

'You can look if you want,' she says.

'No.'

'Why?'

'Because I can't.'

She jumps onto the bed, half naked. 'Look at me.'

'I won't.'

'Look at me.' She puts a hand either side of my face, turns my head towards her. 'It's normal to look,' she says.

I stare at the ring through her belly button. She pulls me

towards her. I can't resist her warmth. Nuzzle her stomach. Feel the hard muscle against my lips.

'Higher,' she whispers.

'I thought you had to go.'

'It can wait.'

'So can I.' I break out of her embrace. Sit up. Catch a glimpse of her tiny, perfect breasts.

'See. It's not that difficult, is it?'

I grab her arms and throw her onto her back, kneel over her.

'No, it's not that difficult, Birdie.' I kiss her. 'But I want to resist.' I kiss her again. Make sure I don't touch her naked torso. 'And I will resist until I'm ready.'

She laughs at me.

'How strong you are, Adam. How powerful.' She pretends to try to wriggle out from under me. 'Do it to me. Now.'

'No.'

I get off the bed. She turns onto her stomach and stares at me while I pull a pair of jeans on.

'You're not even changing your boxers? Yuk.'

'I'll shower when you've gone.'

'Are you cross with me again?'

'Not particularly.'

'Not particularly. Nah, nah, nah.'

'Honest.'

'Why?'

'I must be getting used to you and your extremes.'

'Good.'

Ten minutes later she's gone, back to London. And I'm so frustrated I'm throwing books against the wall.

Spring comes and goes.

I tell the people I work with that I'm going on a six-month sabbatical in September. No one questions me. No one insists I can't go. So much for being indispensable. I don't tell anyone where I'm going. But then none of them ask. We're all islands, really, all alone.

Birdie. Birdie. Always back to Birdie. Always back to trying to figure her out. I give up, because there's no working her out. She's unique, unpredictable, tiring, and trying. Some nights we're together, more not. We don't ask each other about the nights apart. I've got nothing to tell. And what she does is none of my business.

It's a quiet time, this. There's no rushing around, just a quiet sense of anticipation. She keeps herself in check. I keep reading, try to figure out what to do with all the data she's given me. I double-check the figures and try to find more info on the net. She carries on painting. It's not always the Antarctic, not always about her obsession. Sometimes it's the graffiti, when she comes back with spray paint on her clothes. Sometimes it's just what's in her mind, when she's compelled to throw a picture into the open from her thoughts. When I go to her house and look at the new canvases, I can see some sense of calm in them; deeper, richer colours, lines less jagged, less abrupt.

It's a lazy time, too, for me. I start turning down work when summer comes. I play more cricket. Who knows when I'll play again? I enjoy standing in the sun, revel in the banter, the carelessness of it all. There's an unreal paradox in chasing a ball around a field when the world's in turmoil, when a friend of mine is killed in Afghanistan and others are losing their jobs, when I'm about to go away for over half a year to the coldest place on earth. Maybe it'll be my last season. I ache for days after every game. I might want to stay south once I get down there. If they let me.

The best part of it is that I've got a secret at last, one I tell no one about. Of course people ask me about Birdie, because that's what people in villages do – ask about everything. It's not really nosiness; it's just them keeping themselves informed about what's going on in their village. I tell them she's just a mate. We make up a name for her – Jasmine; let

77

people think she's some dippy middle-class wannabe. It fits in with the way people probably think of me, too. So all prejudices are satisfied, all stereotypes observed. It's nice and clean that way.

It's a hot summer. I sit in the sun and read Scott's journals. I notice how he grows from someone who uses words in an awkward, almost childish way, into a man who knows how to use his words to the best effect. The power of his writing takes me by surprise, overwhelms me at times. And, in the end, it moves me.

I try again to work out exactly where the tent might be. I come across hypothesis after hypothesis, published paper after scientific paper, and, then, finally, something useful. The ice moves northwards at about 800 metres a year, one kilometre maximum, they think. The tent was located at 79 degrees 50 minutes south, according to the records. Assuming one kilometre a year, it'll be 94 kilometres further north than when it was found. But did it move in a straight line? The thing is, no one knows exactly, and climate change has taken the certainty out of science.

What about the depth of the snow? I still can't figure out why Birdie might ever think of uncovering the thing if we should find it. It would take lots of people and machines to do this. I read on through what I've found. It gets worse. Some people reckon that there's an average 30 centimetres of snow a year, but that the pressure of the weight compacts the layers further down and turns them into ice. So the tent would be encased in ice, not snow. Hard, blue ice. Bollocks. That makes it impossible.

The day after my last game of the season, and my last big – too big – drinking session with the boys, I phone her, shaking with the hangover and depression.

'It's impossible,' I say.

'You sound like shit.'

'I feel like it.'

'Shouldn't drink so much.'

78

'I know.'

'No booze on the Ice.'

'You've told me before.'

'Is that it?'

'I said it's impossible. Even if we find them, we won't be able to get to them.'

'But do you think you've worked out where they might be?'

'To an area of about five kilometres in radius.'

'Can't you get it any more precise?'

'I'm not a miracle worker.'

'Try.'

'I'm sick and tired of going through the same thing over and over.'

'One last try, and then I'll let you come and see me again.'

'Oh, *you'll* let *me*?' I have to laugh, even though it makes me feel sick.

'Yes. *I'll* let *you*. You know what I mean.'

'Whatever … Do you really need me to go through the calculations again?'

'It'll take a week or two to search the area, even if it's down to two kilometres. And I'm not sure how much time we'll have.'

'OK. Just this once. But no more after that. And not today.'

'Fine.'

'And you're ignoring the fact that they'll be frozen into the ice.'

'Doesn't matter.'

'What do you mean, it doesn't matter?'

'Exactly what I say.'

'There's no point if we can't get to them.'

'Let's find them first. Don't be so bloody anal.'

'I'm not. I just don't see the point.'

'There is a point. There will be a point. Just leave it. You're getting hung up over nothing.'

'Thirty metres of ice is nothing?' I say.

'I'll deal with it, I said.'

'Fine. Bye, then.'

'Bye.'

I put the phone down. Back to the spreadsheets and programs, even though I said I wouldn't, back to staring at a screen in a darkened room. Life hasn't changed that much really, has it? I can feel yesterday's sun still burning on my skin, the booze sweating out through it. I should leave the curtains open, really, to let in the sun. Summer won't last forever. But I can't stand the light right now. Strange how happiness leads to excess and regret.

It takes me over a week to get the calculations to point us at a smaller area. And it's all guesswork. Who knows how the ice flows, really? We're not real scientists, not glaciologists. And even they wouldn't know. They don't watch every part of Antarctica all the time. The change in the world's temperature is unpredictable. All this is based on is generalisations and theories. We'll be lucky to find anything.

The sugar beet harvest has started and the leaves are turning red. I like this time of year. Harvest always makes the village seem more alive, reminding me I live in a place where the land is still worked, where the weather determines most people's work cycle, and there's a harmony between nature and people. It makes me a little melancholy.

But I decide, with absolute certainty, I'm going. I'm more nervous than I thought I could be. And I don't know why. This is the twenty-first century, and we're not explorers. We're tourists, and if anything happens, there'll be lots of people and technology on hand to get us out of trouble. So there's nothing to worry about.

When I get to Birdie's house, she's not there.

Chapter 11

I don't like this. She's normally at the door within about half a minute of me ringing the bell. Where the hell can she be? I ring again. Nothing. I'm afraid. Has she changed her mind, decided that, after all this, after all her efforts, I'm not the one she wants to take with her? No, can't be. I texted her when I got on the train. She said she'd be here. What, then? What if something's happened to her? OK, there haven't been any fainting fits lately, but I know she doesn't feed herself properly when I'm not around. What if something's wrong, something bad?

The studio faces onto the main road behind the house, and there's no way for me to get to it from here. I run back the way I've come, towards the traffic, sprint round the corner. The red brick facade of the old factory is covered in graffiti, and the narrow strip of no man's land behind the low fence is unkempt. I vault over it, find an overturned dustbin, push it up against the wall, and climb onto it, puffing and panting. I stand on tiptoes, unsteady, and pull my eyes level with the small window that's up there. It's one of the library windows. I can see all the way through to the studio from here. The world grinds into silence around me. The studio walls are now bare, and there's a small shadow curled up on the floor. It's not moving.

The bin falls over with a clatter as I jump off it. My trousers get snagged on the fence as I try to jump over it again. I ignore the ripping sound and the pain in my leg to race to the front of the house. I try the door. It won't budge. I take a step back and try to shoulder-charge it. And bounce off it. I take more steps back, a proper run-up. I clatter into

81

the door. There's a little crunch, and it shifts, but not enough. Again, I run up and try to hit the door with as much of my side as I can manage. There's more movement this time. It always looks so simple when they do this on the cop shows on telly. One last try. The doorframe splinters, and I'm in.

The silence overpowers me after the noise of breaking in. I slip on the wooden floor as I run through the hall and the kitchen. The shadow's Birdie, a tiny huddle of clothes and limbs. I go down on my knees next to her. I can't see her breathe. I put my ear next to her mouth. All I can hear is my heart pounding. Sweat drips into my eyes. It runs off my nose onto her face. I'm sure she's dead. What ... what? I feel for the pulse in her neck. Oh, there's a flicker there. This isn't the same as catching hold of her when she fainted on the train. How long has she been like this?

As I move her, more of my sweat drips onto one of her closed eyes. Her eyelids move. A rattle climbs up out of her throat. Her eyes open and look at me, vacant. They don't know me. Oh God, oh God, oh God. I put my hands under her back and start to roll her over. She feels really heavy this time. No, no, no. I try not to think.

Once she's on her side, I dial 999 on my mobile. The ambulance will be here in ten minutes, the voice reassures me after I've given the address. And I ask the voice what to do. Just stay with her, it tells me, try talking to her. So I talk. It's the longest monologue of my life. 'Please, please, don't die. I do love you. I want to be with you. I'll do anything you want me to. Listen to me. It's not your time, it's not time to go. You belong here with me. I can't do this on my own. I can't be without you. I need you. You're all I ever wanted. Please, please, please.' Over and over again. But she's incapable of hearing. Although her chest is moving up and down with sharp, fluttering, irregular breaths. Like her body's having to work too hard to keep going, like it could give out any second.

I kiss her forehead. I take her limp hands and stroke their bony fingers. I long for them to have that hard touch about them, that muscular, powerful grip, but they stay still and heavy. I kiss them. I talk to them, to her, to her closed eyes, to her matted hair, to her face. And all I hear is my voice bouncing back at me, because this empty place has become a theatre of echoes.

'Where are you?' A shout from the house.

'In here,' I shout back.

'On our way.'

Just as the paramedics put their cases down next to her, she splutters and shakes. Her arms and legs draw irregular circles on the floor. Her nails scrape crooked shapes into the wood. She heaves and retches. She opens her eyes, and screams. The men are on their knees, trying to hold her down, and trying to calm her. The screaming doesn't stop. Her neck is tight with the effort, the veins rigid along the sides. I can't look, but I have to look. What else can I do? I try to calm her with my thoughts, but I don't think it's working.

'Shhh, shhh, shhh.' I don't even realise I'm saying it and swaying as I say it until the men look at me. And then she stops screaming and looks at me. She's afraid. Her lips move. They form the same shape, over and over again. She tries to sit up. The three of us help her. One of the paramedics straps a blood pressure monitor round her arm. She doesn't resist.

'What's her name?' the other one asks me.

'Birdie.'

'Birdie, can you hear me?' he asks her.

'Mm ... yes ... can.'

'Can you feel your arms and legs?'

''Course,' she slurs.

She stares at me. She doesn't stop staring. She doesn't look at the others.

'Can you lift your arms?' he asks her.

She lifts her arms. The colour starts to come back into her face.

'What day is it today?' he goes on.

'How should I know?' Her voice isn't so slurred now.

'I think we should take you to the ambulance and do a few tests.'

'Fine.'

'D'you think you can walk?'

She shakes her head.

'Blood pressure's fine,' the other guy says. 'I'll go get the chair.'

'Do you want your husband to come with you?'

She shakes her head again.

'I'm not her husband,' I say.

'I suppose you'd best wait here, then.'

I nod. I can't do anything she doesn't want me to. I don't follow when they wheel her away, just lean against one of the empty walls. I can't fathom what's happened to the paintings. Has it got anything to do with her collapse? She can't have been robbed, can she? The front door was locked. Nothing seems to be disturbed. My leg's hurting. I hobble into the library. There's nothing missing here. I shake my head. I wander slowly through to the kitchen, get myself a glass of water, and drink it down in one. Then I fidget with the tap and the glass and pour myself some more water. I can't stand still, can't sit down, can't stay here any longer.

The door's open, so I leave the house to stand next to the ambulance. I listen to the muffled voices, but can't make out what they're saying. I lean against the white metal. The voices carry on speaking. The sun's too hot for me, but I don't feel like moving. Then the back doors open. One of the paramedics climbs down out of the van.

'She's fine,' he says before I've a chance to ask him. 'Low blood sugar. But it's a good job you called us.'

'Anything I can do?'

'Persuade her to eat more.'

'I've been trying.'

'She needs to understand.'

'I'll keep on trying.'

'Best thing you can do is to go get her a couple of bacon and egg sandwiches. They'll boost her sugar better than cakes or anything, and stay in her blood for longer.'

'There's café just down the road.'

'We'll be here for another quarter-hour at least, so you've got time now if you don't want to leave her on her own later.'

'We need to get the bloody door fixed as well.'

'One thing at a time,' he says. 'You can call someone out for the door when we've gone. The sandwiches are more important.'

'OK.'

Less than ten minutes later I'm back. They're still in the ambulance with her. I take the sandwiches into the kitchen. Then I'm by the ambulance again. At last they come out with her. At least they're not having to carry her. They just hold her by the arms as she climbs down.

'I've got sandwiches in the kitchen,' I say.

The paramedics smile. 'Good,' one of them says.

'Just what the doctor ordered,' says the other. 'We'll be off, then.'

'Thanks very much,' I say.

'Nothing to thank us for.'

I take Birdie's arm. 'You all right?'

She nods, tries to smile. The ambulance leaves. The siren goes before it reaches the end of the street.

'I wasted their time, didn't I?' she says.

'Not really. You just need to learn to eat.'

We walk slowly back into the house. I sit her down at the kitchen table.

'You've got to eat those now.' I plonk a glass of water down next to her.

'I'll try.'

'Do more than that.'

I watch her. She almost recoils from the food.

'Birdie, you'll die if you don't get over this attitude to food.'

'I don't really hate it. I just can't be bothered most of the time.'

'Then start being bothered – please.'

I hunt out the phone directory while she tastes her first mouthful. She's still chewing it when I've found someone to come and fix the door.

'You'll have to do better than that.'

She drinks and says nothing.

'They'll be here to fix the door in a couple of hours.'

'Good,' she says and stares at the sandwich as if it were going to attack her.

'Come on – more. You'll love it, after a while.'

'Not sure about that.'

'I am.'

She soldiers on. It takes her almost an hour to eat one sandwich.

'Can I have a little rest?'

'Go on, then,' I say. I sit down next to her. 'What happened to the paintings?'

'Part of the deal.'

'What deal?'

'Us getting out there.'

'Eh?'

'I've given them to the art gallery in Christchurch.'

'What's that got to do with us going down there?'

'There's a charity down there that looks after all the huts on Antarctica. It needs a load of money, mainly for Scott's place at Cape Evans.'

'I know all that.'

'So all the money raised from the exhibition and sales is going to go towards the project.'

'So that's what you meant when you said it was just money.'

'Yes.'

'And you're fine about it?'

'I wouldn't have done it otherwise.'

'I guess not.'

'Do I have to eat this other sandwich?'

'Yes.'

'They taste like shit.'

'But they're good for you.'

'Whatever you say.' She starts eating again.

She eats through the noise and mess of the doorframe being fixed. She doesn't object to me paying for it on my card. She's on her last bite when I close and lock the door.

'Thank God that's done,' she says.

'Yes.'

'Are you angry with me?'

'What about?'

'The paintings. The fainting.'

'I'm worried about you. The paintings aren't any of my business. It's not like you to ask me about something that doesn't concern me.'

'I must be feeling weak.'

'Not surprising, really.'

'I s'pose not.'

'How much are you hoping to raise with the paintings?'

'A million quid, maybe.'

'In New Zealand?'

'Yup. It'll work out.'

'Are they still going to let you go out there?' I say.

'What do you mean?'

'After today.'

'Why not?'

'It's not exactly good health, is it? I'm surprised nothing came up when you did your medical.'

'I made sure I ate lots and told the doctor lies. And there's

87

only a week to go. It's too late for anyone to change anything.'

'And you're happy to go?'

'Why not?'

'It doesn't worry you – today?'

'No. It won't happen again. Adam, I promise ... I'll be a good girl.'

'I've been thinking ...'

'What about?'

'That I've got a week to teach you how to cook.'

'I can do the microwave stuff.'

'I mean properly. Basic stuff, anyway. You're going to have to cook over there. Real food.'

'I'm not a very good learner.'

'It'll be fine.'

That night is the first time since we've been sharing a bed that she doesn't wake me with her kicking and shouting. Instead, I spend most of the night awake listening to her breathing, worried every time it becomes irregular. I lie on my side, stare at her sleeping face in what little light the night gives. I put my hand on her belly, and feel her warmth through the thin shirt, make sure I don't let her take the weight of my arm, and make sure I don't wake her. In her sleep, she burrows the top of her head into my armpit. It makes me strangely happy. Such a simple thing.

I must have fallen asleep. The sun on my face wakes me. She's still asleep. My hand is still on her flat stomach, her face still snuggled up to me. I breathe in. I can't get enough of her scent. I manage to disentangle myself from her. When I look at her, I change my mind about getting out of bed. The warmth is too enticing. When I wake up again, it's almost midday. She's still asleep. This time I do get out of bed and fetch two glasses of juice. By the time I come back, she's awake. Sitting up in bed.

'Drink,' I say.

'Thanks.'

'And then we go shopping.'

'Why?'

'Food. I'll teach you how to cook a decent breakfast.'

Many burnt rashers of bacon later, we sit down to a very late breakfast. It's not bad. And she eats it rapidly.

'Much better when you've done it yourself,' she mutters, egg dripping down her chin.

'Yes.'

'Thanks.'

'You're welcome. When you get married you'll be able to tell the lucky man you owe it all to me.'

'I won't get married.'

I shrug.

'You're an idiot,' she says.

'Let's wash up.'

'I'm not finished yet.

'When you're finished.'

The week passes quickly. Between cookery lessons and shopping tours, she fills the studio with the heavy scent of oil paints again. She starts a handful of new canvasses. So she has something to come back to, she says.

We make sure we've got all the clothes we need, and all the other gear, like sunblock, sunglasses, films, cameras. Everything's packed tight into bags, not suitcases. We drink red wine in the library after she's finished painting for the day, in the gloom after the light has gone. I rejoice in the sound of her voice when I can't see her clearly.

One night we go to see John so I can tell him what I'm planning. For once, he doesn't bluster about my idiocies. He wishes me luck, us both luck. He gives Birdie a hug as we're leaving. 'Take care of him,' he tells her, and winks at me. He likes her. She likes him. I'm relieved.

We leave tomorrow. The bags are downstairs in the kitchen,

and the passports on the table. Everything's sorted. We're all set.

'Are you nervous?' she whispers in the dark.

'A bit. You?'

'Nervous and excited.'

'I ...' I bite my tongue.

'I like you, too.'

She kisses me and turns over.

Chapter 12

Kathleen Scott was a sculptress, a mother, a wife, but, most of all, an independent woman. She was determined to travel to New Zealand to meet her husband after he had returned from the South Pole. All her plans were made. No news was good news. No news was no cause for concern. All was well.

Kathleen Scott was leaving her boy. She kissed him. When she felt the tears coming, she shooed him off to play with grandmother, and then quietly let herself out of the house in Henley. To start her journey from Liverpool to America and then to New Zealand. Christmas had just passed, 1913 just begun. England was mired in the January fog. The statues in her studio in London stood unfinished, gathered cold dust.

By the time she reached New York, she was reconciled with the fact that her Robert hadn't been first to the Pole. She even attended a dinner for Amundsen. There were no storm clouds on the horizon. She spent a week with cowboys on a ranch near the Grand Canyon, rounding up cattle and cooking cornbread. All the while she thought of her Robert, her Con, as she called him, her bird of prey, her handsome Falcon. All was well. And always would be. Let the world mutter. She loved him.

The men at Cape Evans were worried. January was nearly at its close, and there was still no sign of the *Terra Nova*. They had started again with the killing of seals to give themselves sufficient stocks for a third winter. But nature was having her say again, too, for the wild animals had learned to shun the men by now, and each kill grew more meagre.

To pass the time, they organised expeditions to

Shackleton's hut at Cape Royds, where they could feast on buttered Skua gull eggs, be scientists again and observe the penguin colony. It was from here they climbed the smoking Mount Erebus and nearly lost their lives in one of the volcano's many unannounced eruptions.

But now they were all back at the hut at Cape Evans as the first anniversary of Scott reaching the Pole passed. 17 January 1913, and still no ship, and the smell of winter in the air. What if the ship had sunk? Who would save them then? They would not be able to live out their natural lives on this frostbitten patch of the world. Cherry and Wright sat together outside after all the others had retired to their beds.

'What if no one comes?' asked Cherry.

'Then we must make the best of this place for winter. I'm sure another ship will come if there is no news of us in six months.'

'Are you sure?'

'Why shouldn't I be? We can't just be left here. No one even knows the Owner is dead. The government would come to his rescue. Mrs Scott would see to that.'

'Maybe they don't want us to leave.'

'Have you heard them again?'

'I have talked to them every night, even if I cannot hear them. I have dreamed of them – and heard them singing in my dreams,' Cherry added.

'Just our five?'

'No, no. I have seen whole hosts of men and women and children dancing across the ice. Smiling, smiling, always smiling. With open arms.'

'And waking?'

'My friend, I don't know whether I'm awake or asleep anymore.'

'You will sleep better in the dark when it comes.'

'And you, Charles?'

'Not for a while, though sometimes I think I hear a word

or two and begin to listen. But then there is nothing but silence.'

'I hope the ship comes soon. I want to go home.'

'Maybe next week.'

That night they slept uneasily; mindful, as always, of the five empty bunks which now scarred the hut.

The next morning, preparations began in earnest for their third winter. The implacable Barne Glacier glared at them, a white shield against the blackening sea. Behind the hut, out towards the little hill where the weather station cowered in the inexhaustible wind, the snow turned red with seal blood. But still they didn't have enough meat for the winter.

Tryggve Gran's mittened fingers scrawled Norwegian words into his diary. The only Norwegian on Scott's expedition, he was sitting on his favourite rock, scarred by ages of moving ice, the sun on his face. He looked up from the page to think, and thought he saw a dark shape where the glacier met the water. He blinked. Mirages were common here. A few more scribbled words, another glance out towards the glacier's edge. The shape had grown, grown into the familiar shape of hull and masts and sails.

'She's here,' he shouted and threw his diary into the dirt. 'She's here! We're saved.' He skidded into the hut. 'Come out. *Terra Nova* is here.'

They all ran to the edge of the ice to watch the anchor chains roll out and crash into the lazy water.

'Are you all well?' Teddy Evans called through the loudhailer from on board the ship.

'The polar party died on their way back from the Pole,' Atkinson called back.

Silence.

'We have their records.'

More silence. Some hurried movement on the ship. And then a boat was gently lowered into the sea and approached land.

'How very sad,' Evans said as he stepped ashore. He shook Atkinson's hand. 'Where did you find them?'

'Eleven miles south of One Ton. We buried them there.'

'As it should be. Thank you. I should have been here. I was the second-in-command.'

'You almost died of scurvy. We had no choice but to send you home.'

'Nevertheless.' Evans walked towards the hut.

'The diaries talk of unexplained oil shortages at the depots.'

'You mean they ran out of fuel?'

Atkinson nodded. 'That's one of the reasons they died, I think. They couldn't cook the food they did have, towards the end.'

'Damn it.' Evans pushed open the door to the hut. 'We had dreadful weather. That's why we're so late. Best to start loading her as soon as we can. Don't want to risk getting caught in that weather.' The missing oil was never mentioned again.

Twenty-eight hours later, and the men thirty-six hours without sleep, the ship was fully loaded. Just before they closed up the hut, Gran scrawled a thank you onto the side of his bunk with red paint. Much was left behind in the hut, as if someone still lived there.

The beds on the *Terra Nova* which had been covered in white linen for the polar party were stripped. The letters from home meant for the dead men were sealed, to be returned to their wives and mothers. Only Cherry looked back as the ship slowly made its way out of the bay. Alone on deck, he thought he saw five figures run from the hut to the shore and wave. After a moment's hesitation, he waved back.

The *Terra Nova* did not leave Antarctica immediately. She made several stops on the way to McMurdo Sound, where Scott's first expedition had landed years earlier, to pick up geological samples and scientific instruments. Once in the

Sound, Atkinson, Cherry and the rest of the search party decided a monument should be built for the polar party. Observation Hill, almost 1,000 feet tall, and from where there was an unrestricted view south towards the Pole, was the ideal spot.

On 20 January 1913, a heavy cross made of jarrah wood was sledged across the ice and then carried up the steep hill. Two days later, it was finally embedded in the hill's summit. They carved into it: *To strive, to seek, to find, and not to yield*, and the names of the five dead men. Cherry was the last to leave the summit, and the only one, nine miles out to sea, to watch the five shining figures dance around the cross, hand in hand.

For the next three weeks, most of the men who had spent two winters on the ice did nothing but sleep. That sleep became more and more fitful the closer the journey took them to New Zealand. The light changed, too, and by the time they saw land, the nights were almost dark. And finally, on the tenth day of February, at 2.30 in the morning, darkness not yet lifted, *Terra Nova* crept into Oamaru harbour on the east coast and dropped anchor well away from the shore.

What ship are you? the lighthouse asked. No answer was made. Instead, Atkinson and Pennell rowed ashore in a small boat. They made their way to the post office, roused the postmaster and sent a telegram to London. When dawn rose a few hours later, everyone knew that Scott and his men had died. Everyone except Kathleen Scott.

Kathleen had left California at the end of January. She revelled in the warm weather, because she knew it would be winter in New Zealand when she got there. The ship's new wireless lost reception after a few days.

She loved these weeks at sea, when she became one with the creaking ship, with the rolling gait of the vessel. She would often wait until night had fallen before she walked the deck. Nothing could shake her faith in Con, in life, in herself.

Now, the coolness of the bed enveloped her. Not long. She would soon be there. And then Con would take her in his arms, his strong arms. He would tell her how much he had missed her. They would read the letters they had written to each other and never sent. And then they would find the cool linen of another bed, marry each other again, become one again. One body, one soul, and a life together. She closed her eyes and saw his earnest face. She fell asleep and dreamed of his kisses.

Valentine's Day 1913. The whole of London in black. Crowds in the February frost around St Paul's Cathedral. At noon, a memorial service for Scott and his men. And still Kathleen knew nothing. England mourned, while the widow thought she was still a wife.

The cool morning sun caressed her as she reclined in the deckchair. She needed the sun's warmth on her. The wretched cramps would not leave her. It was the same every month. Even having a light breakfast had not helped. She stretched. They had just passed Tahiti. She closed her eyes and tried to calm the pain with the power of her mind, to make time pass more quickly. *My Con, my Con, we'll be together soon.*

'Excuse me, madam.'

She opened her eyes.

'My dear Captain,' she smiled. 'I must have dozed off. I hope you didn't have to call too often.' She sat up and shielded her eyes.

'Not at all, madam. Could I speak with you in my cabin, please?'

'Of course.' Maybe there had been a message from Con. Maybe he was in New Zealand already.

The captain offered her his arm. She took it playfully. Felt it tremble. She was an attractive woman, and would have expected nothing less, even though she had dined at his table several times. The world was in love with her, and she with it.

Once they reached his quarters, he asked her to sit down. He went to his desk to pick up a piece of paper, then sat down next to her. His hands shook.

'I have some news for you, but I don't see how I can tell you.'

'The expedition?'

'Yes.'

'Well, let's have it.'

He passed her the telegraph paper.

Captain Scott and six others perished in blizzard after reaching S Pole Jan 18th.

'Oh, well,' she said, without thinking. 'Never mind. I expected that. Thanks very much. I'll go and think about it.'

'Is there anything I can do?' He was confused by her calmness.

'Please don't tell any of the others about this.'

'You have my word.'

'Thank you.'

She rose, numb, folded the paper, shook his hand, and left the room. She needed to carry on as normal. She had to make sure she didn't collapse. She couldn't, not in the public eye on this ship as she was. So she followed her routine. First, she endured Spanish lessons for an hour and a half. Over lunch, she discussed Australian politics with friends. All the while, she kept herself in check, wouldn't allow herself to think of what she now knew. After lunch, she read *The Sinking of the Titanic*. She had always been good at coping with other people's grief. Now she would have to teach herself how to cope with her own.

The day wore on. It was too hot in the cabin, too cloistered, claustrophobic, too replete with thoughts and memories, and fears. She didn't want to be contaminated by grief, nor by the objects of his with which she had surrounded herself. All day on deck, in the sun, she wrote her notes, made her sketches, watched and listened and talked. And all the while she understood it was up to her now to make the most of this, her life, to enjoy it to the extreme, before she, too, froze and stopped breathing.

What she knew, what she felt, what she held on to, was that they had married for love, for a passion beyond most people's comprehension, that they didn't need each other all the time, not physically. They lived, one within the other, to the exclusion of all else. Death brought them closer together, not because they believed in a life after death, but because she carried his influence with her now, because she believed they had shaped each other. And she would carry his power with her forever, because she still loved him, because she would always have loved him, alive or dead.

The heat slackened a little towards evening, yet she remained on deck. She slept up there, wrapped in a plain cotton dress, her long hair tied up to afford her air. She dozed fitfully, plagued by happy dreams, until they docked at Rarotonga. She would not be distracted from the necessity of living.

She found an island adrift in a rain storm. All that day she perched on a coral reef, kept company by a young man from South America who didn't speak her language, who didn't know what had happened to her. He didn't precipitate the anger and grief which ebbed and flowed inside her, didn't ask her questions she couldn't, wouldn't, answer. Slowly, she asserted her control over herself. She would not become a widow hamstrung by tradition. She would rejoice in Con and in the joy he would have wanted her to experience. In her son Peter she had a part of him.

And so the journey continued. The only thing plaguing her now was not the caustic grief of being abandoned, nor the pain of loss. What grieved her most was that she knew nothing more than the fact her Con was dead. She didn't know how he had died, nor how much pain he would have endured, nor how he endured it. That was all she thought of, all that mattered. For she did not want him to have suffered. When they had last been together she had given him a pencilled note to carry with him at all times. She had told him he should take risks with his own life if he felt he had to, if he felt he needed to, if he wanted to. Because she didn't want him to feel guilty about exploring, about daring to explore. Because he was daring. Because, because, because ...

And then, one night, within range of the wireless stations, the deluge came, the flood of messages of condolence, concerned messages, loving messages. But she didn't want them, not because she didn't care, not because she didn't need them, but because they stopped her from getting the press cables, the cables with the detail she needed to build her defences before she even got to New Zealand. Finally, a pause, half a minute of silence before the tapping began again. This time it was Con who spoke to her.

For my own sake, I do not regret this journey ... We took risks, we knew we took them ... That was all she needed. She gloried in the courage of his message to her, to all his fellow humans. He had suffered, but now that suffering was over, and he could rest.

Atkinson was nervous. He watched Kathleen's ship approach the quayside. She would be on it, somewhere. He shaded his eyes with his hand, tried to pick her out in the crowd lining the deck. He couldn't find her. Perhaps she wouldn't want to disembark until everyone else had, so she would avoid the gaze of publicity. He wasn't sure.

With him were Kathleen's brother, Wilson's widow and Teddy Evans. But it was Atkinson who would hand her the package he had carried with him night and day since he had found it in the tent. He adjusted his tie. It had been so difficult getting used to wearing a uniform again these last few weeks, being an officer again on the outside, instead of just a man.

The lines went out and were made fast. The gangplank came down with a crash which sent the autumn dust up into the air in a fast flurry. He still didn't see her. And then, all of a sudden, she was beside him, wrapped in a dark coat, her hair in waves down her back and over her face.

'Hello, Edward,' she said.

'Madam,' he said, bowing his head.

'Kathleen, please.'

'I have something for you, Kathleen,' he said, obeying her.

'Con's diary.'

'And letters.' He handed her the package, held together with rough string. 'He expressly asked that these be given to you.'

'How?'

'He left a note with instructions.'

'So organised to the end.'

'Indeed,' he said.

'But then he did have Birdie with him, didn't he?'

'Birdie and Uncle Bill Wilson.'

'And the others?'

'Oates and Evans were lost on the way.'

'Oh, yes. So there were only five of them, not six. The wires were wrong.'

'Thank God.'

'Whomever we have to thank is not for me to judge, Edward. I am just glad his pain is over and his worrying done.'

She walked across to the others in the group. She took each one by the hand, and smiled her brightest smile. She reserved a hug for Ory Wilson, whose eyes were red with misery and despair. Former conflicts were forgotten. Kathleen would always be centre stage.

That evening, she read his diaries and copied parts of them into her own. And then his letters. His last letter to her. She steeled herself, let the words flow into her, made sure she understood what he was saying. Because, when she finished reading it, her new life would begin.

To my widow
Dearest Darling ...
... cherish no sentimental rubbish about re-marriage –
when the right man comes to help you in life you ought to
be your happy self again ...
I hope I shall be a good memory ...
You know I have loved you ...
You must know that quite the worst aspect of this
situation is the thought that I shall not see you again ...
What lots and lots I could tell you of this journey ...

Chapter 13

We step out of the bright, air-conditioned corridors of Singapore's airport into dark humidity. The smokers' room is a rooftop garden. A multitude of yellow lights pierce the heavy night. I drag on my first cigarette for over half a day and it makes me feel dizzy.

'You OK?' she says.

'Yeah. Fine.'

'Fancy doing some shopping?'

'Why not? I like shopping.'

'Come on, then.'

I buy cigarettes. She tells me off. I stop next to a shop that sells anything made of silk. I go in. There are some very beautiful clothes in here, with bright colours and soft textures. I run my hands along them. She elbows me.

'What are you doing?' she whispers.

'Just feeling the material.'

'What the hell for?'

'I like to.'

'Why?'

'Because that's what I do when I shop.'

I pull a two-piece, skirt and top, from the rail. It's a size 36 – tiny. I hold it up against her. She pushes it away.

'Stop it.'

'Why?'

'Because.'

'What?'

'I'm not your wife.'

'I know that.'

'So why bother?'

I hold the crimson and pale yellow fabric against her aggressive body again.

'Has anyone ever bought you clothes?' I ask.

'Yes, me.'

'Someone else, I mean.'

'I don't want people to buy me clothes. It's just a way of trying to change me.'

'Shit, is that what you think? Sorry.' I hang the outfit back. 'I didn't mean to upset you.' I start to walk away from the rail, towards the exit.

'Wait a minute,' she calls.

I turn around. She's holding it in her hand.

'D'you really think it would suit me?'

'Why else would I have shown it to you?'

'Just let me try it on, then.'

When she reappears a few minutes later, I'm speechless. She's even more beautiful in it than I thought she'd be. The pale yellow matches her hair, the rich red blends with the brown of her eyes. She looks timeless and elegant, graceful and controlled.

'Give us a twirl,' I say.

She does, with a broad grin on her face. 'It looks great with my boots, doesn't it?'

'That's what makes it. You look wonderful.'

'When am I going to wear it?'

'Anytime.'

She just grunts and walks back to the changing room. When we get to the checkout, I insist on paying for it.

'A thank you,' I say and give her the bag.

'What for?'

'Everything.'

'Oh, stop being so soft.' She grabs my hand and squeezes it.

'And what was that?'

'Oh, nothing.' Now she does let go. 'Come on. Get your smoke done. It's time we moved on. And try to get some more sleep on the next leg. Otherwise you'll be no good for anything.'

'But I tried already.'

'Try again.'

This time, the plane really is blacked out as we fly across territory I know nothing about. I sleep after two glasses of wine. Fitfully. At one point, I wake up and open the window blind just in time to see a shooting star fizz across the sky. I don't recognise a single constellation. As I close the blind, I hear her move next to me.

'It's wonderful, isn't it?' she says.

'What?'

'Being in limbo. In a timeless zone.'

'Yes.' With you, I think.

'Sleep.' She closes her eyes again.

Christchurch airport isn't as big as I'd imagined it to be. It's light now, but I'm still not sure of the time of day. I'm a zombie. She drags me along the corridor. We're met by a guide.

'Hi. I'm Shane, and you look like you need some coffee, mate,' he cheerfully shouts at me.

'Yeah, story of my life, pal.'

'Your bags are priority, so all we need to do is pick them up and then you can have that coffee.'

'We've got a cab waiting,' Birdie says. 'We'll get coffee at the hotel.'

'Fair enough,' he says.

We get in the cab. Shane puts all our gear in the boot and hands me his business card. Bit sexist, really, seeing as it's Birdie who's paying for all this. She's not bothered, though. She shrugs and winds down the window, despite the chill.

'It's gonna turn to custard later,' the cabbie says as he pulls away from the kerb.

'Eh?' Birdie raises an eyebrow and shoots me a secret smile.

'Muggy,' he says.

'Gotcha.'

I think I'll let her do the talking. I can't transmogrify into a Kiwi like she just has.

'So whatcha down here for?'

'Just a holiday.'

'Just married?'

'Nah, mate. Just good friends.'

'Fair enough … No harm in asking.'

'None at all.'

'Posh digs, though.'

'Luck of the draw.'

'Good customers of mine.'

'Even better.'

We're down the long straight road from the airport by now. The city is scattered in the wake of a range of hills, green, dotted white with houses. We move gently along the road, and I get a sense of us missing Christchurch out altogether, and just motoring on up the hills. But we suddenly come to a stop in the middle of a huge park populated by enormous trees. They're pine trees, he tells us, as we're waiting for the traffic lights to change. There's one in there that's 137 years old. He tells us to make sure we find it. The lights change, and we're there. After London, this place seems more like a village than an international city. And I like it.

I think the cabbie's too old to help us with our bags, so I lug all our gear through into the hotel lobby, and tell the hovering porters I don't need any help.

'I gave him a twenty-dollar tip,' Birdie says when she catches up with me.

'Why?'

'Such a nice old bloke.'

'I'm surprised he's still driving.'

'He obviously wants to keep going.'

'Not like you to be so generous.'

'Must be the company I keep.'

'Ha.'

She checks us in, and we carry our bags into the lift. The doors close without a sound. Posh digs, indeed.

'Why the separate rooms?' I ask.

'Wouldn't want anyone getting the wrong idea, would we?'

'S'pose not.'

'Oh, stop being so grumpy. It's just so we've each got our own space.'

We dump her stuff in her room. Mine's next door.

'Very nice,' she says.

'Not bad at all.'

She jumps onto my bed, my double bed.

'I'll get my stuff later.'

'What?'

'I'll get my stuff later.'

'I don't understand you.'

'You just see everything in black and white when there's no need to. Just go with the flow.'

'I'm trying to.'

'You think too much.'

'So how do I stop?'

'If I knew, I'd have told you by now.'

'Can't you ever be serious?'

'I'm serious about finding that tent.'

'What about feelings?'

'They're not important. Not now. Come on, Adam, leave it. We'll talk about all that when we've done what I came here to do.'

'We're not quite there yet.'

'I know.'

'So what now?'

'The guys from the Antacrtic Trust are going to have dinner with us later. And tomorrow we go to their office and get kitted out.'

'I hope that works out. I'm sure I've put on weight since we sent our measurements.'

'You're so full of shit.'

'But I have.'

'Rubbish. Anyway, they'll have more than just one size of things, won't they?'

'How should I know?'

She stands on the bed. She starts bouncing, then jumps off with a little scream.

'Come on,' she says. 'I need that coffee now.'

I touch her shoulder as she walks past me. She turns and puts her arms round me. We kiss, a long kiss. She strokes my face. She looks at me and smiles. There's a sadness in that smile I can't fathom.

When we get downstairs, the guy at reception waves at us. We go across to him.

'Mr Wheeler has arrived for you. He's waiting in the bar area. He told me not to disturb you until you came down.'

'Who?' I ask.

'He's the bloke from the Trust,' Birdie says. 'You should pay more attention. He's the one who's taking us out there.'

We wander across to the bar. There's a stocky guy with dark hair on one of the bar stools drinking what looks suspiciously like booze to me.

'Neville?' Birdie asks.

'Ah, Henrietta.' He jumps off the stool. 'Nice to meet you at last.' He shakes her hand. 'Call me Nev.'

'Hi, Nev,' she squeaks.

'And you must be Adam.' He turns, shakes my hand, too. He's got a good, firm grip.

'Hello, Nev. How you doing?'

'Good, good.'

'So, what brings you here before the appointed time?' Birdie asks him.

'Just thought I'd see how you're settling in.'

'Fine,' she says. 'Let's sit over there. Adam, can you get me a double espresso, please?'

'Try a Long Black,' Nev says. 'Speciality here.'

'And what's that you're drinking?' I ask Nev.

'Lemonade with bitters and fruit. Dead refreshing.'

'I thought it was booze. Sorry, mate.'

'No worries. Too early for that ... You wanna try the local beer, though.'

'I'll leave that till later, too. I need some caffeine.'

'Are you very tired?' he says as we sit down.

'I'm not too bad,' Birdie says. 'But I think Adam's struggling a bit. Just can't take the pace, these oldies.'

'I'll be fine. Just a bit disoriented. Never been in the Southern hemisphere before.'

'You'll get used to it,' Nev says. 'I think it's great you reckon you'll be fit enough to have dinner with us later.'

'You try and stop us,' Birdie says.

Our coffees arrive. Bliss. I excuse myself so I can take mine outside and have a smoke with it. Old habits, and all that. It's warmer now. The sun's threatening to come out. I wander round the car park with my smoke and my coffee, nose around a bit. The park looks interesting. And immense.

'... and the weather's a bit unsettled, as well,' I hear Nev say as I walk back into the hotel.

'Is that a problem?' Birdie asks.

'It could escalate to a Condition One, in which case we won't even take off if we know about it. Or we'll get boomeranged when we're in the air.'

'How will we know, if we're still on the ground here?' she says.

'Scheduled take-off is 9 a.m. every day. That means being there by seven. So I'd pick you up at about 6.30. If we get bumped, you'll get a bump call at about 5 a.m. or so.'

'From you?'

'Me or Warney. He's the guy in charge of logistics, and he usually knows before me if there's a problem. You'll meet

108

him tomorrow when you get your gear. That'll be your last day of getting up late, because I won't be picking you up till 8.30.'

'So what happens if we get bumped the day after tomorrow?' Birdie asks.

'24-hour delay.'

'And if we get bumped again?'

'Same thing.'

'Jesus. It could go on forever, couldn't it?'

'You never know,' he says. 'Although normally bad weather only lasts three or four days.'

'So what about Scott's ten days in that tent?' I say.

'No one knows,' Nev says. 'That's why you're here, isn't it?'

So she has told him. I look at her. Why? She avoids my stare.

'Apparently,' I say and finish my coffee. 'Apparently so.'

Chapter 14

'Why the hell didn't you tell me you'd come clean with the Trust?'

'Because I didn't.'

'So it's OK for me to look like a total dickhead, then?'

'No. I just assumed you'd reckon I'd talk to them, because you prefer things to be played straight.'

'How am I supposed to second-guess you? You always do what you want anyway. I've got no influence over you whatsoever.'

'More than you thought, obviously.'

'Might as well be none, the way you carry on.'

'Oh, please ... you don't tell me everything.'

'Not about the rest of my life, maybe. But about this project or whatever you want to call it I do.'

We're walking through Hagley Park opposite the hotel. It's a warren of pathways and bushes and those immense trees. You could get lost in here. And you can shout without being overheard.

'Birdie, we've got to be able to trust each other a hundred percent on this. Not just because we're looking for something that's important to us.'

'Why, then?'

'We might only be going on a jaunt, but it's dangerous out there, no matter for how long anyone goes, or where they go. People still die out there, you know.'

'And?'

'It'll be even more dangerous if we can't rely on each other, if we're bearing grudges because we've not been open with each other.'

'I'm not bearing any grudges.'

'You know what I mean.'

'I don't, actually. You're the one making a big deal out of this, not me. You're the one who's banging on about it all the time.'

'I wouldn't call an hour all the time.'

'Oh, come on. You're like a broken record. Just leave it. If you don't like the way it's going, you can just stay here when I fly. Or swap your ticket for an early one home.'

'Jesus wept. You make your own bloody rules and expect people to do just as you want.'

'That's because I'm selfish and focused.'

'You admit it, then?'

'I've never denied it. You know I haven't.'

I shake my head. I don't know what to say. We walk along in silence. Suddenly she stops.

'Adam, I'm sorry I didn't tell you. Maybe I even thought I had. And I wanted to make sure this was a bona fide project for the Trust to be committed to rather than us just swanning over there like tourists. I didn't want to lie anymore.'

I shrug.

'Look at me,' she says. 'Look at me.' She spreads her arms. 'This is me. This is the way I am. But … This is difficult. I'm … I'm changing, and it's because of you. And that's not easy to cope with, not easy to accept.' She looks up into the tops of the trees, then back at me. 'I need my secrets. I need all sorts of things. It's weird, asking myself new questions, up here.' She runs her hands through her spiky hair, starts pulling at it. 'And it confuses me. It's not something I'd reckoned on. I … I'm not very good at this, am I?'

'At what?' I ask.

'Explaining myself. I've never had to. Never. And now I feel like I have to, and I don't like that. It makes me feel vulnerable.'

'Don't. I don't want to hurt you. I don't even want to change you. I'm not even trying to.'

'Maybe that's what's so scary. I don't want you to think I'm just looking for a surrogate father.'

'It never crossed my mind,' I say.

'Really?'

'Really.' I reach for her hand. Kiss it. 'Let's start again.'

'Yes, let's.'

We walk back into the hotel hand in hand.

Dinner is fun. Nev brings along a group of people I've never heard of. Birdie obviously has, because she greets them all by name. I can't help admire the way she handles herself in company. I can't do this small talk chatter and smiling routine. I'm too shy for it. Even though my hands are still warm with her touch. Even though what she said to me in the park has given me some sort of stupid hope for what might become of us when we go back to England.

Once we're sitting down, I feel less out of it. As the evening wears on and the wine flows, I relax. We talk of nothing but the Antarctic, past, present and future. I sense that all of us – the ex-mayor, the director of the local museum, Nev's assistant, Nev – are addicted to that continent brooding out there, 4,000 miles south, and to everything to do with it. Everything we talk about that's happened here, in this real world, has some sort of parallel out there, has somehow been touched by what's happened out there. I realise that its presence extends beyond its physical boundaries, that Christchurch is connected – by an umbilical cord, almost – to it.

I take to these people, especially Welland, the museum director. He and Nev are like brothers. Birdie said to me on the plane that she liked Kiwis better than Australians, because they were more upfront, but more laid back. That they wouldn't do you over. I can understand that now. And I like the feeling of being able to talk with them about what

112

the hell I feel like talking about without having to think too hard about how it comes out of my mouth. The evening ends too soon, really. Although I'm flagging by now.

'I'll just have another glass of wine with my last smoke,' I tell Birdie when we've seen them all off in the lobby.

'See you in a minute or so, then.'

'Ten minutes.'

'I might be asleep.'

'Good. It's been a long day.'

'Yes.'

Outside, the night is fresh, a hint of warmth in the air. Spring is on its way. Strange to think the Antarctic spring is colder than our winter. I savour the few minutes of solitude after all the talking. I can't quite get used to being here. And when I go back in, it's obvious the porters have now heard why we're here, because they wish me luck on the Ice when I say good night to them. Somehow it makes me feel really proud, like I'm a real explorer, although I know I'm not one, makes me feel ridiculously happy.

There's a note under my room door. *Gone to bed. I figured we could both do with some decent sleep. I know I always keep you awake, so don't be offended. Just thinking of you. Bx*

I can't argue with her thinking. I'm dog-tired and half drunk by now. And I don't feel very attractive. I look at myself in the mirror in the bathroom, and my body looks bloated. But my arms look like a strong man's from a hundred years ago. That's worth a little smile at myself. At least I like one part of my anatomy.

When I wake up the sun's already out, but my bedside light is still on. I must have fallen asleep fairly rapidly last night. All the tiredness has gone, and I'm out of bed in a flash. I have a quick shower, then head downstairs. Birdie's already in the restaurant having breakfast. Typical.

'Why didn't you wake me?'

'I reckoned you'd get up in good time. If you hadn't been

down here fifteen minutes before Nev was due to pick us up, I'd have woken you.'

'Thanks.'

'You're welcome.'

I barely have time to wolf down a couple of slices of toast and a coffee when Nev arrives to pick us up. Dead on 8.30, just like he promised. And I thought Kiwis were supposed to be laid back and easy-going. Especially after the drinking last night. Not the first time I've been wrong.

The Trust's office is out by the airport. As we turn off the main road, I see a huge plane sitting outside one of the hangars. It's got an American star on the side.

'That's the C-17, then, is it?' I ask Nev.

'Yup.'

'Isn't it supposed to have taken off by now?

'Condition One out there now. I didn't want to spoil your breakfast with the bad news. I wouldn't be surprised if we didn't get to fly out tomorrow.'

'Bugger,' Birdie says. 'Any sign of it getting better?'

'No way of telling. Like I said yesterday, sometimes it's crappy for two or three days, and sometimes it blows through real quick. They only just managed the round trip yesterday. And then the weather got much worse overnight. Nothing we can do about it.'

'Bugger, bugger, bugger,' she says. 'I suppose I'll just have to try to be patient.'

'That's the ticket,' Nev says as we get out of the car. 'I've learned that, too, since I've been doing this job. And I've been lucky. Not missed a trip in ten years. Even if some of 'em have been shorter than planned.'

We walk towards a low-slung white building. It looks very American in design to me, long and narrow. And sure enough, the Trust doesn't just share it with Kiwi government agencies, but with the Americans, too, and the Italian Space Agency. Nev hands us a spare key fob each so we can get through the security barriers without him.

'Not that you'll need them,' he says. 'But just in case. Specially the smokers amongst us.' He grins at me.

Dan, a government bod, has asked to meet us, so we're given coffee and cake in his office. Good, because I'm still hungry. Birdie's getting impatient, but she's political enough to understand she needs to humour the bureaucrats if she wants her plans to work. She's very adept at avoiding his most probing questions. He doesn't know who she really is; just that she's someone who's working on the Cape Evans hut restoration project. And Nev's sworn to secrecy.

Once we're finished with Dan, we head back across the corridor to Nev's office. We're living on coffee. We pile into his room. He pulls out a huge map and folds it out onto the table.

'Right,' he says. 'The stuff you sent me suggests that One Ton is about here.' He points at a spot in the mass of white. 'You reckon that, because it's nowhere near the edge of the ice yet, the movement's about 600 metres a year, and that it's moving north-north-easterly. So it's moved about 60 kilometres since 1913. Same goes for the final camp, which is somewhere here.'

'Spot on,' I say. 'Although we can't be sure of precisely what direction the ice has moved in. Lots of the research papers I read talked about lateral ice movement, so I tried to include some in the calculations, but there's still a lot of uncertainty.'

'We're aware of that, but I reckon it's worth taking a punt. If you find anything with the radar, you'll do some exploratory drilling and get a video scope down there without touching anything. If it is the tent, you'll mark the site, and we'll send a TV crew out there next season to do a programme.'

Birdie nods, her lips tight.

'Why not this time?' I ask.

'To be frank, the risk's lower this way, financial and other. If you don't find the tent, we've lost nothing. If you do find it, we'll have guaranteed funds from just about anyone to do a Scott series, and that'll raise more money for the hut.'

'Suits me,' Birdie says. 'I don't want to be in a film. But there's something you're not telling us, isn't there, Nev?'

He's a bit embarrassed by the question. Too nice a man by far.

'Thing is, if you don't get out there this week, there aren't any seats till January, because we've already got lots of people booked to do projects out there, seeing as your project was a last-minute add-on. And that means you'd only have about six weeks before the last flight before winter.'

Birdie goes really pale. She has a bright red spot on each cheek. And she's gripping her chair so tightly, her fingers have gone white. 'Well, then I just hope the bastard weather picks up. For fuck's sake!'

'Sorry,' Nev says.

'That doesn't help. It doesn't help at all. Who do I have to slap to get out there? It's not like we're fucking immortal.' She's jumping up and down. 'And don't take that personally.'

'I won't. Come on. Let's get our kit.'

'Waste of bloody time,' she says and kicks her chair over as she gets up.

She's still chuntering away to herself when we walk across the grass to the logistics department. It's a grey, squat, uninviting place. Nev clatters in through the swing doors, Birdie and I in his wake.

'Where are ya, Warney?' he shouts.

'In the briefing room, mate,' a voice shouts back.

We round a couple of corners. The room's full of old sofas, an old coffee table, and a mountain of empty coke cans.

'Been waiting for ya,' the giant lying on the sofa says and sits up.

116

'You know Dan, mate. He can talk the arse off a donkey,' Nev says.

'Well, yer here now, so I can get this briefing over and done with.'

'What?' I say.

'You'll get used to this,' Nev says. 'Antarctica is one briefing after another.'

'God save us,' Birdie chips in.

'Procedure, ma'am,' Warney says. He bends down. She's about half his height. 'And it's actually for your safety rather than my entertainment.'

She laughs at him. 'That's all right, then. I'm all ears.'

Chapter 15

Warney drones on and on. *Don't do this, do that. Don't forget your earplugs. Make sure you've got your ice boots on, otherwise you won't get on the plane. Ditto if you don't bring your boarding card and passport.* I know it has to be done. I just wish I didn't have to sit through it. There aren't any windows in this room.

'And that's about it,' Warney finishes. He looks at me. 'You haven't listened to a single word I've said, have you?'

'Oh yes, I have,' I say, and recite his list of dos and don'ts back at him.

'Look, boys, can we stop all this messing around and get our kit sorted out?' Birdie interrupts. 'I can do without all this alpha male bonding crap.'

So we go to the kit room. There are hundreds and hundreds of coats, boots, trousers, shirts, hats, gloves; racks and racks and racks of every possible item of clothing anyone could ever need. Everything except underwear. Understandably. That's why we've brought our own.

I lose count of how many different things we try on, because, although they've already laid out gear in our sizes, there's always something wrong. Salopettes too tight or too loose; shirts uncomfortable; boots pinching when we've got thick socks on; neck gaiters scratchy; gloves too small. And so on.

By the time we've finally found the stuff that fits, we're sweating like pigs, because we've got five or six layers on, and huge boots to match. Everything has to be just right for the supervising Warney, because he'll feel responsible if

118

anything goes wrong, and because it's important to be comfortable, and warm, and safe.

Birdie looks swamped by her massive outfit. And cute. Her small face is hidden under the wire-reinforced hood of the anorak. She pulls the hood back. Her hair is totally flattened and dishevelled.

'Strewth, there'll be nothing left of you if you keep that stuff on for much longer,' Warney says.

'I can take it off now, can I?'

'Be my guest.'

She retires into the cubicle. It takes an age for her to get out of the clothes. But I take even longer. And then we have to practise packing it all into two small canvas bags. Naturally, she does it in two minutes flat, while I'm still floundering fifteen minutes later. By that point, she's laughing so hard she can hardly stand. And then, at last, she comes across to me and helps.

'Right, guys,' Warney says. 'Last thing. You know it's a Condition One out there at the minute. Odds-on that you won't be flying out tomorrow. But the pick-up's still scheduled for twenty past six in the morning. If the weather's fine, you won't get a call from me. If the flight's cancelled, I'll call you at about five.'

'You'd better not bloody call us,' Birdie says.

'We're due at the museum in half an hour,' he says.

'Are we?' she says.

'Don't tell me you've forgotten. Welland will be gutted if I tell him.'

'Then don't tell him.'

'You're a hard woman.'

'I try to be.'

Nev and Warney shake their heads. They can't work her out. That makes three of us. At least they're not in love with her. That would be even more confusing.

The museum is all grey stones and white arches. A square tower tops the building, makes it look like a castle. The round window above the entrance is a rose, like the ones at the ends of churches. We walk out of the sun into the quiet building. Welland's waiting for us. I hadn't noticed yesterday that he's even taller than me, and definitely a lot thinner. And he's got a tan like he spends all his time outdoors. He's a handsome man.

'I've got a real treat for you today, children,' he says, rubbing his hands together. 'Something not everyone gets to see. Follow me.'

Birdie skips into step with him. The two of them wander off ahead. I don't mind. Quite the contrary. I walk behind her, watch her tight shape, and rest my eyes on my favourite part of her, that tender spot at the nape of her neck where the hair ends and the skin begins.

I missed her last night. I wanted her to keep me awake. I hoped to listen to her talking in her sleep, to hear her breathing, to watch her silhouette rise and fall in the dark and feel the warmth of her body next to me. I hope we'll be in the same bed tonight.

Funny how we've spent so many nights together and never seen each other fully naked. Maybe I'm wrong to want commitment first. Maybe I'm wrong to be so obsessed. I should just give in to my want for her. Maybe I'm wrong to be here. This is all a mistake.

'Here's our Antarctic gallery,' Welland says, and drags me out of my regrets.

We've moved from the low, artificially lit galleries into a tall hall full of natural light. It must be a modern extension at the back of the Gothic mansion. The space is sparse and harsh and aggressive, sharp edges to every object, every simple single thing. It knocks the breath out of me.

Birdie slows down. She brushes against me as if by accident. I catch her scent again; fresh lemons warmed by the sun.

'You OK?' she whispers.

'Yeah, I just feel a bit out of it.'

120

'You worry too much. I know what you're thinking.'

'Do you?'

'This is fantastic, Welland,' she says loudly.

'Wait till you see the best of it.' He smiles. 'But you need to look round this first. There are artefacts here from before Scott and Amundsen right through to Sir Edmund Hillary's joint expedition with Sir Vivian Fuchs in the fifties. I'm sure you'll love it.'

'Thanks,' she says, and she's not being facetious.

I just want to get this whole thing over and done with. I want to get out there and find the tent, reach a conclusion, and get her back to England. I want to build a proper relationship. I want to be with her. I want to live in a house that always smells of lemons and sunshine.

She stops in front of every exhibit, reads every sign. She absorbs it all. Stuffed penguins and seals stare back at us from behind glass. The walls are littered with paintings and photographs. The one that affects me most is an enlargement of Tryggve Gran's photo of the cairn they built over the tent after they'd buried Scott, Wilson and Bowers. I've seen it so often in so many books, but its size transforms it. It's almost nothing but different shades of white. The cross of skis and the sledge are the only black objects in the frame, the cairn a white pyramid merging into the horizon, a desolate, disappearing mound, a fresh grave to the three men buried beneath, three men frozen into the continent that killed them. And all around the cairn, a chaos of footprints. The left corner is the lightest, the sun about to burst out from behind the cold clouds, with no hope of warmth, no hope of revival.

'Reckon we can find it?' Birdie asks me.

'It won't look like that now.'

'I know that. But there'll be something inside it that we can locate with the radar.'

'I hope so. Something metal. Even if we find one of the sledges, or just a trace of a ski binding or a belt buckle, we'll be able to find the tent.'

'There will be something, Adam. There will be. There's got to be. I can feel it.'

'We won't know until we find it.'

'Or till our time runs out. Bloody weather! Bloody bureaucrats!'

'And if we don't go?'

'I don't even want to think about that.'

'And what if we don't find anything?'

'We will, we've got to.' She stamps her foot. 'God, why the hell is this so bloody complicated? It's just a five-hour flight away, for fuck's sake.'

I shrug.

We stop in front of a scale model of four men hauling a sledge and a fifth pushing. Although they're only small figures, plastic figures, they make the physical effort of man-hauling suddenly real.

'God, I'm glad we won't be doing any of that,' I say.

'It might do us some good.'

'I doubt it.'

'Where's your sense of adventure?'

'It doesn't outweigh my appetite for life.'

'And cigarettes and booze.'

'OK, and cigarettes and booze.'

'We all die in the end.'

'Not yet, Birdie, not yet.'

She smiles, stretches. I catch a glimpse of her stomach, of the ring through her belly-button. The veins in her neck stand out with the effort of living, of keeping awake, her body still in the wrong time zone.

We move through into an even larger room. A staircase at the far end reaches up to another floor. The sun bounces down to us from the partition windows.

'What's up there?' Birdie asks Welland.

'Some of our archives.'

'Is that where you're keeping the surprise you promised us?' she asks him.

'Could be.'

He's flirting with her. He's very good at it. I smile at the floor.

'Should we?' he asks and offers her his arm.

'Yes, let's,' she says and takes the offered arm, glides elegantly up the steps at his side. They make a fine couple.

He opens the glass door for us. As we file into the room, the first thing I feel is a change in temperature. It's almost cold in here, even compared to the coolness of the Antarctic Gallery down there. I shiver.

'We need to keep the temperature fairly low in here,' Welland says, 'on account of the fragile nature of these things. Come.'

He gestures at a U-shaped arrangement of tables, covered from end to end by white cotton cloths and an array of old manuscripts, books and notebooks. Two nervous-looking women in white coats stand behind all this. They're wearing white gloves.

'These are my lovely curators.' He smiles at us and them at the same time. He could charm blood from a stone, this bloke.

'And these are my lovely guests, girls,' he goes on. 'Now don't worry. They won't break anything. Nev is vouching for them with his life – and his wallet.'

Nev ignores him and goes to stand by the window. He's probably used to Welland's performances. I find it hugely amusing. Birdie's already over by the tables, ignoring us. She wins the women over by helping herself to a set of white gloves and standing back, waiting. If I got her back to England, and if I got her to be with me, could I ever get used to the chameleon she is? My head's not convinced by my heart.

'Come on, then, Welland, tell us all about this stuff. Can't hang around all day,' she says.

'What do you want to know?'

'Can I open this?' She points at an oversized notebook covered in stains.

'Go ahead.'

'Please use the white card to separate the pages,' one of the conservators says.

'Sure thing,' Birdie says.

The spine is loose, the pages fragile and frayed. Birdie places her left hand flat on the cover, lightly pushes the white card under the inside of the cover and turns it over. She gasps. I touch her shoulder.

'What?'

'This one's for you, Adam. It's Frank Worsley's, from the *Endurance*. The guy who sailed the *James Caird* to South Georgia with Shackleton. Dear God.'

Inside the front cover, in copperplate writing: *Lieut. F. A. Worsley R.N.R. commanding s.y. Endurance on a Voyage of discovery to the Antarctic. Work Book.* Amazing.

'And it did go all the way with them,' Welland says. 'He wrote in it every day, even when they thought they'd never get saved.'

'Tough bastards,' Nev says from his window spot.

'They must all have been. All those who've been down there,' Birdie says. 'We can't compete with that.'

'But you can help take their message back to the modern world,' Welland says. 'Young people don't understand about endeavour, respect, dignity and honour.'

'I'm not old,' she says.

'But you're exceptional, my dear,' Welland says.

She doesn't even blush. She just nods. I wish I was as sure of myself. Welland smiles. They're two of a kind.

We make our way round the table to look at more manuscripts from Shackleton's time. I love the way the paper crackles and rustles when we turn the pages, the paper's weight has reduced with age. I ask Welland if they've scanned all this stuff into a document management system.

'Of course. But we hope we can find ways to preserve the paper, too, because it would be dreadful to lose it.'

'Sorry to be geeky,' I say.

'You're not,' he says. 'It's good to know someone else cares as much as we do.'

There is an original copy of *Aurora Australis*, the book that was created on Shackleton's 1907 expedition, when he got to within ninety miles of the Pole. It's one of only eighty copies printed, full of schoolboy humour. Funny, but not funny. Not when I think of the real reason we're here. But it's still history. Where do we draw the line? What we scribble today may be artefacts in a hundred years. Birdie's paintings definitely will be. Those of us with no talent will be lost in the drifts of history.

We've looked at just about everything on the table. I'm about to walk off when Welland stops me.

'Hey, you'll miss the best piece I could find,' he says.

'What?'

'Here.' He points at a small notebook at the end of the table. It's undistinguished, but in fairly good condition. I hadn't noticed it.

'What is it?' Birdie says.

'Frederick Hooper's diary,' he says. 'He was one of the search party that found the tent.'

'But haven't all the diaries been published?' she says.

'Hooper's started as a letter to his fiancée. It wasn't long enough to be published. And, to be honest, all of those that have been published are nothing compared to Scott's.'

'True.' She picks the book up. Opens it. 'Does he mention finding the tent?'

'I believe so. You'll have to leaf through it, though.'

I stand close to her as she turns the pages. She's trembling. The scrawl is almost indecipherable. Then she stops shaking and stands motionless.

'Here it is,' she says. I look over her shoulder as she reads out loud.

10th November – 1 Ton Depot. A dull morning and bitterly cold wind, face badly frostbitten, surface getting much softer.

She skips the rest of that day.

11th, 12th. We found the Pole Party this evening about 11 miles south of 1 Ton Depot. We noticed what we thought was a cairn ... When we got up to it we found it was a tent badly drifted up. We dug it out & lifted the tent off & I shall never forget the sight that met our eyes. Capt. Scott was lying with his head opposite the door, half out of his bag, both of his arms were thrown across the other two bags which we found contained Dr Wilson & Lt. Bowers. It's apparent they have died of starvation.

We had a service over them & buried them as they were absolutely stiff, frozen in every limb. It was an awful sight to see our dear comrades in such a state, a sight I shall never forget in a hurry. I forgot to say that a blizzard kept them at this place. It lasted over 8 days. It looked very much like Dr Wilson and Lt. Bowers died while asleep, but Capt. Scott must have been awake when he passed away, his eyes were wide open & he looked as though he must have been in great pain.

Birdie puts the book down and turns to me. She's crying. 'We have to find them.'

Chapter 16

Cold fog rising. Spectres emerged, frozen mouths wordless, faces jagged, their rigid eyes open. Behind them, a veil of ice.

'Speak to me,' Cherry cried out.

No answer.

'Are you well?' he called.

Silence.

'Please, please.'

He thrashed about him blindly and screamed. Frozen, broken hands reached for him. There was no escape for him in his delusions. He was waiting and waiting at One Ton, the horizon edging away, his glasses icing over, waiting for them to appear from the white distance.

'All's well. All's well,' Scott should have answered. They should have survived. There was nothing now but Cherry's rage in the cot of a small cabin on a mail steamer bound for Italy. He blamed Scott for killing the two men he loved above all others, and felt guilty for his anger.

The voices on the Ice had been tempting, delicious and friendly. They had made Cherry want to give up his life and stay. Now they taunted him. They burrowed into him with hatefulness and spite, and imbued his existence with dread. They serrated his nights and days, scratched sores into him he never would be able to erase, that would never heal.

Distance brought no relief. Throughout the long voyage, he picked over the expedition. He went through his notes page by page, over and over again, replayed in his mind the days at One Ton with Dimitri, tried to piece together his minutes and hours and days. Should he have needed his friends before they died? By the time the ship docked in Naples in late April 1913, he had still found no answer, and no redemption. This was his life now; a slave to the past's questions.

His mother and sisters met him in Naples. Outwardly, he looked older, more mature. He was a man now, not a boy any longer. Inside, he was broken, but couldn't show it. He hid his pain, his rage, his emptiness. How could he write the story of that expedition, that death march? Would he find the words to do them all justice?

When they finally reached the family home, Lamer, with May almost upon them, he walked straight into his study. Carefully, he sat down on his chair and listened for its familiar creak. Four years ago, he had spent a thousand pounds, a fortune, to join an expedition he knew next to nothing about. Three years ago, almost to the day, he had left without understanding the real dangers of the south. Was he any wiser? Doubt grabbed at him, made him sway. There were no answers in a changing world.

He walked across to the window and looked out into the garden. At least here nothing had changed. His trees were still there. Things were as they should be when a traveller returns home, except for the silence without the voices of his companions, without the wind shrieking up to the windows from the Pole, without the cold. He leaned his forehead against the cool pane, bit his lip. He could do nothing but move on, force the pace of his life, immerse himself in activity, and try to forget. No, he wouldn't just try, he would forget.

That afternoon, he began to deal with all his business correspondence. It was past midnight when he finished sorting through it. Just before he retired for the night, he put his diary into the top drawer of his desk, and pulled out one solitary piece of paper. He dipped his pen into ink and scribbled one line onto the noisy paper. *Polar exploration is at once the cleanest and most isolated way of having a bad time which has been devised.* He put the paper in the drawer with his diary and locked the desk. The rest would have to wait. There were other things to do for now, more important things.

But the past would not rest. A succession of trips took Cherry into London to raise funds for what was now a bankrupt expedition, and for the relatives of the dead. In June, he met the *Terra Nova* at Cardiff, finally returned from New Zealand. He would never see her again. And then the most painful trip to receive his Polar Medal at Buckingham Palace, another duty he didn't enjoy. Yet he fulfilled it, because his life now was one of duty and honour. He was sincere when he asked his friends to come to Lamer whenever they wished. Many of them did so that summer, to celebrate an age which had passed too swiftly. Amongst them Ory Wilson, Edward Wilson's widow.

'You must have it back,' she said, and pushed the green leather book into Cherry's hand.

'I gave it to Bill as a gift. He liked to read Tennyson. You must keep it,' he said.

'Then how shall I repay you?'

'For what?'

'For helping me through this. For helping me to sort out his things. For looking after him that winter.'

'Oh, my dear Ory. He looked after me. He saved my life. Maybe I could have saved his.'

'Don't say that. You know that there was nothing you could do. They were still five days away from their final camp when you left One Ton. You could not have reached them. You would have died, too.'

'But I am starting to believe what the papers say; that my failings led to the disaster.'

'We all know differently. Let the others lie to save their own reputations. In the end, the truth will not be hidden.'

'I hope you are right.'

'I am. And you must listen to me. You must tell the real story in your book.'

'When I write it.'

'You will. I know you will. I trust you.'

They remained friends for the rest of her life. She never remarried.

When Cherry went to the Natural History Museum in London to deliver the precious penguin eggs he'd harvested with his lost friends Bowers and Wilson, he was pushed from pillar to post, from one curator to another, ignored and patronised. Their ignorance and arrogance hurt him deeply. It took him a day to get a receipt for the eggs. And then they were put in some cupboard and forgotten. When they were finally examined, they contributed nothing to the advancement of science. The journey, the hardship, the friendships, had been for nothing.

As Cherry's delusions grew more vicious, he was increasingly crippled by stomach cramps. By now he was a stranger to sleep, the mental and physical torture too much for his body, the veil of fog and guilt more difficult to penetrate, the spectres impossible to identify. What he saw was skeletal; yellow frostbite, skin flaking from bone, a frozen hell.

Life fragmented. He spent a lot of time with Bowers' elderly mother and sister. But nothing could bring Bowers or Wilson back. The years at Cape Evans had been the best of his life, the worst of his life, the most fulfilling, the most wasted. And still that piece of paper remained locked in his desk. He had no use for it.

Then came the first of two world wars, a needless war. He served in Flanders, but his stomach wouldn't let him see it out, and he was invalided home. Many of his Antarctic friends died in the devastation of Europe. He grew more alone and more withdrawn. He was a man out of time, a man lost, a man without future and without love.

130

Kathleen came to stay with him. She recognised his anger, his depression, his need.

'Don't give up,' she said one night, after Peter, Con's son, had gone to bed.

'I'm not giving up.'

'It seems like it to me.'

'There is too much to think of, too much to grab hold of and put into one place.'

'Make notes. Just write without it making sense.'

'But it has to make sense.'

'Not when you first write it, it doesn't. You can always edit it later.'

'I'm not sure I have the will to.'

'You have. I know it. Con knew it.'

'Ah yes, Con.'

'He made mistakes like everyone else.'

'But he was the leader.'

'Can leaders not make mistakes, too?'

'I suppose they can. I suppose they must. To be human.'

'And he was human.'

They listened to the fire.

'Were you never afraid of him not coming back?' he asked, looking at her long hair, permanently in motion.

'Not really. I told him to do what he thought was right.'

'Did you ever think you pushed him too hard?'

'What?'

'That he might have overstretched himself to please you?'

'No. Never. He had a mind of his own, you know.'

'I didn't mean you forced him. I'm just trying to make sense of it all.'

'There is no sense in it, Cherry, my dear boy. No sense at all.'

'How then can I write a book about it?'

'To put it all into perspective.'

'But many of you don't want me to write the truth.'

'What do you mean?'

'The oil shortages. The fact that his orders grew muddled. That the dogs went nearly four hundred miles further towards the Pole than he had planned. That he didn't change his orders despite taking the dogs so far. That I didn't have enough food for the dogs to take them further south than One Ton to meet him and Birdie and Bill. All that.'

'Some people think it would do harm to mention his errors, she said.'

'But why?'

'Because he is such an example to the troops just now. Because his diaries are an inspiration to the men in the trenches.'

'But shouldn't the truth be told?'

'Only if it is of use.'

'I don't think I could live with myself if I didn't tell the story the way I saw it.'

'I think you must do what you will. It is obvious you won't listen to me, or any of the others.'

'Do you really want Teddy Evans to be able to avoid the fact that Con wanted him off the expedition? Do you really want him to carry on parading half-truths to the public in his lectures?'

'That's not my decision.'

She looked at him and sat up straight, her back against the hardness of the chaise longue in the Lamer library. Dared him to contradict.

'And it's not my decision either,' he said. 'I shall write my book. I shall be honest. And I shall publish it myself.'

'Let's not become enemies over this.'

'I have no intention of becoming your enemy, Kathleen. Even my grief pales beside yours.'

'Do you know, Cherry, maybe it does. But I can't judge that. I can't comprehend your grief. As little as you can comprehend mine.'

'Are we agreed, then?'

'I have no influence over you. You know that. I wish you luck.'

'I miss them all, you know. Not just Bill and Birdie. Con, too. And all the others who have gone since.'

'I understand. I really do.'

He lit a cigarette and inhaled deeply. It was his only pleasure.

'Cherry?' she asked.

'Mm?'

'If I tell you something private, will you keep it out of the book?'

'Unless it affects the truth, yes.'

'A month or so before they set out for the Pole, I had a bad dream about Con.'

'Go on.'

'I can't really remember the dream, but I woke with a start. And then Peter came into the room with that determined little walk of his. And that serious face under the cherub's smile.'

She drew breath, took a sip of her red wine.

'And?' Cherry asked.

'He came up to me, really close up to me. I was shivering. And he said, quite emphatically, *Daddy won't come back.*'

'And you remember nothing of the dream?'

'You don't seem surprised.'

'Why? – should I be?'

'People seem to think dreams are just so much poppycock.'

'I don't.'

'And premonitions figments of the imagination.'

'I don't.'

'Why not?'

'I may not believe in God –'

'Neither did Con.'

'I may not believe in God, but I believe there are greater forces at work than we can ever comprehend, that there is motion in the universe which we can't foresee, and which may link us to each other or to events we should rationally know nothing about.'

'I did tell Con about Peter and the dream in a letter, but he never got it, of course.'

'Of course.'

'Does it shock you that I half believed that Con would die? And that his death came as no real surprise to me?'

'No, it doesn't. But I don't know if that's because you knew he was going to do a dangerous thing, or because I believe in the power of the spirits.'

'You are a strange man.'

'I am a contradiction, even to myself.'

'Did you see anything out there to persuade you that spirits were at work?'

Cherry hesitated. Lit another cigarette. 'Yes and no. I can't explain it.'

'But you carry it with you?'

'Yes. And the doubt and the guilt.'

'Stop the guilt. There is nothing to be gained from it.'

'And the doubt?' he asked.

'Doubt is healthy. It will keep you alive.'

'And destroy me from the inside at the same time.'

'Only if you let it.'

'I am not as strong as you.'

'I'm not sure about that.'

'Can I ask you something that you won't pass on?'

'Of course.'

'Did you hear any voices in that dream?'

'No one spoke, if that's what you mean.'

'But?'

'I'm sure I heard someone sing.'

Chapter 17

When Birdie starts crying, I don't know how to react. I nearly put my arms round her, but I'm not sure that's the right thing to do. Has she told them about our weird relationship? God knows. So Welland is the first to do something. He steps towards her, and pulls a perfectly folded handkerchief from his perfectly pressed trousers.

'It gets a lot of people like that,' he says quietly, shielding her from the rest of us. 'To read it from a source you've never seen. From an actual diary written there and then.'

'Sorry,' she says as she wipes her nose.

'Don't be sorry.' He doesn't ask for the handkerchief back. He's probably got loads, anyway, in a perfectly ordered dressing-table drawer. 'I promise what I've got to show you next won't make you cry.'

He takes us out of the room by a door at the back, one I wouldn't have noticed if he hadn't led us to it. Out in the windowless corridor, he rummages through his pockets again and gets out a key to open a heavy metal door.

'Storage cupboard,' he says conspiratorially.

'And what exactly do you keep in here?' Birdie asks.

'Everything that's not out there. Everything precious and fragile. Our conscience.'

'Why do you say that?'

'You think it's just a turn of phrase I've practised?'

'No.'

'And it isn't. Museums are repositories of living things, not just shelves full of dead history. Good museums make history live again. It's just that governments and bureaucrats don't always give them enough money. Every time I come back here, I feel the pulse of memory, the heartbeat of history, the quivering timeline that binds together all ages.'

'Nice speech,' she says.

'I mean it.'

'I can tell. But I have my own spirits to find.'

'I hope you do.'

'Come on, then, show us what there is.'

We walk past row after row of metal shelves until we reach a gloomy corner of this immense cupboard. He bends down to the bottom shelf, pulls out two wooden boxes. He lifts them, with an audible wheeze, up to the metal trolley and puts them down with a crash.

'I hate history being so fragile,' he says. 'Dive in,' he laughs.

Birdie approaches the boxes with care, as if she were expecting something unpleasant to leap from them.

'It's fine,' Welland says. 'They're framed photographic plates. And they're just brilliant.'

She picks one out and holds it up towards the nearest neon light.

'Bloody hell,' she says. 'It's Cherry.' Turns to Welland. 'Are these original?'

'Yes,' he says. 'All of them.'

'Unbelievable,' she says. 'Unbelievable.'

'Digitised?' I say.

'Not yet,' he says. 'So much to do, so little resource.'

There are hundreds of these plates. Photos of Shackleton, of Scott. There's one plate of the northern party after their winter marooned in the cave. They must have washed and brushed up before the photo was taken, though, because they don't look dirty or bedraggled. We spend over an hour going through the plates one by one, and exchange only the occasional word, the odd question. We know these people. We're familiar with their faces. We've lived with them through the books we've read. They're like our family. Even I have to swallow hard to make the emotion drain away before it reaches my eyes.

We finish going through the boxes of the past. The wood feels smooth under our fingers. We help Welland put them back onto the shelf. How long till they're looked at again? I can't help thinking that all these things need a bigger audience to become really alive again. New Zealand is so far away from the rest of the world. Even what's in the glass cases out there needs more people to see it, to appreciate it, and understand it. To remember what it was like before life became so easy. Before we could use our satellite phones to be rescued from mountain tops and deserts.

Where do these things really belong? Out there, on the Ice, in the huts? Or should they be continuously journeying from museum to museum, around the world, so the world can remember them? I don't have an answer. I don't have a bloody clue. Perhaps I will when we've been to the huts, especially Scott's. If we ever get there. Bloody weather. That's one thing that's changed. When they sailed there, the weather was just another obstacle, to be seen out. For us, it's a show-stopper.

'Great stuff,' Birdie says, fully restored. Back to her impatient, lithe, hungry self. 'Let's go there now.'

'But your exhibition opens tonight,' Nev says.

'Oh, what fun,' she says. 'I'm supposed to be going, aren't I?'

'Yes, you are.'

'As long as you don't tell anyone who I am.'

'We won't. No one else actually knows.'

'Good. It wouldn't do to destroy the mystery.'

'What made you become Storm Moon?' Welland says.

'My parents. Me getting pissed off with them and their obsession, initially.'

'That's perverse,' he says.

'I thought they were ignoring me, that they'd looked past me as a person, lumbered me with the name of someone I had nothing in common with. So I made up my own persona, and started running wild with spray cans. Childish things at first. No thought of becoming a cult.'

'And then?' he says.

'I started reading about the expedition, about their deaths, saw Wilson's work, and the colours of the ice. Found out that governments weren't doing anything to preserve, conserve, protect. Not the buildings, not the continent. It made me angry. And then I came across Blek le Rat's work, and started spraying images of ice and stencilled slogans.'

'Sex on the ice is hot.' Nev snorts. 'That's quite some political statement.'

'You taking the mick?' she says.

He holds his hands up. 'No way.'

'It's about climate change,' she says.

'Oh yeah,' he says.

'Seriously … And I guess it must be quite exciting to –'

'I believe you,' he says.

'We all know global warming's one of the main reasons for the work at the huts,' Welland says. 'The freeze and thaw cycles getting more extreme, the wet wood splitting when it freezes.'

'That's what gave me the idea to support you, not just because I wanted to get out there, if we ever bloody get there.' She grinds her teeth. 'And with the Pole centenary coming up there's a great opportunity to create public awareness of how real global warming is, and to kick those politicians' arses.'

Nev shakes his head, smiles.

'But you've still got a soft spot for Bowers?' Welland says.

She nods. 'I've got his name, haven't I?'

'Although he was a bit of a jingoistic old boy?'

'Yes, despite that. Whatever he thought, and whatever kind of man he was, he carried the weight of that expedition. The planning, the packing, the observations. His resistance to the cold. He was an astoundingly resilient man. He never kept still, apparently. He was always doing something.' Her eyes light up as she talks of her namesake.

'No one can argue with that.'

'It's just sort of weird that nowadays he's considered in this narrow view of what his politics were, almost, rather than being thought of in the context of what he achieved, and what he almost achieved.'

'What do you mean – what he almost achieved?' I say.

'No one's ever done what Scott and Bowers and the others tried. There's never been a completed walk from Cape Evans to the Pole and back.'

'But there've been people who've skied across the whole continent on their own.'

'It's not the same. That journey's never been made and completed.'

'D'you think anyone will ever try it?' I say to Nev.

'I don't think so,' he says.

'Why?'

'Well, no dogs or other animals are allowed, for starters. And that's one reason no one's ever tried Amundsen's route either.'

'And the fact that where he started from doesn't exist anymore.'

'Well, yeah, but they could start from an approximate point.'

'Anyway ...'

'Anyway. To reconstruct Scott's walk properly, leaving aside the dogs and ponies, you'd have to spend two years out there. You'd have to lay depots one summer, and then do the walk the next.'

'Couldn't you just get planes to do the depot-laying?'

'I suppose you could, but that wouldn't be an exact reconstruction then, would it?'

'If there's no dogs, you might as well have planes.'

'And, besides, I'm not sure the Yanks or the Kiwis would support it.'

'How's that?'

'Well, rescue effort-wise and stuff like that. I don't think any government would like people to go over there and die.'

139

'But is there anything to legally stop them?'

'Not really. But it'd be bloody expensive.'

'So why didn't you do this trip privately?' I ask Birdie. 'Wouldn't it have been easier than involving any bureaucrats?'

'It would have,' she says. 'But if the weather's shit, I wouldn't have been able to force them to fly either. And it wouldn't have been giving anything back. It wouldn't have helped the huts or made a statement about climate change. It would've been something really selfish to do. And I didn't want to do it that way. I want something good to come from my search for an answer.'

'And we're very grateful,' Nev says.

'Don't be,' she says. 'If not me, someone else would've done something.'

'Not any government,' Welland says.

'Why?' I say.

'It's not strictly politically correct, is it, to celebrate Scott or anything that happened during the Empire? That's why the anti-Scott brigade have been so successful.'

'Well, fuck them,' she says. 'It's all bollocks. If more people remembered what happened then, or were taught about it objectively, maybe they'd learn from it.' She shakes her head. 'It pisses me off.'

'That's why you're here,' Nev says. 'And we're lucky enough to know a cult hero.'

'Quite,' Welland adds.

'D'you think I'll make a difference?' she says, suddenly fragile again.

'I hope so,' Welland answers. 'Otherwise everything we're doing is wasted.'

Back at the hotel, I knock on her door.

'Hang on,' she shouts.

'OK,' I shout back.

A minute later, she opens the door. She's wearing the silk

outfit I bought in Singapore. It doesn't cover very much of her body. Her skin looks even paler than usual against the brightness of silk colours. And her hair even more blonde. She's gorgeous. Part of me just wants to grab her now, love her now.

'What?' she says.

'Nothing.'

'Liar.'

'You look amazing.'

'You think so? Honestly?'

'Yes. You know that's what I think.'

'I know nothing for certain. I can't read people's minds.'

I sit on her bed. It's still light outside. Spring here seems much more cheerful than spring back home.

'What do you want me to do tonight at the gallery?'

'Nothing. We're just visitors. No one knows who we are.'

'Do you really do this all the time – go to your exhibitions anonymously?'

'Always have. Always will. I don't want people to make judgments based on me. I want them to judge what I paint. I don't want someone to like my pictures just because they fancy me, or to hate them because they don't like the way I look. I want the paint to speak. I'm not important, really.'

'But you're the painter.'

'I'm a medium no more important than the canvas or the paint.'

'That's a weird thing to say.'

'It isn't, really. I am talented, OK, I know that, but that's not entirely the point. For writers and painters what's important is the message, to get their voices heard. And I think my voice would get lost if people started judging me, my appearance, my body, instead of the paintings.'

'But do you think your voice is heard? And what do the paintings mean? Don't some people think you're just ripping off Wilson?'

'Some people do think that. I don't. I'm interpreting him

in my own way. What I do is different to what he did. It's on a much bigger scale. But without the experience of having been out there. And it's not all based on Wilson. More and more of it is about something else.'

'So what is your voice trying to say?'

'Art doesn't always have to be beautiful. We don't always have to paint things that are nice to look at. There is beauty in ugliness, redemption in horror.' She sits down next to me, and leans up against me. 'Getting in front of the public, though, that's a question of luck. And if it happens, you've just got to keep going. Be focused. Think of nothing else. Rely on the fact that we all read different messages into different things.'

'I suppose we do,' I say, enjoying the weight and warmth of her body. 'I'm just not a very arty person.'

'You don't have to be,' she says. 'All you have to do is feel, not think.' She reaches out and takes my hand. 'Lie down here with me for a moment.' She stretches out on the bed. 'Come on.'

'Why?'

'Don't ask. Just do.'

I stretch out next to her. On my back. She nestles up to me. The last rays of sun make a pattern of sparkle and shadow on the ceiling. I never want this moment to end. I just hold her hand and say nothing. I've never been quiet for so long. I've never been this happy. Time stretches out ahead of us. I close my eyes and disappear.

'Adam,' she whispers.

'What? Shit, we'll be late.'

'No, we won't. Plenty of time for you to get changed.'

'What do you mean, get changed? I've got nothing else to wear. You didn't tell me I'd need to get poshed up.'

'We don't. I don't. I just wanted to wear what you bought for me.'

'Sorry I can't match you.' I sit up.

'Maybe you can. Just have a rummage in the wardrobe.'

Intrigued, I get up. I can't keep up with her. She makes me feel slow. I open the wardrobe. It's almost empty. Except there, hidden on the left, there's a suit bag.

'Go on, take it out,' she says from the bed.

'How did you –?'

'Don't ask, just do.'

I lay the plastic bag on the bed to unzip it. Soft, pale green material shimmers at me.

'Go on, put it on.'

I pull the material gently out. It's a silk suit. Its green ebbs and flows in the light.

'How d'you know it'll fit me?'

'I read you measurements, remember. And what you didn't write down, I guessed.'

I turn for the bathroom.

'Don't be stupid. Try it on in here. Don't pretend you're embarrassed. You're not in bad shape.'

I strip down to my boxer shorts and socks. I'm very conscious of the grey hair on my chest.

'Oh, hang on,' she says. She jumps up, skips across to her dresser and pulls out a black T-shirt. 'Forgot to put this in the bag with it.' She hands the shirt to me. Kisses my chest before I've a chance to pull it on. 'You smell nice.'

'Thanks.'

I get dressed as quickly as I can. The cloth feels wonderfully smooth on my skin. And the suit fits. Perfectly.

'Cool,' she says. 'Have a look in the mirror.'

So I have a look. I don't really see anything different to normal. Just an average man in a posh suit. I must admit, though, that I look thinner than I expected.

'Now you're as gorgeous as me,' she laughs. 'What a couple we make.'

'We do?'

'For sure.'

'You shouldn't have bought this.'

'Yes, I should. I wanted to.' She wraps her arms around

143

me. Pulls my face down to hers, and kisses me. 'Now stop asking stupid questions. It's time to go. I just hope this is our last night in Christchurch.'

'Together?'

'Together.'

Chapter 18

I've not skipped since I was a child. Yet here I am, skipping through Christchurch with a beautiful blonde elf, holding hands, laughing, shouting and singing. We dance along Hagley Park's boundary down to Welland's museum, then off towards the city centre.

Birdie disentangles her hand from mine, runs across to the stone walls of the old university, and presses herself flat against them, palms down.

'Come here,' she calls. 'Feel this.'

I stand next to her and copy her. The warmth floods from the stones through my body.

'Isn't it wonderful?' she says.

I nod and push harder against the wall. It feels almost malleable, solid but changeable. I can't help smiling. It's what I've become. And I never thought I'd change. I take off my glasses, close my eyes, and let the sun warm my whole face. I feel Birdie's hand on mine.

'Have you ever felt like this before?' she says. 'So excited and carefree?'

'No. Never. And you?'

'I don't think so. And I don't know why.'

'We forget the shortness of life too easily, I say.'

'Oh, don't spoil it.'

'Sorry. That came out wrong.'

'What was it supposed to come out as?'

'Life's too short, so we must enjoy it now. Take the present we have, not the past or the future.'

'That sounds almost revolutionary for you.'

'You're obviously teaching me well.'

'I don't think I could teach you anything.'

The wall lets us go, and we stroll a few paces further. Then we see the gallery. It towers above the town houses around it, an array of glass and metal curves, like the shapes of the wind.

'Nice,' she says.

'You mean that?'

'Yes, why shouldn't I?'

'Because I can never make you out. Because you're such a contrary modernist.'

'You make me too complicated. You make everything too complicated.'

'So you keep telling me.'

'No bluff or double bluff with me, Adam. I mean what I say. Especially what I say to you. And especially now. Let's go and have a laugh.'

Huge red banners sway from the flag poles outside. *Ice for a Warming Age – A Storm Moon Exhibition*, in plain black type.

Once we're past security and ticket office, we both grab a glass of champagne. The tall foyer lifts the buzz of voices and languages into a pealing echo.

'Cheers,' she says, clinking my glass.

'Cheers. Here's to your paintings.'

'Thank you. I hope they raise lots of money.'

'Bound to. Infamous painter and all that.'

'We'll see.'

Almost the entire ground floor of this place is given over to her exhibition. That's three adjoining halls. I count almost a hundred canvases when we do a quick walk-through. She's built a relentless cascade of Antarctic images, from epic to miniature. I'm breathless.

'And that's not all of it,' she says as we get back to our starting point, which has become even more crowded since we first arrived.

'Meaning?

'There's one more thing. I'll let it be a surprise for you. We've got time to go for a slow mingle now.'

There's no point arguing or asking. I find it intriguing that none of the crowd here turn and look at us. But then only Nev and Welland and I know it's this tiny, hyperactive, silk-clad woman who's created all the visions on these walls.

We push our way through the crowds in the galleries. The rest of Christchurch must be deserted.

I decide to stand by one of the paintings, to eavesdrop near the route back out to the foyer. She stands on the other side of the doorway.

'D'you think she'll turn up?' a middle-aged American asks a woman who must be his wife.

'No. She never does,' she says.

'I thought she was supposed to come to all her exhibitions. Just that no one knows what she looks like.'

'Someone must do. And she's probably as ugly as sin. That's why she never shows herself.'

'Maybe.'

'And old.'

Birdie grins at me through the crowd. Sticks her tongue out at me. *Told you*, she mouths. *OK, OK*, I mouth back. Shrug. *Told you* looks so much like *love you* when you're lip-reading, and you're not very good at it. Love and reading lips, that is.

Welland, taller than anyone here, steers his stately course towards us. He's carrying two glasses of champagne. As the sea of people parts, I catch a glimpse of Nev carrying another two glasses.

'I thought you might need some more refreshment,' Welland says to Birdie. He hands her the glass with a slight bow.

'Thank you,' she smiles and curtsies.

'Here you go, mate,' Nev says to me. 'Reckoned you'd need a top-up by now.'

'Cheers,' I say.

'Happy with the turnout?' Birdie says.

'Sure thing,' he says. 'They've all paid five hundred bucks to get in. We got the gallery and the booze for nothing, because the folks here want to support us. And there's at least two hundred payers here, so we've made a hundred grand already.'

'Cool,' I say.

'And the gallery gets twenty-five percent of the sales, you-know-who gets five, and we're getting seventy percent.'

'And a hundred percent of tonight's auction,' Welland adds.

'Oh yeah?' I say. 'Is that what you were talking about before?' I ask Birdie.

'Yes, but it's staying a secret,' she grins. 'No point otherwise.'

'Fair enough,' I say. 'And when's this happening?'

'In about half an hour,' Welland says. 'And I'm the auctioneer.'

'That should be exciting,' I say.

'Not for me. I'm perspiring too profusely already,' he says. 'It's ruining my shirt.'

'You'll be fine, Welland,' Birdie says. 'You can always use one of your perfect hankies to mop your brow, can't you?'

'It's not his brow he's worried about,' Nev laughs.

'See you later,' Welland says. 'I think I'll go to prepare for my public humiliation.'

'You're such a bullshit merchant,' Nev says. 'You've done this hundreds of times.'

'That, my dear boy, is entirely beside the point,' Welland says and stomps off.

'I'd better go with the big man,' says Nev. 'No knowing what he'll do if I don't look after him. Now make sure you get yourself a good spot. Although there's telephone bidding, there's a bloody fleet of private jets at the airport, so God knows which glitterati are here.'

'Who cares?' she says. 'As long as you get lots of cash. That's what matters.'

'We will,' he says. 'Don't you worry ... See ya later.'

She leans against the door frame.

'Come here,' she says.

I walk right up to her. She hugs me. Looks up at me. Pulls me down and kisses me. Then she kisses me again. It must be the drink.

'What's got into you?' I ask.

'Nothing. I'm just happy.'

'Good.'

'Why don't you know anything about today ... or about our trip, really? I thought you Googled everything.'

'I gave it up once I knew I was coming here with you. I don't really care much about anything else right now.'

'You're weird.'

'Not really. Knowing lots about lots of things sort of lost its attraction when I met you.'

'That's a bit like putting all your money on one horse.'

'I don't care ... Anyway, I thought you said to stop thinking, and now you're thinking too much.'

'S'pose so.'

'Let it go. Enjoy.'

'That's what I'm supposed to say to you.'

'Whatever. Come on.'

We wander through to the foyer again. They've set up a stage there now, with a lectern and a microphone. She drags me in the opposite direction, up an escalator, onto the next floor. It's almost deserted up here. The balcony looks down on the auction setup.

'This is the best place, I should think,' she says.

'I hope so.'

'Storm Moon – are you here?' Welland's voice booms through the mike. Laughter rises from the crowd. 'Well, ladies, and gentlemen, is she here or isn't she? I guess we'll never know, will we? But, from wherever she is – or could she be a he hiding behind a girl's name? – she has donated a marvellous piece to go with the paintings you've already seen.'

Welland pauses and pulls out one of his handkerchiefs. Mops his face. Exaggerates all his movements to attract everyone's eyes.

'Does anyone wish to put in a bid before we actually find out what this piece is? Come on, folks, all the money goes to the Antarctic Trust, and they really do need the money, because what they're trying to save is a precious piece of history.'

'A thousand bucks,' someone shouts from the crowd.

'That won't even buy you a look at it,' Welland shouts back. 'Why don't we start at fifty thousand? And I'm talking American.'

One of the official numbered bidding cards goes up, and we haven't even seen whatever it is that's up for auction.

'There we go. I knew that wouldn't take long. Now – let's see how far we get before we reveal all in five minutes. Enough to get to a quarter of a million, do we think?' He laughs. 'Of course we do.'

The crowd smiles at the actor down there. There's a sparkle in his eyes, and he moves with a grace not many men have. Another card goes up. Sixty. And another. Seventy. We're at a hundred and fifty thousand before two minutes are gone. And the phones haven't even rung yet.

'Why are they doing this?' I whisper.

'Dad told me to always be a mystery, to hype it like that. And not just because of the money, but because it was better not to be known, because that way no one could ever take anything away from me. It's a game for really rich people. That's all. It's got nothing to do with the art.'

'One minute to go, ladies and gentlemen, and we're just ten thousand short of two hundred and fifty thousand. Come on, be brave someone? Do I have 250k? The gentleman at the back there – thank you very much.' He lifts his auctioneer's gavel. 'Going once ... And that's all there is, because there's nothing. Going twice ...' The hall falls silent. 'Only joking, because ...' He looks up. 'Because here it is.'

We all hear whirring from just under the roof high above us. A huge canvas comes down, suspended on steel wires. I can't make it out yet. It's still moving. 'Here is *The Cairn* by Storm Moon.'

The canvas stops just above him. There are gasps from the crowd. It's about twelve feet high by twenty feet wide. It's entirely in black and white. Just like the photo we saw in the museum earlier, the one Gran took when they'd built the cairn over the tent. Except I recognise her brush strokes. And those loose strokes have created something frightening, something dark and primeval, almost repulsive. Each piece of snow those men carved to make the cairn, each dark, recessed footprint in the snow around the tent, has been turned into a skull. The cairn is a mountain of skulls, an ossuary. The Antarctic plain has become a necropolis on a massive scale. The gasps die away. A brittle silence takes their place. And then the phones start ringing.

I look round. There's no one too near us. I move close to her.

'Where did you paint that?' I whisper into her ear.

'I got someone to hire an old hangar somewhere for me. The factory's too small for this kind of stuff,' she whispers back. Her hair tickles my face.

'It's amazing. But a bit big for a living room.'

'Whoever buys it won't be keeping it in a living room.'

The auction cards are going up and down like jack-in-the-boxes, from people in the crowd, and from the line of phone handlers. There's amazed chatter from those not bidding, a constant buzz from the phones, and, above it all, Welland is keeping pace with the bids that fly around the room.

'Five hundred and fifty,' he calls. 'Five sixty.'

The madness goes on for five more frantic minutes before the bidding slows down. We're over one million now. And then it's only the phone bidders who are still in. The price creeps towards one and a half million. Birdie can't watch. Covers her face with her hands.

'One million four hundred and fifty thousand,' Welland says calmly. 'Any of you phone bidders want to make it a nice round one and a half?' He waits for what seems like an age. 'No? Going once, going twice ...' One of the bidders raises his card and spreads all the fingers on one hand.

'One million five hundred thousand. Going once ...' Welland looks down the line of phones. They all shake their heads. He picks up the gavel. 'Going twice. Going three times.' Smacks it down onto his lectern. 'And gone for one and a half million to the mystery bidder on line five.'

The crowd goes mad. There's whistling and stamping and clapping. It goes on and on. And all the while Birdie's still got her face covered. I put my arm round her. Her warmth seeps into me. I don't move until she does. Her eyes are red, but she's smiling.

'Job done,' she says. 'Time to go.'

Chapter 19

'Don't you miss a painting when it's sold?' I say as we wander back along the dark streets.

'Yes, a bit. But I take photos of them all.'

'And *The Cairn*?'

'I won't miss it. It's creepy.'

'Then why did you paint it?'

'I don't decide what to paint, you know. It just happens. I guess the cairn was on my mind when I started sketching my idea for a painting to auction off here. And once the idea was there, I couldn't stop.'

'You didn't have to paint it that big, though.'

'I did. I started to imagine what it would be like if we got to where the tent is now and everyone had been wrong, and that the snow hadn't covered it, and there was no ice, and it was still there like it was the day Cherry and Wright and all those men left it.'

'Not very likely, though, is it?'

'No, unfortunately. But that's not the point. If you visualise something – doesn't matter if you're writing or painting – you're much more likely to be able to take your audience with you. If you just make something up that you don't really believe in, then it doesn't mean a thing.'

'So where did those skulls come from?'

'From nowhere. Nothing really decomposes out there, anyway, so it's a figment. I guess it's a parable. How many dead people are out there now?'

'Who knows?'

'I suppose there must be a count somewhere. But one thing I've always wondered is if there were people in

Antarctica before it froze. And even after it froze? People who got there before those explorers we know. Or if it would have been totally impossible.'

'Totally impossible, I should think. Surely Scott or Amundsen, and others since, would have found traces of anyone who'd been there before.'

'But would they? If the snow covers all traces, won't all traces from other ages have disappeared?'

'I see what you mean, but I still don't think it's likely.'

'Yeah, you're right. Anyway, that's not what we're going for.'

'If we go tomorrow.'

'Don't be so pessimistic.'

'I'm just being realistic.'

'Oh, I know. I just don't want to be reminded. I don't want to wait.'

She pulls me tight to her for the rest of the way. She's desperate to get out there, and I wish there was something I could do. But I can't. The weather will decide. All we can do when we get back to the hotel is to make sure that all our gear is packed, and that we've got our passports.

'Sleep in my bed tonight,' she says.

'You sure?'

'I'm sure.'

'Then I will.'

We both have a glass of wine before we go up. She surprises me by asking for one of my cigarettes. She stands outside with me, takes small sips of smoke, and nips at her wine. She looks up at the dark sky and says nothing. We're just two shadows under strange constellations, waiting to pass into the land of ice. When we turn to each other, her eyes glint with faraway light.

'There is always hope,' she says.

'Yes,' I say, but I don't know what she means.

When the call comes at five the next morning, we are wrapped around each other. She stretches for the phone.

'Yes?'

I can't hear the voice at the other end of the line, but I guess it must be Warney.

'Fuck it. Any chance of tomorrow?'

The buzz of a voice.

'No, it's fine. I'll call him.'

She nods.

'I'll call Nev later. Bye.'

She puts the phone down and turns back to me. 'You heard that, I guess.'

'Yeah. You'd better call me, then.'

'Ring, ring.'

'Thanks.'

She sighs. Turns her back on me. I put my arm round her.

'Don't,' she snaps.

'Sorry.'

'Just leave it. Go back to your room.'

What the hell is she doing now? A minute ago we were almost lovers.

'Just go, for fuck's sake,' she says. 'I need to think.'

'Fine.'

I get out of bed and pull on my clothes, make sure I have the card for my room, but say nothing. I don't understand. But I won't, and can't, push her. She knows best for herself. Maybe she'll explain. Maybe she won't.

My bed is cold, too tidy, and without scent. I turn on the TV, switch it to the music channel, and lie down. I watch the empty ceiling drift, put my arm over my eyes, and enjoy the warmth from the crook of my elbow. I want to be in the next room with her. I'd almost persuaded myself it would be a good thing to sleep with her, to give in to my overwhelming need. That then she'd grow to love me the way I love her. But she's escaped me again. Strange how little things, meaningless things, change our destinies. I fall asleep imagining her skin against my fingertips. This city has us for another day.

I'm woken by a knock on my door. I jump out of bed. It's bound to be her. I open up. Shit. It's only Nev.

'Whoa, old feller. Yer could've got dressed first.'

I realise I've only got my boxers on.

'Ah. Sorry, Nev, mate. Thought it might be good news.'

'No such luck. We'll have to try again tomorrow. Gusts of sixty knots over there.'

'Bollocks.'

'Yeah. Hey, d'you know where she is?'

'No. I mean … what time is it?'

'Just gone eight. She called me at six. Asked me why the fuck we couldn't just arrange for something else to take her out there. Gave me a serious ear-bashing.'

'She does get a bit impatient now and again.'

'A bit? Anyway, I arranged to come over here for eight, got the guy downstairs to phone up to her room, and there's no bloody answer. And he says he's not seen her.'

'Get a spare key, then.' God, I hope she's not gone and collapsed again. My heart's racing.

'Already done that. Thought it'd be best if you did the door-opening, though. You know her better than I do.'

'Not much.'

I run to her door in just my boxers.

'Gimme the bloody key,' I hiss.

I open the door, jumpy. Rush to the bed. Eh? It's made. She's not here. False alarm. Thank God. But where the hell is she?

'Mobile, let me get my mobile.' I say to Nev.

'Calm down, mate.'

'I am calm.'

I find my mobile. Try to call her. No answer. I text her. *Where r u?*

'Might as well have some brekkie while we wait, eh?' says Nev.

'Not sure I can eat.'

''Course you can.'

I get dressed and we go down to the restaurant. We've just loaded our plates when my mobile rings. I answer it without looking at the screen.

'Hello?'

'I'm sorry,' she sobs.

'What for?'

'Being horrible.'

'I'm used to it.'

'You shouldn't have to be.'

'Oh well.'

'Why don't you hate me?'

'Because I can't.'

'Why?'

'You know why.'

'Tell me again.'

'Nev's here with me.'

He starts to get up. I signal to him to stay. He sits down again.

'So say it anyway,' she sniffles.

'Because I love you.'

'Adam …?'

'Yes.'

'I think I love you, too.'

'Then tell me where the hell you are.'

'I'm in Lyttelton.'

'How'd you get out there?'

'Cab.'

'And now what?'

'I'm eating.'

'I was about to.'

'Then eat.'

'I'll get Nev to drive me over to you now.'

'No. Eat first. I still need to get used to the idea of loving you.'

'That could take some time.'

'I don't think so.'

'You know best.'

'You won't change your mind?' she asks.

'What about?'

'Everything.'

'No, I won't.'

'Then I want you to think about something.'

'What's that?'

'Will you marry me?'

'What?'

'You heard me.' There's no laughter or mockery in her voice.

'I don't think it's something to talk about on the phone.'

'That's why I said you should think about it.'

'I don't know what to say or think.'

'See you later, then.' She hangs up.

'Erm, I can see things are a bit complicated,' Nev says.

'Just a bit.'

'I had no idea that you –'

'You weren't supposed to, because it wasn't really like that.'

'Hey, listen, tell me to mind my own business.'

'No, no, I don't mind. There wasn't anything to hide, you see. Just a possibility. A forlorn hope on my part.'

'And now?'

'She thinks she loves me, after all.'

'Oh, shit.' He laughs, embarrassed. 'I meant that in the best possible way, of course.'

'Naturally.' I push my food away. Change my mind. Pull it back to me. Eat some of the egg and toast. Drink the orange juice. Autopilot.

'Where is she?' Nev asks.

'Lyttelton.'

'Why didn't I think of that?'

'What d'you mean?'

'I should've reckoned she'd have gone somewhere that's got a real link to the Ice.'

'Because that's where all the expedition ships left from. God, we're idiots.'

'So, what now?' he asks.

'Would you mind taking me down there? She can't be that difficult to find.'

'Not difficult at all. There's only one café in the main street there. And then I'll leave you to it.'

'Brilliant. Listen, would you be very offended if I asked you to wait down here while I just give a friend of mine a ring from upstairs?'

'No worries, mate. I'll have another coffee.'

'Thanks, again.'

I get up and rush upstairs. Use the speed dial on my mobile. It rings for ages.

'Yeah?'

'John, it's Adam.'

'Oh, hello, pal. Wasn't expecting to hear from you.'

'Wasn't expecting to call you till this was all over, mate.'

'Problems?'

'You could say that.'

'Go on.'

'Well, the weather out there's shit, for starters.'

'Yeah, but you knew that could happen. Cut to the chase.'

'It's Birdie.'

'Spit it out, man.'

'She's asked me to marry her.'

'Bloody hell. She must be mental.'

'Oh, thanks.'

'Sorry.' The hiss of the static. 'So what d'you want me to do about it?'

'Tell me what to do.'

'Don't be stupid. You've got to do what you want to do.

You were busy telling me how right she was for you before you upped and left.'

'I still think that.'

'Then stop bloody thinking about it, and do it. Tell her yes. If you think you can put up with her for the rest of your life. And if you think she'll put up with you for the rest of her life. You're not exactly young.'

'And that's it?'

''Course that's it. Why the hell do you have to ask questions all the bloody time? Why do you always have to doubt? Commit for once in your life. And if it doesn't work out, drink yourself to death.'

'Like you, you mean?'

'Nah. I drink because I'm happy.'

'Oh, right.'

'You should try it.'

'Maybe I will.'

'Are we done? It's late here and I'm losing valuable drinking time.'

'Yes, we're done. Thanks, old friend.'

'That's what I'm here for, dickhead. Take care.'

'I will. Eh, I miss you.'

'You, too, you soft old bugger.'

Half an hour later, Nev drives me in to Lyttelton. It's a small place. It reaches down from the hills into the round bay, the crater of an extinct volcano. The early day is hot, not a cloud to be seen.

'So where is this café?' I say.

'In London Street, of all places.' He smiles. 'Just about unchanged since the explorers. All the men were billeted with families round here. Big party here the night before Scott and his lot left.'

'I guess these folks still feel part of all that, do they?'

'For sure. You know, I always get the shivers when I stand quayside and look south, because there's not really anything

160

between here and the Ice. It's like the Antarctic starts here, if you know what I mean.'

'I get you,' I say.

'The museum here's got some great stuff, too. Either stuff from Welland's reserve collection, or stuff that's been donated by lads who were with Scott and Shackleton.'

'Is it open today?'

'Should be. I'm dropping you there anyway. Here we are.'

I jump out of the car. We're just about on the quayside, outside an old, miserable-looking white building.

'This it?' I ask.

'Sure is.'

'Thanks, mate.'

'No worries. You've got my mobile anyway, haven't you?'

'Yes.'

'Just give me a call if there's a problem with anything. You're our guests, after all.'

'Thanks. Means a lot, that.'

'See you later.'

'OK. Where's this London Street?'

'Just up the hill. On your left. You'll have no trouble finding it.'

'Right. Better let you get to work.'

'Yeah. No peace for the wicked.'

The sun's on my neck as I walk the short distance up the hill. The museum can wait. I need to find Birdie. I'm confused and excited and nervous. I follow Nev's instructions and come to a straight road carved into the side of the hill. I stay left, out of the sun. It's a relief. It's too hot for me to think.

There are seats out in the street, parasols, and the smell of coffee in the air. I can see her blonde hair from here. She's facing away from me, staring across the road. She's in the shade, looking out into the brightness. I walk up behind her and lightly put my hand on her shoulder.

'Hello, Adam,' she says, without turning round.

161

'D'you want another coffee?' I say.

'Please.'

I walk into the shop to get the coffees. I struggle with my New Zealand money and get a smile from the girl serving me. Yes, I'm a tourist. Not difficult to spot an impractical Englishman, is it? I go back outside with the coffees, put them on the table, sit down, face her. She looks awful. She's got bags under her eyes, black rings round them. Her pale face has two angry red marks on either cheek. She looks like she hasn't slept in days.

'Talk to me,' I say.

'What do you want to know?'

'Why did you ask me to marry you? You said before we came that you couldn't get into a relationship, that you had to focus on finding out what happened in that tent before you could even contemplate anything else.'

'I changed my mind.'

'You threw me out of your bed this morning.'

'I was just pissed off,' she says. The red marks on her cheeks deepen.

'You can see what I mean, can't you?'

'Yes, I can. I lay there, angry as hell with all the crap, all the delay, all this shitty waiting. And then I called Nev and shouted at him for being useless, for his government being useless, and the Yanks being useless. And he didn't say anything. He just listened till I ran out of breath. And then he said he couldn't change anything anyway, and did I really want to risk my life and others' lives for something that's been waiting for nearly a hundred years? And wouldn't it be more sensible to be patient and wait to do it the right way, and find out what I was going to find out safely? So I told him to stop being so fucking sensible. And all he said was that it's his job to be sensible.'

'And that's what made you want to marry me?'

'No ... no. I lay there and tried to imagine what it must have been like in that tent. Who would have hurt the most emotionally? Scott and Wilson who had wives they'd never see again, or Henry who'd never loved anyone, never been loved by a woman? What would be worse – to love and die with that love in your heart, or never to have loved and to die never having experienced it? And the more I thought about it, the more I realised that to die without having loved must be the most desolate way to die. Because, even if you believe in God like Henry did, it's love – it's the bond between lovers – that delivers redemption. And Henry died without that. And I don't want to die without it.'

'You're still young, for heaven's sake.'

'But I could die any time. And I don't want to keep denying what I feel for you. I don't want to keep being that selfish bitch. I want to have to share. I want to have to consider others. I want to be with someone who'll make me a better person.'

'I can't change you. That's down to you. Marrying me won't make you a better person.'

'But it'll help me. It'll guide me.'

'And love?'

'I do love you, Adam. I'm just not good at showing it … yet. But I'm getting better, aren't I?'

'I suppose your monologues are getting longer,' I laugh.

'So, do you want to marry me?'

'I've told you before – it has to be forever. There'd be no way back. All or nothing.'

'I know,' she says, slowly. 'And that's what I want.'

'I'll die before you.'

'There's no certainty in that either.' She reaches out and holds my hand. 'This week?'

'Here in Christchurch?' I ask.

'Why not?'

'We might fly out tomorrow.'

'Nothing to stop us asking Nev how it might be done. And if we can't do it before we go, we can always do it when we get back.'

'Are you sure about this?'

'Yes, I am,' she says. 'The surest I've ever been. I've never been in love before.'

I look at her. She is so unbelievably beautiful, so full of life, full of contradictions. How could I not want her? All of her.

'Adam?'

'I will,' I say. 'Yes, I will marry you.'

Chapter 20

'I'm going to cry now,' she says.

'I already am.'

'Foolish man.'

'I know.'

'Let's go, then,' she says. 'There's something on the quay I want to show you.'

'Museum first, please. Nev says we shouldn't miss it.'

'OK.'

My heart's racing. My mind is filled with all the days to come, my heart with the unbearable pain of living. I hold her close, wrap my arms around her. She'll never be mine, though, despite all this, will she? Not like I've been hers since the first time we met. I don't want her to be. Then she wouldn't be the woman I fell in love with. I don't do control. I can't do control. I care too much.

When we get to the museum, it doesn't seem such a sad, white place as I thought after all. The glass doors are open. The heat of the day stretches into the old place, warms the lino that looks like it's been there since the day it first opened. Our steps echo as we walk in. It's free, just a contribution requested, so I stick a fifty-dollar note in the box because I'm feeling generous. We ask the old man behind the glass where the Antarctic collection is.

'Up the stairs. You can't miss it.'

'Thanks.'

Upstairs, we walk through a room full of old uniforms and stuffed animals. And then there's a glass door with a handwritten sign: *Antarctic*.

'Shouldn't I be buying you a ring?' I say before I push open the door.

'That's up to you,' she says. 'Maybe we could look this afternoon. Nev'll know where.'

'I guess you're right.'

'Let me in, then,' she says. She tries to squeeze past me so deliberately awkwardly that she has to put her hands on my chest. 'Come on, lover boy.'

'I'm afraid that will have to wait till after the wedding.' I laugh.

'Are you being serious?'

'Yes. I want to do it properly. There've been too many one-night stands and meaningless relationships in my life for me not to mean it.'

She hugs me. 'I'm glad,' she says. 'Even if it's old-fashioned.'

'That's me. The old-fashioned one. Let the world laugh. I don't care.'

And then we go in. And stop dead. Because it's so different to where we were yesterday. Because this isn't a museum at all, it's a memorial, a chapel of remembrance, a still, quiet old space that reverberates with memory. The huge windows look out over the bay, and the light through the windows is suffused with the blue of the sea and the gold of the sun. The curtains scatter dust. Here is history at its warmest.

We wander round the room. Our slow feet tap on the wooden floor. There's treasure in every display case, and so much that's not in boxes, so much out in the warm air. We can touch it without feeling guilty, without gloves on. I'm covered in goose bumps despite the temperature.

A sledge from Shackleton's Pole attempt spans one of the walls. Under it is the head of a dog from Scott's last expedition, called Beck. And next to him, a brass plaque commemorates the dead men. I look at Birdie, but her eyes are fixed elsewhere.

'Look at this,' she whispers. 'Can you believe it?'

'Eh?'

'Look at what you're leaning against.'

'It's a bench, that's what it is.'

'What's the sign say?'

Saloon bench from Terra Nova. 'Oh, hell.' I pull my hand away and stand up straight, blushing.

'Come on, then,' she says. 'Let's sit down on it.'

'That's not right, surely.'

''Course it's all right. It wouldn't be here otherwise, would it?'

We sit down. She leans up against me.

'It's not the same as being there, though, is it?' she asks.

'I don't know. I've never been there.'

'You know what I mean. These are just reflections of the past. I want to be immersed in it. What's there left to be learned?'

'We're always learning. Who says we won't come across something new that someone's just forgotten to document? That's been lost somewhere but that'll help you find out what happened in that tent?'

'I suppose so.'

'Maybe it's just because you're excited.'

'What about?'

'Everything.'

She burrows her head into my shoulder.

'Mmm. But about what the most?' she asks.

'You tell me.'

'I asked first.'

'Probably about the trip,' I say.

'Yes and no.'

'About getting married.'

'Yes, but you make it sound like I was getting married to someone else. Not to you.'

'I'm just shell-shocked.'

'But excited?' she asks.

167

'Very. I just want to get everything organised now.'

'Mr Sensible strikes again. It'll get sorted soon enough. Don't worry.'

'I'm not worried.' I get up. 'What was it you wanted to show me?'

'Just another echo. Out there. You still want to see?'

'Yes.'

We walk out of the museum hand in hand. We head down to the quay, across concrete paths, past modern ships.

'That's Quail Island over there,' she says. 'Where Scott and Shackleton trained their dogs and ponies.'

'D'you want to go over there?'

'No. There's only one ferry a day and we haven't got time.'

There's an old tug moored here. She rises and falls with the gentle swell, and her side rubs quietly against the tyres protecting her from the seawall. It says *Lyttelton* on both sides of her bow. The gold writing reflects in the calm water.

'Is this what you wanted to show me?' I ask.

She nods. 'She's not in bad shape, is she? She's probably over a hundred years old.'

'And what makes her so important to you?'

'She took all the ships bound for the Antarctic out of the harbour.'

'So *Terra Nova*, too?'

'I think so.'

'Cool.'

'That's what I thought. And she's still working.'

'Shame *Terra Nova*'s lost.'

'Yes. Anyway, that's it.'

'I'll give Nev a call, then. To pick us up.'

'No. Let's get a cab.'

The whole way back, her legs won't keep still. Her whole body's in motion and just can't stop. I put my hand on her thigh, but still it goes on.

'All sorted?' Nev says, grinning, when we get to his office.

'I think so,' we both say, as one.

'Nothing I can do, then?' he asks.

'Tell us where there's a decent jewellery shop,' Birdie says. 'We need some rings.'

'You're joking,' he says.

'No,' I say.

'Wait till Welland hears about this. He'll be spitting blood that I found out first.'

'Why?' I say.

'Oh, he's a sucker for a love story with a happy ending,' Nev says.

'He can be a bridesmaid, then,' Birdie says.

'And you can be my best man,' I say.

Nev comes over to us, gives us each a hug. Shakes his head.

'You're gonna need a licence from the Department of Internal Affairs,' he says. 'That'll take a day or so. And you have to give them three days' notice of when you want to get married.'

'And how long's the licence valid for?' I ask.

'Three months.'

'So we could get married after we get back, if we end up going tomorrow?' Birdie asks.

'Sure thing. It's not looking good, though. Still really high winds and hardly any visibility.'

'Hang on a minute,' Birdie says. 'Let's just cut the crap. How likely is it we'll get out there tomorrow? Nev, be honest.'

'Less than ten per cent, I'd say.'

'We might as well go home then,' she says. 'I can't stand just sitting round here. I've got to do something.'

'You're not thinking of going the Argentina route, are you?' Nev says.

'I wouldn't do that to you.' She sits on his desk. 'Could you do me a favour, though?'

'Like what?'

169

'Call Internal Affairs and get them to waive the three days' waiting, get them to marry us tomorrow.'

'Why?'

'No more waiting,' she says. 'Not for anything.'

'Can't make any promises,' he says. 'Give me a minute.' He shoos us out of his office and closes the door. Ten minutes later the door opens. 'They're thinking about it,' he says. 'They'll call back later.'

'What did you do?' Birdie says.

'Nothing.' He shrugs. 'Come on, there's something I want to show you while we wait.'

He takes us into a huge hall in the basement. It's the Trust's warehouse and workshop, and it smells of oil and sweat and freshly cut wood.

'This is where we keep some of the stuff that's come back from the huts, and we've not been able to deal with yet.'

'Like what?'

'All sorts. The stuff on the shelves is interesting enough, but it's not as exciting as what we've got in the freezers.'

'In the freezers?' I ask.

'Some of this is so fragile, we bring it back from the Ice frozen, and keep it frozen until we can process it.'

'Why not just leave it out there?' Birdie asks.

''Cos it might get lost again. We find a lot of artefacts under ice that we've chipped away, or under snow we've cleared and dug out. And some things can't be left over there.'

He opens one of the freezers.

'Here's a shirt we found at Shackleton's hut at Cape Royds. Probably Murray Levick's from the 1907 expedition.'

'Not important,' Birdie shrugs.

'I knew you'd think that,' he says. I don't think she'll ever manage to shake this solid Kiwi. 'And that's not why you're here.'

He digs deeper down into the freezer, carefully, but with

170

purpose, and pulls out a big package. He closes the freezer and unrolls the package. It's a sleeping bag.

'Reindeer bag, as usual,' he says. 'Found it at Evans last season. And look at this.' He turns out the top of the bag. There are some very faint markings on a white tag.

'What does it say?' Birdie asks.

'Can't you decipher it?'

'I think I can, but I don't want to guess,' she says, and takes the bag from him. She puts her nose right into the opening, sniffs, pulls a face, and stares at the tag. 'If I didn't know better, I'd reckon there were three letters on there.'

'That's what I think,' Nev says.

'Can you be sure?'

'Once we've worked on it. But it all takes time,' Nev says. 'Too much time. Better late than never, I suppose.'

'D'you really think it's Cherry's?' she says.

'I think the letters are *AC-G*, but I wouldn't say so publicly. I can't find any records anywhere saying he took his bag with him when he left the Ice.'

'Incredible,' she says. 'And it just goes to show how crazy we are to get addicted to this stuff. Wild theories.' She laughs. 'I'm really glad we got to see it.'

Nev's closing the freezer when his mobile rings. He looks at it, shakes his head, walks off into another room to answer it, comes back out a minute later, a broad grin on his face.

'OK,' he says. 'You've got it. Ten o'clock tomorrow morning. Better get moving.'

Birdie runs up to him, nearly knocks him off his feet when she launches herself at him, legs around his waist. 'Thanks, thanks, thanks,' she shouts, smothering his squirming face in kisses.

'That'll do,' he says, embarrassed, and levers her off him.

I just shake him by the hand.

'Listen, folks,' he says. 'I've got shitloads to do. This weather's cocking everything up out there. Should we meet for dinner tonight?'

'OK,' I say.

We look for lunch in Christchurch and get it from several shops. After we've bought our rings, we find bookshops and books and time to read. In the sun, and with sticky hands from the cakes, we eat as we read. We don't need to talk to be together, and holding sticky hands is fun. Shit, I feel like I'm about eighteen again, but without the uncertainty or the fear.

Around each familiar corner, we discover the unexpected and new. A market today where yesterday was emptiness, songs where there was silence, crowds where there was loneliness. The day passes without withering. It's evening before we have drawn breath. Is this what real love is like?

We sit outside for dinner, Nev, Welland, Birdie and I, in the centre of Christchurch, almost in the shadow of the statue of Scott made by his widow, Kathleen. Strange to be here, eating, drinking, being happy, when he reminds us of thirst, starvation and death. Welland does most of the talking. He's so excited you'd think he was getting married.

After dinner, Birdie and I sit outside the hotel in the crimson dusk. She's borrowed another cigarette from me.

'Separate rooms tonight,' I say.

'Why?'

'Mustn't spend the night before the wedding with you.'

'Superstitious old git.'

'Some things never change.'

'I'm glad,' she exhales her smoke. 'How can we resist each other?'

'Common sense?' I say.

'Anticipation?'

'Respect?'

'Love?' she says.

'Probably.'

She rubs her eyes. 'I'm exhausted.'

I think she looks scrummy. I pull her towards me and take a deep breath of that lemon scent.

'Hey, old man, I thought we were going to wait.'

'We are. I just want to feel you close to me.'

'You might get carried away.'

'I'll rely on you to stop me.'

'I don't think you can do that. I'm relying on you to stop me.'

'Ha.'

One kiss lasts an age, two kisses an eternity. I lose myself in our embrace.

Alone in my room now, I'm about to turn the light off when Nev phones.

'You all set for tomorrow?' he says.

'I think so,' I say. 'That's why I'm shitting bricks.'

'Don't. Just enjoy it while you can.'

I can hear the laughter in his voice, and the excitement, and some emotion. It's strange to have made an unexpected friend. I don't make friends easily. And it's odd that John's not here, although he told me not to be such an arse when I phoned him to tell him so, and when I started crying because I felt like I'd betrayed him by not getting married in England. He told me it wasn't important, that he'd probably have his hands full sorting out my domestics when we got back. Because that's what he's used to doing – picking me up when I'm down. There will be times, he said, there will be. And I'll have to find my way through those. Except it'll be different, because there'll be no real escape. Because vows are just that – vows, promises, pledges. For always.

Chapter 21

I'm cold in my bed, despite the warmth outside. Will she show up tomorrow? I'll leave here at eight, have a coffee and breakfast somewhere else. Welland will pick her up at nine, and she'll walk into the registry office, where I'll be waiting, at about half past.

I lie on my back, wait for sleep to come. All I can see is that painting of hers, all those skulls, all that unhappiness from back then, and her pain at something I know nothing about. It hurts me, too. I decamp out to the veranda with my cigarettes when the restlessness becomes too much.

Back in bed, the skulls are still there when I close my eyes, along with the fears of tragedy gone and tragedy to come. They're illusions. There's nothing to fear, I keep telling myself. My Antarctic bags taunt me from the table across the room. *You won't make it,* they whisper to me. *Not this time. Not ever.* I close my eyes, turn onto my stomach, and hide myself under my pillow. They can't mock me now. Seconds pass as minutes, minutes as hours.

The phone wakes me. It's half past three. Warney never sounds any different.

'Thought I'd call you first for a change,' he says, wide awake. 'Even though you're not flying today.'

'Cheers, mate,' I say. 'I'd only just managed to get to sleep.'

'It's a hard life,' he says. 'Good luck today.' Another man who specialises in afterthoughts.

'Not as hard as it could be,' I say, but he's already hung up.

The next thing I know, the phone's ringing again.

'Wakey, wakey,' Nev's voice shouts. 'It's your wedding day.'

'I only just put the phone down on Warney,' I mumble.

'Bollocks, mate. That was four hours ago. I'll see you downstairs in ten minutes.'

'Great.'

I shower as quickly as I can. I grab my fags, my wallet, my key.

Nev's waiting outside the lift when I get downstairs. 'Come on, mate. Can't risk you seeing the bride before the appointed time. You look like shit.'

'Thanks. I love you, too.'

'Wrong person, mate. Save it till later. You got the rings?'

'Yeah. Put them in the suit before I went to bed.'

'Just check, will ya?'

I put my hands in my pockets. Yes, there they are. I'm not that disorganised.

'OK, mate. Let's go have some breakfast.'

'Where?'

'Anywhere but here,' he says. 'And we're walking.'

The registry office is just a block past the art gallery, so he walks me briskly away from the hotel, past the gallery and the registry office, and into Cathedral Square. There are lots of places to eat here.

'What d'you fancy?' he asks.

'I need coffee and cake.'

'No worries.'

I'm starting to shake now, and chain smoke. I'm getting nervous. He sits me down. Gets me a coffee and a piece of cake. Sits down opposite me, then leans back and smiles. A long, slow, broad grin that lights up his face.

'Listen, mate,' he says. 'Stop worrying. Enjoy the day. It'll be the best day of your life. I've never been happier than since I've been married. Honest. And she was late.'

'I've forgotten to get flowers,' I say, cursing myself.

'Her bridesmaid will have gotten her some, you can be

sure of that. Welland wouldn't miss out on a chance to get a beautiful woman some flowers.'

'What about us?'

'I put in an order yesterday for us. It's all sorted.'

'I'm useless at this, aren't I?'

'No, just nervous. Why'd you never get married before?'

'Never got round to it. Always fell in love with the wrong women.'

'I know what you mean. Been there. But I saw the light when I was still young.'

'Thanks for making me feel older than I am.'

My stomach knots with the coffee and the cake. I feel worse than I did when I woke up.

'Just breathe deeply,' he says. 'And maybe one day you'll be saying that to her.'

'Eh?'

'Babies,' he says. 'Maybe you'll have to talk her through giving birth.'

'I don't think so.'

'We'll see.'

We walk across to the flower shop to get our red roses. He even pins mine on my lapel for me, because I can't do it. And then we make our way back to the registry office. I feel my legs getting heavier with every step. Will she really show up? Stop it. She loves you. You love her. What more can you want? What other proof do you need?

We're waiting in the anteroom. It's half past nine. She should be here. I look at my watch again. The seconds tick away too quickly all of a sudden. Where is she? Twenty-five to ten. I'm starting to sweat. The suit's too heavy for me. I sit down. He doesn't look worried. *Women's prerogative*, he whispers. Whatever that means. It doesn't make me feel any better. Twenty to.

Welland walks in. He holds the door open, stands straight.

'For the very final time, I present Miss Henrietta Birdie Bowers.' He bows.

In she walks. She's wearing the silk outfit from Singapore. And she carries a huge bunch of yellow roses with just one red one right in the middle. Her hair is spikier than ever. And she's wearing the boots, those boots she wore when we first met. She looks at me. Tears are running down our faces. She blows me a kiss. Takes Welland's arm.

The door into the registrar's office opens.

'It's time,' the attendant says. 'Are we all here?'

We all nod in unison. I'm ushered in first with Nev. Birdie and Welland follow. The room is a sea of sunshine. My breaths come quickly.

'Mr Caird? Miss Bowers? Please step forward,' says the registrar, a stern-looking woman with grey hair.

Birdie hands her flowers to Welland and reaches out to me. We walk to the desk hand in hand.

'You have both declared that there is no legal impediment to your marriage. Can you confirm this?'

'Yes,' Birdie says.

'Yes,' I say.

'Have either of you prepared any words to say to your partner?' the registrar asks.

'I have,' says Birdie.

'Please proceed.'

Birdie turns to face me. Shit, I haven't thought about this at all.

'Adam Caird,' she starts. 'I have loved you since you saved me, but I have denied that love for too long. I will deny it no longer. I want to walk the long road of life with you, to share with you all the goodness and brightness life brings. I want to protect you and carry you through any darknesses life may bring. I will remain with you through all challenges. And I will love you beyond death. These are my vows to you on our wedding day.'

I swallow deeply. I can't not cry. I try to think of something.

'Mr Caird?' the registrar asks.

'Birdie, my Birdie, I have no words to describe my love for you. My life was a waste ground before *you* saved *me*. I can imagine no one else whom I would want to share my life with. I love you despite our failings, because of our failings, and I will love you for as long as there is breath in my body and light in my soul. These are my vows to you.'

'Have you any rings?' the registrar asks.

I fish them out of my pocket.

'Please say the official words now. You first, Miss Bowers.'

'I, Henrietta Birdie Bowers, take you, Adam Caird, to be my legal husband.' She puts the ring on my finger.

'I, Adam Caird, take you, Henrietta Birdie Bowers, to be my legal wife.' I bend down and slide the ring onto her finger.

'You are now legally husband and wife,' the registrar says. 'If you could sign the Particulars of Marriage, along with your witnesses. And then, Mr Caird, I will allow you to kiss your wife.'

We sign the paper and get our copy. Welland has brought a camera, so we get photos with the registrar, and she even takes pictures of the four of us. And then I kiss Birdie. And she kisses me back. Grabs me, as if she'll never let go. We don't stop till Welland taps me on the shoulder.

'Erm, folks.' He coughs. 'Nev and I thought it would be a splendid idea to buy you both lunch to celebrate. There's a great place out at Sumner. Not very romantic, but ...'

'Sounds good to me,' I say.

'You sure you'd rather not retire to the hotel?' Nev asks.

'No, no, too much to think about. It'll keep, won't it?' I say.

Birdie looks up, as if she's waking from a dream. 'Ooh, lunch at ten in the morning. That's what I like. I'm starving.'

'Didn't you feed her?' I ask Welland.

'She said she couldn't face it. I've never been known to force a lady ...'

'I'm sure you haven't,' I laugh.

'Come on, guys,' Birdie says. 'Let's get down there.' She grabs me again. Kisses me. Touches the ring on my left hand. Whispers in my ear. 'We belong to each other now.'

In Sumner, right by the water, we sit outside in the sun. It burns into me. We're on a pier, and it's like I'm on holiday. There's a whiff of wood and heat.

The first round of drinks arrives. Welland, bless him, has ordered a bottle of champagne. It's only eleven in the morning.

'To Mr and Mrs Caird,' he toasts us. 'May they live long and fruitful lives.'

'Hear, hear,' Nev says, and takes a slug, a whole glass in one mouthful.

'I've been thinking,' Birdie says.

'Dangerous,' Welland smirks.

'Seriously, guys,' she says. She never stops being practical. Maybe that's why I like her so much, because she likes to get things done. She leans back, wrinkles her face, smiles a faraway smile. 'Maybe we should have a honeymoon.' She looks at me. 'What d'you think, husband?'

'I'm disappointed,' I say. I'd expected her to lose her temper again. And I'm not expected back at work, anyway. 'But it would give us some time to do some more research.'

'Is that what they call it nowadays?' Welland asks.

'Very funny,' she says. 'And I'll have time to do some more painting now you've got all my old ones.'

'You calling it off now, then?' asks Nev.

'Yes,' she says. 'And we'll be out of your hair. For now. We'll be back in January. It's only six weeks, although it'll feel like six years.'

'What?' I say.

'We need to find out more about Amundsen,' she says. 'Everyone ignores him, although he was first to the Pole. And no one's considered the possibility of him and Scott having met on the Ice.'

'Teddy Evans did suggest that they might work together once they found out he'd come south,' Nev says.

'But everyone says it never happened,' she says. 'And since then it's been all smoke and mirrors. What if they did meet?'

'Are you saying Amundsen caused Scott to die?' Welland asks.

'No, not at all,' she says. 'But wouldn't it be interesting if they had met and decided, however much they liked each other, to go their separate ways?'

'I don't think the timelines add up,' Nev says, frowning.

'That's why we should research it,' she insists.

'Wouldn't that change your mind about this project?' Nev asks.

'Don't be silly,' she says. 'I've made a promise. I've signed my name. I'm committed.'

'Thanks,' Nev says.

'Don't thank me. This is something I believe in. But I want the truth, too.'

'You'll find it,' Welland says. 'I know you will.'

Although he tries to persuade us to let him buy dinner as well, we eat quietly on our own in the hotel, in a corner, in semi-darkness. Then we go upstairs, after she's cancelled my room and we've moved all my things into hers.

'I'm shy now,' she says.

'So am I.'

'Turn the light out.'

'No. Not until I have seen all of you.'

She pulls back the covers. She is perfect in her nakedness. I bury my face in her hair. She pulls me to her, runs her hands down my trembling back. I'm immersed in her scent, filled with her freshness, enveloped by her. Time halts. There are no words, just touch. Nothing has ever felt this real.

'Come to me,' she whispers, draws me closer. 'Be mine.'

Slowly, gently, we intertwine, skin on hot skin, hand to

hand, face to face, eyes open, staring into each other, nothing between us, strangers no more, never. We are one double-hearted body, two souls in one vessel. We are one another.

Chapter 22

'Do you want me to carry you over the threshold?' I say to her when the cab has dropped us off outside her front door.

'Do you want to?'

'It would be kinda nice,' I say.

'Go on, then.'

She's as light as she was a year ago. I kiss her as I carry her in. I kick the door closed behind us, and carry her to her bedroom.

'So what exactly is for sale at this auction?' I ask her the next morning when she tells me there's an Amundsen auction at Christie's in a week.

'You know Amundsen's last lover, Bess Magids?'

'Only as a footnote to his story,' I say.

'She went over to Norway from the States expecting to marry him, but he'd already gone missing trying to rescue some Italian general from an ice floe in the Arctic.'

'And?'

'His family gave her lots of his things – silver trinkets, things he'd had with him on the Pole trip, and a load of cash, and then she went back to the States.'

'And that's what's being sold at the auction?'

'Some of it.'

'And you reckon it could be of some significance.'

'Yes. The more we know, the better.'

'You're right.'

'And we can't stay in bed all the time.'

'Isn't that what honeymoons are for?' I say, laughing.

'Not very long ones.'

'Will you ever learn to rest?'

'Not until I've done what I need to do.'

She wins the auction, of course. I never doubted that, not once she'd got it into her head that she wanted to get under Amundsen's skin. And two days after the auction, four wooden packing boxes arrive. I carry them into the factory, put them down in the middle of the floor.

She empties the boxes, her face like a child's at Christmas, puts everything on the floor, still wrapped. She's so careful it takes an age just to do this and, by the time she's finished, there's no room to move on the studio floor.

'OK,' she says. 'Let's do this systematically.'

'Systematically? Us?'

'Yes. Us. I'll unwrap, and you can write it down.'

'Isn't it all documented?'

'Yes, it is, but there's always something new in these things that someone's not picked up on when they've been cataloguing it.'

'Like what?'

'When it's a private sale like this, of heirlooms I suppose you could call them, folks haven't always turned small containers upside down or gone through books to see if there's anything in them.'

'There always has to be a mystery for you, doesn't there?' I say.

'Life's boring without a mystery,' she says. She looks up at me. 'People will say it's a mystery how a girl like me managed to get a man like you.'

'Don't be silly. The other way round, more like.'

'I'm not arguing, and neither should you.'

I grunt.

'Don't fret, Adam, please,' she says. 'I just want to get this done.'

I open my notebook. 'Come on, then.'

She opens the first package. 'Dear God,' she says. 'It's a matchbox holder, like the one of Scott's we saw at the RGS.'

The next package is a silver spoon, the one after that a

bayonet. There's even Amundsen's sledging medical kit, with an English provenance. And so we go on, and the number of packages on the floor seems never-ending.

'You had enough yet?' I say.

'No. Have you?'

'It doesn't look like we're going to find anything interesting, does it?'

'Be patient,' she says.

'That's rich.'

'You know what I mean.'

She unwraps what must be a couple of hundred photographic slides; the note with them describes them as glass lantern slides. They're of various Amundsen expeditions, including some from the Pole, in which he looks totally and utterly wasted.

'His book says they put on weight when they got back to Framheim from the Pole,' I say.

'Perhaps he did, after the photo was taken,' she says.

'But he looks dreadful, and the trip back can't have been much easier than the one getting there.'

'Perhaps he lied,' she says. 'Perhaps he just pretended to be a hero.'

I shake my head. 'Weird. Hasn't anyone told the truth, ever?'

'Have you? All the time?'

'I suppose not,' I say. 'Although I always try to. And I always will to you.'

'You don't always have to qualify things just because we're married now,' she says. 'It's understood we'll be honest with each other and that the past doesn't matter.'

She's automatically unwrapped the next thing that came into her hands.

'*Sydpolen*,' she says. 'It's a first edition by the look of it. And it's got his signature in it.' She stands up, picks up the book, one hand at either end of its spine, and begins to shake it.

'You'll break it,' I say.

'No, I won't,' she says. 'This is the only way to make sure there's nothing in it.'

'How about just going through it carefully, page by page?'

'Too long-winded,' she says. She keeps shaking it. Nothing. 'Dammit,' she shouts, and stamps her feet. She drops the book on the floor.

'Hang on,' I say. 'Do that again.'

'Which bit? Throwing it onto the floor?'

'No. Just shake it again.'

She picks it up and shakes it again. 'Now what?'

'Give it to me,' I say.

'What is it?'

'Something odd about it.' I put the book flat on the floor, closed, and flick the pages through my fingers. Once, twice, three times. Yes, I'm right. There are a couple of pages that don't flick properly, where the thickness sliding through my fingers is denser than all the others. I do it one last time, and stop when I feel the resistance. 'Here,' I say. 'Two pages stuck together or not cut.' I show her. 'I told you we should leaf through it. Good job I'm such a bore.' I start laughing.

'Bastard.' She laughs with me.

'I'll get a knife,' I say. 'Let's do this slowly.'

I hand her the knife. 'Go on.'

'I think the pages are stuck together,' she says. 'Not uncut.' She carefully loosens them from each other.

'This is crazy,' I say as she lays the book on the floor, a yellow rectangle of paper now visible on the white paper. 'What is it?'

'I don't know,' she says, and picks up the rectangle. It's folded sheets of paper. 'A letter?'

She unfolds the paper, stiff with age. There are two sheets, covered in tight lines of tiny black scribbles. She turns them over and over.

'Can you make any of it out?' I say.

'Only that it's dated the sixteenth of June 1928. That's

the day he left Oslo for Bergen, two days before he disappeared. And his signature.'

'What about the rest?'

She shakes her head. 'Do you know anyone who speaks Norwegian?' she says.

'No. Do you?'

'I do, as it happens.'

I'm intrigued, but she's giving nothing away.

'We're going to church,' she says.

'What *are* you going on about?' I say.

'There was a man, once. I thought I loved him. But I didn't, really. He was Norwegian.'

'Bloody hell.'

'I went to his church with him a couple of times. The Norwegian Church in Rotherhithe. The vicar there's really nice.'

'How long ago was that?'

'Long enough.'

'So how d'you know if the vicar's still around?'

'I check the website now and again.'

'And the bloke?'

'No idea. Does it matter?'

'I s'pose not.'

'We're married now.'

'I'd gathered that.' I pull her towards me. 'Won't it hurt you? Going back there?'

'Why should it? I'm happy now.'

'And you weren't then?'

'No, I wasn't,' she says. 'I was torn in too many directions, too young to understand about love and lust and the things lust makes us do.'

'And now?'

'Now? I love you and I lust for you. And most of all I'm greedy for knowledge.'

'I'll teach you.'

'I'm sure you will.'

'Come on, then,' I say. 'Let's get this over with.'
'Won't you teach me some more before we go?'
'Do you want me to?'
'Oh, yes, please.'

The inside of the church is all wood and coffee scent, warm after the damp rain outside. It's not like an English church. The nave starts halfway into the building, and before it is a wide hall with low tables and chairs. It's more like a community centre than a church. And in the left-hand corner, there's a sort of shop selling Norwegian food and newspapers, a young girl behind the counter.

Birdie walks across to the girl. 'Hello,' she says.

'Can I help you?' the girl says.

'Is Helge here today?'

'Yes, he is. Is he expecting you?'

'No, I don't think so, but I'd love to be able to see him if he has time.'

'Does he know you?'

'From some time ago.'

'I will go and ask him. Can you tell me your name, please?'

'Henrietta Bowers,' Birdie says. 'I don't know if he'll remember.'

'Please wait. I will be back in a few minutes.'

We sit down. I like this place. There's an intent to its silence, a purpose to its warmth. I might almost start believing if I had a church like this to come to. One that's welcoming, not spartan and puritan like our cold English churches where we go to be punished rather than forgiven.

'Henrietta,' a voice echoes through the room. 'I thought I'd never see you again. What a lovely surprise.'

He's all in black, dog collar scraping against his five o'clock shadow, and probably ten years older than me. His black hair is flecked with grey and, behind his glasses, his eyes are kind and inquisitive.

187

Birdie gets up, ready to shake his hand. Instead, he envelops her in a bear hug, pats her back.

'And who is this?' he asks.

She laughs. 'This is Adam. We were married a few days ago.'

'Congratulations.' He pumps my hand. 'You're a very lucky man.'

'I know.'

'How can I help you?' he says.

'I'd like your advice on something important,' Birdie says.

'We'd better go through to my office, then. Although I cannot, of course, promise I can help you.'

On the way through a side corridor he grabs a silver kettle and some cups. 'Norwegian coffee,' he says to me. 'We brew it in the kettles. I'm sure you'll like it.'

His office is small. There's a modest cross on the wall behind his desk.

'Sit, sit,' he says, pours the coffee. 'Now, talk to me.'

Birdie gets Amundsen's note out of her bag.

'We found this,' she says. 'I don't think anyone else knows it exists.'

'So why bring it to me?'

'We'd like to know what it says.'

'Can't you read it?'

'It's in Norwegian.' She hands the papers to him.

Helge raises an eyebrow, turns the pages over in his hands. 'Where did you find this?'

'In a book I bought,' she says.

He unfolds the sheets. His voice falters. 'Amundsen. What *is* this?'

'I don't know,' she says. 'Can you translate it?'

'And then?' he asks. 'What then? This belongs to the Norwegian people.' He looks up. 'I thought everything that could be found about him had been found.'

'The Norwegian people shall have it back,' she says. 'But first I need to know if it tells me something I need, something I've been trying to find out since before I first came here.'

'I will do my best, Henrietta. And I will tell no one of this until you give me your permission.'

He starts to read in Norwegian, aloud, into the gloom of the late afternoon. He has a melodic, calming voice. I can't understand him, but his voice makes me think I can. After a few paragraphs, he stops, coughs, and begins again in English.

Chapter 23

16. juni 1928 – Stemmene

16th June 1928 – The Voices

I woke last night to what I thought was a voice calling. It was a familiar voice, one which I had hoped I would never hear again.

I had planned never to tell anyone of this, never to commit to paper some of the things that happened when I won my way to the South Pole, but now, this morning, as I prepare to save an enemy from the Northern Ice, I feel compelled to do so, just as I feel compelled to save my enemy.

There are no voices, of course. Nature is a barren beast, bereft of the thoughts and feelings which separate the human from the wild. All our lives are spent keeping that beast from our homesteads, proving that we can tame her. That base instinct is not what makes us heroes, but our intellect, our will, our determination to succeed at all costs. We can never fail, nor shall we, for to fail is to allow those charlatans of nature and the supernatural to take over the world with their softnesses and petty ideals.

But I must tell this story, tell of what happened to us when we strove to conquer the Pole for our country, to demonstrate the superiority of man over nature.

Our first attempt was ill-fated, and I was afraid, for the night before we set out, when I thought the Antarctic spring had begun, I heard the same voice I heard again last night. It whispered to me as I lay awake then, as now, words I could not decipher and sounds I could not understand put a song into my brain which I could not, and cannot, shake from me.

Then, on 7th September 1911, it drew me South, pulled me and the men towards the goal I had chosen and invited me to come and grab my prize, my glory, my reward. Out we went, with our dogs and sledges, along tracks we had driven many times before to lay our depots. We went so well I believed this was fated to be our destiny, to achieve the Pole and return to Framheim before Christmas.

The song, the sounds, overwhelmed me out there. They made me want to rush up onto the Polar Plateau, on and on, sparing not the men nor the dogs nor myself, to chase and chase and not to rest until I had succeeded. I even forgot about the cosiness of Framheim, about the warmth and protection the mother country would offer us when we returned. They made the Pole seem home to me, a destination from which I might never want to return.

Johansen, my second-in-command, foisted upon me by the old man Nansen, started to ask questions when the weather grew cold, probing me for weaknesses. Could he tell how those sounds were depriving me of sleep, did he know I stayed awake every night waiting for something to materialise, something to give body to these noises which awakened urges in me that I refused to recognise? I knew he didn't want me to be the leader, that he thought he should be striving for glory with his old master, the master he claimed to have shared a sleeping bag with in the Arctic winter. He was such a small man with so much bluster, yet so little intellect.

There is nowhere to begin. There is nowhere to end. We wander around this globe without finding where it begins or ends. Because it does not. It cannot. There is an endless path etched into the surface of this imperfect sphere which spirals its periphery. There is nothing but an abstract goal planted into deserts of white, an eternal mirage of sea, a vast plain of sand. This haunted planet turns on its crooked axis. This is where we are. This is where we will always be. There are no prayers for the victors and none for the vanquished. There is only lament.

The cold began to crush us, and still I urged us on. Johansen accused me of being afraid of nature and, in my fear, taking leave of my senses. He told me we should turn back before we lost everything, that the cold was draining the life from the dogs and the men. That night, as he and I stood outside arguing in low voices, I was sure I felt something grab for me, for my heart, and begin to drag me towards a different existence: a new, bright beginning without the pain of living. The last thing I remember is kneeling in front of Johansen and begging for mercy, the next awaking in my bag the following morning. I let Johansen persuade me to find the next depot, and then turn back to Framheim. I wanted to kill him for doubting me. He said a voice had told him he would die because of his selflessness. I couldn't believe that.

On the way back, I jumped onto Wisting's sledge and didn't look back. I thought I heard sounds begging me to stop fleeing, but I did not look back, I did not turn my head, for all I wanted was silence and warmth. We were the first back to Framheim, Wisting and I, nine hours before Johansen.

I knew then that I would never make the Pole with Johansen, that he would poison my mind against my goal, that he was vain enough to try to prevent me from achieving the fame which he thought should be his. I told him and all the others that only five of us, not eight, would travel to the Pole. There was no mutiny. I saw to that. And still Johansen laughed at me. I could see it in his eyes.

The frostbites were cured, and the days permanently light by 19th October, so we left without so much as a farewell. Nothing had disturbed my sleep during our weeks back at Framheim, and I took with me handfuls of candle wax with

192

which to seal my ears to anything out there which might try to goad me again. This time, there were no hindrances to us reaching our goal.

The day after we arrived at the Pole, when we had set up Polheim, and the others were asleep after having skied off to encircle the Pole in all directions and returned, I thought I felt the earth shake, thought I saw a bright light there, right ahead of me where the Pole was, thought I heard that song again, those voices, daring me, inviting me, tempting me to stay, to live there forever, amidst the luminescent dunes of white, to let the cold pass into my flesh and freeze me, to free my soul. But I would not give in to them. I will never give in to them.

We left the day after. Bjaaland asked me if I had seen a ghost, and I told him not to be so stupid. How could there be a ghost where no people had been before?

As we shot away from our black tent, I thought I heard a scream. I looked back. None of the others did.

What if it were true, what if there were something else, something otherworldly out there, what if it were here, now, at Uranienburg? I would still be afraid. I am afraid. I fear I shall never return here. God damn nature and her secrets.

Chapter 24

Helge puts down the note and says nothing. The sound of rain clattering against the windows overwhelms this small room.

'There have been rumours, you know,' he says at last. 'That there was a dark side to Amundsen, that he was fearsome and fearful.'

'Do you believe what he wrote?' Birdie asks him.

'I cannot disbelieve it,' he says. 'Although it's not what we used to believe of him.'

'He still reached the Pole first,' Birdie says.

'That's true,' Helge says. 'But he has always been a hero. Arrogant and distant, yes, but not a frightened little boy, not a coward.'

'What was it Cherry wrote about cowards?' I say. 'Oh, yes, "If you are a brave man you will do nothing; if you are fearful you may do much, for none but cowards have need to prove their bravery." Amundsen's fear doesn't belittle his accomplishment; it makes it greater, surely. That he imagined voices which frightened him doesn't mean his efforts count for nothing.'

'But did he imagine them?' Birdie says.

'Exactly,' Helge says. 'It changes everything.'

'So you do believe him?' I say.

'Is there any reason not to?' Helge says.

'Doesn't it go contrary to your faith?'

'I don't see how it can. God does strange things. I can't question what he says, because I wasn't there ... People confuse piety with faith. There is no such thing as a non-believer. We all have faith.'

'But he makes them sound evil.'

'That doesn't mean they were devils.'

'Are you saying they're angels' voices?'

'It's not beyond the realms of possibility. Ghosts are angels by any other name.'

I sit back in my chair and shake my head. I don't understand. The cynic has no answer for the irrational argument of the believer. But then I do believe in love. That's not tangible, either. So why shouldn't it be possible for that lost note to be telling the truth about one of the greatest men of the twentieth century?

'Well, Adam?' Birdie says. 'Couldn't it be true?'

'I suppose it could,' I say. 'But angels? He was frightened.'

'Anything we can't understand frightens us,' she says. 'Cherry came back from the Antarctic a different man, because he was frightened. He was almost sectioned at one point, because some people thought he was going mad. Maybe he heard the same as Amundsen when he was out there.' She reaches out to me and squeezes my hand.

'I see what you mean,' I say.

Helge smiles at us. 'A happiness to last,' he says. 'Make sure the knot stays tight against the rest of the world. The more you pull at the knot, the tighter it will become.'

'I think I understand,' she says. 'Thank you.'

The rain lashes against the windows. The wind has become a storm. I shiver involuntarily.

'OK,' I say. 'Let's take this all as real, not as delusional. Even though, as far as we know, there's no evidence of this anywhere else. Does it have any bearing on Scott's death?'

'Maybe Scott heard them, too,' Birdie says.

'His diary doesn't mention anything.'

'Neither does Amundsen's.'

'We need another source.'

'That's why we need to find the tent.'

'You are looking for Scott?' Helge asks.

'Planning to,' she says.

'You *have* grown up,' he says. 'So certain now. Not a girl anymore. That makes me happy.'

Birdie says nothing. Grips my hand even tighter.

'And you, Adam,' he says. 'What is your goal?'

'I don't really know,' I say. 'I've drifted all my life from one thing to another, never really cared much for anything. And now I'm just enjoying being in love. Why do you ask?'

'I am a priest,' he says. 'My vocation is the exploration of souls, not of continents. There are mysteries in both. As for the saving of souls ...' He shrugs. 'They can only save themselves. I don't represent a vengeful, prescriptive god. No.' He puts his hands on the table. 'I'm a seaman's priest. I have to deal with the real world, not with the abstract world of theologians, not with the theory of faith. Real things. Loss, joy, despair.'

'I suppose you've been round the world, then,' I say.

'Yes, yes,' he says, with his hand on Amundsen's note. 'But never the Antarctic. I don't believe there is much need for Norwegian priests down there.'

'Maybe Amundsen should have had one down there with him,' Birdie says. 'Maybe then there'd be a reliable record.'

'The reality is, though, that no one does understand what happened,' Helge says. 'The letter will change that.'

'How is it you know so much about Amundsen, anyway?' I ask him.

'It's part of our upbringing in Norway, really,' he says. 'Amundsen is a big part of our heritage, one of the great heroes. And because Norway is such a new nation, we treasure our heroes greatly.'

'I hope this doesn't destroy his reputation, then,' I say.

'The fact remains that he got to the South Pole first. He was the first man to be at the North and South Poles. He achieved many things. I don't think the revelation of a man's fears should destroy his achievements. And I don't think they will. He may be judged badly by some but, even before now, many people thought him odd, abrupt and self-centred.'

'That's all right, then,' Birdie says.

'We are all sinners,' Helge says. 'Why should Amundsen be any different? Or Scott? We are all equal in God's eyes.'

'I wish I had your faith,' I say.

'You already have yours,' he says. 'Love is the greatest of all.'

'I suppose we should stop wasting your time,' Birdie says.

'You have not been wasting my time, although there are a few things I must deal with now. Will I see you here again, Henrietta?'

'I think so,' she says. 'It's nice to be here again. So peaceful.'

He smiles. 'It is a sanctuary, this place. It always has been. Quite remarkable, really. I think it was blessed in many ways when it was built.'

'It feels like a home, not a church,' I say.

'If you ever want to come here and have a blessing for your marriage, just call. I understand you're not ready for it now, but the offer is there. As far as I am concerned, you don't have to be a Christian to get a Christian blessing.'

'I'm sure you'll get sick of the sight of us,' Birdie says.

'So, what are we going to do about this?' He picks up the sheaf of paper. 'If you want to keep it until you've reached your goal, please do. If not, I will keep it here until you tell me I can pass it on.'

'Keep it here,' Birdie says. 'We know what it says now, and I don't want it to get lost. I can't think of a safer place than with you.'

'Very well,' Helge says. He puts the note into the top drawer of his desk, locks it, and gets up. 'If you do need it, just call.'

'We will,' I say.

'And let me know how your quest goes,' he says. 'I'm really very interested.'

'We will,' Birdie says, now on her feet. 'Thanks for giving us so much time.'

'You're very welcome.'

Helge walks with us through the church, out through the entrance, down the steps into the noise of the traffic. The rain has stopped, but it's cold.

'Come and see us again soon, both of you,' he says. He hugs Birdie and shakes my hand. He turns, a black shadow, gone.

'I told you he was a good man,' Birdie says.

'He is.'

'What are you thinking?'

'Just wondering how this helps us along.'

'It doesn't. Not really. It's just created more questions.'

'And the frustrating thing is that we can't do anything about it until we get back out there. January seems a long way away.'

'It'll be here before you know it. Now stop dawdling. There's lots we need to sort out at home.'

I've not thought about her house as our home before now. Not even in that briefest of interludes before we came out to the church. I've never really thought about it. What about my place in Suffolk? I don't want to give it up. I won't. We'll have two homes, I guess. Something to discuss. Later. Later.

Being with Birdie feels so different to that succession of short-lived relationships of the past. Is that what marriage does – imbue everything with a sense of purpose, clothe us in a cloak of sensitivity we never wore before, give every moment special meaning? It's odd. Even the bad weather doesn't bother me. I wake up and see her next to me, and that's all I need. It's all I want. There appears to be no drudgery in this, no monotony. How will it be in twenty years? Still like this? Or will the routine of days have beaten the romance out of us? I should stop thinking like this, stop the analysis, and live for now, enjoy the now. Tomorrow will never come. My happy today will last forever.

Weeks pass. We've been up to Suffolk every weekend. And that's what we'll keep doing. I don't want to be an occasional face in a spot that has a permanent place in my heart, that took me in when I fled from London, my heart in shreds, when I stuck a pin in a map, and another fortuitous circumstance brought me to an old cottage with wood-beamed walls a stone's throw from the church. All I've taken down to Birdie's are my computers, a few books and my clothes. The rest can stay up there. It's still my home. Our home, now. I've even turned the brightest room in the house over to Birdie so she can use it as a studio. There's a nice clutter about the place now, a lived-in feel the spartan bachelor's house never had about it. How quickly things evolve.

'Have I changed since you first met me?' she asks.

'In what way?'

'Any way.'

'You're not as horrible as you were.'

'What?' She seems shocked.

'Oh, come on. Don't act as if you don't know what I mean. You said it yourself, over and over again. That you weren't very nice. That you were selfish and hostile.'

'Oh, that,' she mutters.

'I fancied you from the first minute I saw you. I didn't think I'd ever get to know you. I remember thinking you were out of my league.'

'And then I fainted.'

'A flukish coincidence. I couldn't have made it up.'

'Maybe it was meant to be.'

'Maybe it was. But that ascribes power to some greater being. And I'm not sure either of us believes that.'

'Mmm. I'm starting to think there is something to it, you know.'

'Why?'

'You persevering with me. Amundsen's note. Helge. All those things. I don't think it's ever too late to start having some sort of faith.'

'Are you becoming born-again?'

'No … No!' she laughs. 'It's just … so many good things have happened to me I feel grateful to something beyond my understanding. That's all.'

'I don't know what to say.'

'You don't need to say anything. As long as you're happy.'

'I *am* happy. Things couldn't be better. I'm not a miserable bastard any more.'

'That's the most important thing, I guess.'

'Depends on who you are.'

'I am trying, you know.'

'I do know. Stop worrying so much. I wouldn't still be here if you were being an arse all the time.'

'But you still like my arse?'

'Oh, yes. Very much. What's not to like, dearest wife?'

'Just asking,' she giggles as we drag each other upstairs.

'Are you sitting comfortably?' she asks one day.

'Yes.'

'Good.'

'Why?'

'I'm pregnant.'

'What?'

'Do you mind?'

'No … I … I just hadn't expected it so soon.'

She hugs me. Kisses me. Fits her skinny body into the nooks and crannies of my weary bones.

'There are so many reasons I love you,' she says.

'I can't imagine any of them.'

'Fool.'

'And you're even eating properly nowadays.'

'I can't stop.'

'That's good, then.'

'Are you sure you don't mind?' she says.

'Why should I? We're married now. And you? Won't it stop you doing what you want to, what you need to?'

'Painting's not the most strenuous of jobs, compared to some.'

'I guess not. And our trip?'

'I'm not that far gone, so it doesn't make any difference. And I'm not going to tell anyone before we get there. Are you?'

'No. You can always tell Nev once we're on the Ice.'

'Unless we get bumped for weeks on end again.'

'Does lightning strike twice?'

'Yes, it does, actually.'

'Pedant,' I say. Hold her tight.

'That's me.'

'And now?'

'We read all the books again. We think about how we're going to do this when we go back. We focus on the truth. And it's not just about Henry, or Cherry, or Scott, or Amundsen. There's something else out there, and I want to find it.'

'I'm ready. Are you?'

'Yes,' she says. 'We are.' She puts my hand on her hard stomach.

Chapter 25

Hjalmar Johansen was alone. He had been alone since the *Fram* had docked in Hobart, and Amundsen had discharged him from the expedition with only just enough money to travel back to Norway. Now he was wifeless and homeless, an immaterial man whose residence was a cheap hotel. There had been reunions with some of the men from Framheim, but drink was his only real friend.

In Oslo, 1913 had just begun. Iced-over snow cluttered the streets, and night was as dark as the Antarctic winter. In his hotel, Johansen studied the unpaid bill with indifference. There was nothing he could do about it. He slipped on his heavy overcoat and checked the pockets.

When he had completed his short walk to Solli Park along the deserted Karl Johansgate and Drammensveien, he sat down on a bench under one of the largest trees, away from the street. With a sigh, he leaned back and closed his eyes.

He was at the South Pole. His shadow was sharp against the flatness of the great ice plain. He had reached the Pole on his own.

'You have done well,' the voice said.

'I had to try. I wanted to be with you again.'

'You have lived through much pain in so short a time. You deserve your reward.'

'I always wanted only the best for my masters and my country. But they did not understand.'

'We understand. They are your masters no longer.'

'I know I have been a weak man who has not put his time to the best use. I have not resisted temptation.'

'You have been honest and brave, Hjalmar Johansen. It is

a long road to travel, and now you have succeeded. You have been a loyal man with no thought of glory for yourself. We welcome you to our fellowship.'

Johansen heard thousands acclaim him in one voice, with one song, unknown and yet familiar. This was no desolate wasteland. This was home.

Hjalmar Johansen put a bullet through his own head. No more pain.

Chapter 26

It should be easy to recalculate the position of the final camp, but I can't concentrate. It's just a few numbers in a spread-sheet, for God's sake, but my mind's on other things. I can't sit still. I pace around the room, feel like shouting my happiness out of the window into the ragged wind of the English winter. And even when my thoughts threaten to go down that well-worn path of my weariness and gloom, my joy at being married, at becoming a father, takes them away and leads them upwards into a space within myself I never knew existed, where there is always warmth and light, where I finally like myself.

I try the numbers again. But I can't get them right. I'm all over the place. I fiddle with this, fiddle with that. Procrastination is the thief of time, my mother used to say. Well, she procrastinated her life away, sure enough, and never succeeded. None of them ever did. They had chances to move away from where they were, but never took them. Family's more important than anything else, Mum and Dad used to say. We can't be moving away; we're needed here. But they were happy. I think I've reached that stage now, too, and it turns me into a formless shape of repleteness, a fuzzy, muddled kind of happiness. It worries me.

I look out of the window at nothing in particular. It doesn't make sense that a lack of direction and purpose should lead me to being happier than ever, that the very absence of a goal – drifting and dreaming and smiling – gives us our greatest and purest emotions. My reflection grins back at me and tells me that that's exactly what it is, that

that's how it works, and that life gives us most when we least expect it, when we are at our least grasping.

'What are you doing?' she says and puts her arms around my neck from behind my chair. I hadn't heard her come up into this room she's turned into an office.

'Oh, nothing,' I say.

'Come on, tell me.'

'I was just thinking about how happy I am, how lucky I've been.'

'Why didn't you come and find me?'

'I didn't want to disturb you.'

'How could you?'

'Sweet domesticity is new to me, and I'm still not quite sure of how much is too much, and how much is too little. I don't want to smother you, like I've been accused of smothering others.'

She laughs. 'Oh, let the others be the others, let them languish in the past. They obviously didn't bring out the best in you, and probably never tried to.'

She sits on my knees. Wraps her arms around me.

'I've never dared think that; it seemed a bit self-centred, like something I'd tell a mate when I was very pissed,' I say.

'Ah, but that's the difference. I'm telling you, so it's true.'

'Why, thank you, ma'am.'

'My pleasure ... Do you want to know a secret?'

'Another one?'

She strokes my face. 'You feel good.'

'Is that the secret?'

'No. The secret is that I feel so lucky, too. I feel grown up in a good way. And I'm not afraid of tomorrow anymore. That's why I was so angry, I think, because I was always frightened that tomorrow might bring something bad, something to destroy my world. Like when Dad died, and there wasn't anything I could do to change it, to make it better, to make it not real. You've healed me.'

'Don't speak too soon.'

205

'I'm not. I'll always grieve for him, spend the rest of my life wishing he was still around, and that he'd met you, but I won't keep blaming myself for it.'

'You're the most wonderful woman I've ever known.'

'And you, my most wonderful man.'

I bury my face in her lemon-scented hair. I love that smell.

We spend New Year's Eve with John and Karen. We all drink too much. We all shout too much at the fireworks. But who cares? We have a laugh. After all, we're not going to see each other for some time. We fly out to New Zealand in a couple of days, and then on to the Ice. If we don't get bumped again. God knows what we'll do then.

'You sure you're still OK to go?' I say the night before we're due to fly.

'Yes. Why?'

'Just wanted to make sure.'

'I'll be fine. It'll be a couple of months at the most.'

'But what about scans for the baby and stuff like that?'

'I'll only be five months gone when we get back. Why?'

'I've been reading up about it, that's all.'

'How sweet.'

'Not really. I need to understand. I want to be good dad and a good husband.'

'You'll be that without reading any books.'

'I'm not so sure about that.'

'I am.'

'You flatter me.'

'No, I don't.'

I can see nothing in the darkness, just hear her soft voice, feel her smooth skin, touch her heat.

Chapter 27

Kathleen Scott did what she promised Con. She mourned publicly. She grieved privately. She chose life. There was so much of it left. She travelled. She celebrated her existence, her brief marriage, her freedom abroad. Her male admirers, she mostly ignored. They had no place in her heart. She ignored the untrue rumours, too, that she'd been Nansen's lover when Con was dying eleven miles from safety, that she'd had an affair with Barrie and had toyed with other young men. None of that was important. What had drawn her to Con was not the purely physical. It was the challenge of souls, the confrontation of minds, the union of thought. This was what she missed most.

When she escaped from England, she missed her son. Yet she needed to feel she could choose to be alone, to follow her mind's patterns to the extremes they took her when she did not have to bridle them. Only this way could she create the art she wanted to. Only this way could she deserve to think of herself as Robert Falcon Scott's widow.

She knew his weaknesses; she had known them all along. Foolhardiness and too quick a temper may have been among them, and certainly a disposition to brood. Fear was not one of them. She smiled when she recalled how they had brooded together but apart, at either end of a chaise longue, and not spoken for a day. That was when they realised they were meant for each other.

Even now, married to her new husband Edward for twenty-five years, she carried her notebook everywhere: the notebook into which she had copied excerpts from Con's diary in 1913 the night after Atkinson had given it to her.

She never tired of reading the words meant for her. They were her comfort. Edward felt no jealousy. Those days were precious to her, yes, but long gone.

She tried to imbue in her children that sense of urgency with which she enjoyed life, because, as she told them, it could all end tomorrow. Their childhood was all in the past. Now they were grown, she was inordinately proud of them. The present was what mattered, not the future.

Both wars had tested her health, but, as always, she raced through the days until she could stand no longer. Although the wars were now done and she had a sense of peace, she carved her character into each moment to make it her own. Pain she ignored. And she had no fear.

Then, at the end of 1946, she stopped making notes, and stopped writing from one day to the next. She tried to hide her weariness at first, but it grew to the point where she had no strength to leave her bed. On her first visit to the hospital in Paddington, she was diagnosed with leukaemia.

'I shall certainly not write about being ill,' she told Edward. 'I want no unhappiness or misery in my books. Life is a joy, as simple as that.'

'You are a marvel,' Edward said. A few days later he stood by her bed, his hand gently on the back of her semi-conscious head. 'I shall miss you, my dearest.'

She sensed Con sitting at the end of her bed.

'Will you be mine again?' he asked.

'Do you still want me? I married again.'

'I never stopped wanting you.'

'And my new life?'

'We can wind back time and stop it. Come to the Ice with me.'

'I would like that.'

Chapter 28

This time there are no hitches. Nev meets us at the airport. He hurries us through to the other side of the building where our bags are waiting. He's been keeping them in his office since we left last year. It's early morning in Christchurch, and the warmth of January's summer sun clings to our faces.

Birdie hugs him. 'No Welland?' she asks. 'I'm disappointed.'

'He's got a lot on at work,' Nev says, then laughs. 'It's a bit early for him, to be honest. It's only seven, and he doesn't start work till half past eight. He says he'll see you when you get back.'

'So we're really actually getting to go this time?' she says.

'Two hours to lift-off,' Nev says. 'Can't believe it myself.'

'Brilliant,' I say. I shake his hand and add a manly hug for good measure. I'm quite fond of the bastard, really.

'Hi, guys,' Warney's voice echoes out of the open door. 'D'ya remember everything I told ya? Better get your kit on if ya don't wanna miss the check-in.'

'Bloody hell, mate,' Birdie shouts back. 'I'd forgotten how big and loud you are.'

He comes marching out and raises a threatening fist which turns into one gentle paw of a bear hug.

'And how smelly,' Birdie laughs.

'Bugger off, missy.' He wipes his eyes. 'Take care, will ya?' He turns and lumbers back into his domain.

'Don't bother with the long johns and vests,' Nev says. 'Just pull the bloody stuff on over your street clothes.'

We do as we're told. All our stuff still fits. Which is a bit of a surprise to me. I suppose babies don't grow that fast, after all. We're done in about five minutes. I go round the corner for my second cigarette and feel a bit wobbly. I can't smoke near her now, of course, and should stop, really, but I can't. I've brought three months' supply with me, plus the duty-frees I got at the airport on the way here.

When I look round the corner, I see Birdie's face as if it's for the first time. It's alive, so alive. Everything about it moves. She's so excited by this. Her eyes, the corners of her mouth, her hair. It's all in a flurry of motion. And her smile. It's just so … so strong, vulnerable, alive, warm … all those things. There are words in her smile which don't exist. She moves me with her happiness. It's like seeing her for the first time.

'What you looking at?' she says when I stumble across to her, still full of the effects of the smoke.

'Just you.'

'Come on, kiddies,' Nev calls. 'Got a briefing to get to before we get on the plane.'

We groan.

'Listen – you've got tons of briefings to come. Better get used to it,' he says. 'No point complaining. Put up or shut up.' He's smiling. 'Let's go.'

We join the queue. We show our passports, check in our bags. There's a bunch of people in the same semi-dressed state we're in. All with big boots. It seems silly in this heat. The briefing's stuff we know already, and a bit about safety on the plane. Then we're herded onto the bus that's going to take us to the plane.

'Better put your ear plugs on as soon as we get on the plane,' Nev says as the bus heads out across the glistening tarmac.

I can't believe how big the plane is up close. You could drive the bus onto it. When we get out, I'm shaking. This is really where it starts. I can't believe it.

'When you get in there,' Nev says, 'just head straight for the back. There's a door with a porthole there. There aren't any windows anywhere else.'

'What?' Birdie shouts over the noise of the crowd.

'Just follow me,' he says and leaps up the stairs.

He's right. There are rows of seats at the front, and a long line of seats along either wall, but no window. And after twenty rows of seats in the middle, nothing except freight. They had told us it was a freight plane, and would probably be uncomfortable, but I hadn't taken it that literally. I should've done.

Nev heads down the narrow aisle on one side. Most people are choosing the seats in the middle, because they look like airliner seats. We take our coats off, flick the braces of our salopettes off our shoulders, sit down. I get my ear plugs out of my pocket.

'You're sure we need these?' I ask.

'Yeah,' he says.

'But I won't be able to hear you talk.'

'You will, mate. Trust me. And anyway, you're better off getting some sleep. Five hours in here. That's a lot of talking. Sleep's best because, when you get this close, every minute seems like an hour.'

'Do we get to go up into the cockpit?' Birdie asks. She points at the steps that lead up to another level about ten feet above ours.

'Hell, yeah,' he says, 'But they tend to wait till we're over the pack ice, and that's at least three hours away.'

'Oh, well,' she says. She does up her seat belt, and mine. Puts her head against me and closes her eyes.

'You not even going to wait till we take off?' I say.

'I don't think this'll be much different to normal planes, do you?'

'I guess not.'

Nev's shaking me. 'Wake up, you lazy Pommie bastard,' he shouts into my ear. 'We're over the pack ice.'

I stumble over to the door with the window in it and look out. I can see only tiny channels of water. The rest is floating

211

ice, stretching away in all directions, filling the horizon. No big bergs yet, though. To be down there, sailing through it, must be a different experience than just to watch it glide by from up here. *Terra Nova* took a couple of months to travel the distance we're about to cover in hours.

'You'll be able to see better from up top,' Nev says.

Birdie's awake by now. We both walk gingerly to the front of the swaying plane and clamber up the metal stairs. The pilots, even younger than her, are reading their flight plans, checking the lights on the black instrument panel again and again, while the plane steers itself.

'Howdy,' one of the guys says. 'Great view, eh?'

'Amazing,' I say. The sea looks calm, no noticeable swell, harmless, even. 'We're a long way up,' he says. 'It's much rougher down there than it looks.'

'I can imagine,' I say.

Birdie says nothing. She doesn't even smile. After five minutes up there, we climb down again.

'Better sleep some more,' Nev says. 'Landings are normally pretty routine unless there's a penguin on the runway.'

There is a penguin on the runway, though, and a stomach-churning moment when the plane seems about to touch down, only to speed up again and rise back up into the air. I'm nearly sick, but it passes. Five minutes later we're on the ground. Pegasus airfield. We're not on land at all. It's sea ice, thick flat sea ice.

The plane spews us out. The cold hits me in the stomach like a fist. Only when I've recovered do I notice the group of people waiting to get on.

'Quick turnaround, is it?' Birdie asks, pale under the overcast sky.

'Coupla hours,' Nev says. 'Get the freight off, new freight on, and off again. You don't wanna leave a plane that big on the ice for too long. You never know what the weather might do.'

'What about our bags?' I say.

'We'll pick them up at the base,' he says. 'No worries 'bout that.'

We get into a waiting four-wheel drive, white flecked with dried mud. The fan's whirring loudly, and wafts warm air through the car. The radio crackles, and we catch snatches of transmissions between the bases and other cars. It's like being in a cab. Until I start to listen more closely. They're talking about the state of the ice, about where's safe and where not. The anarchy of nature is real. It controls everyone here, where all existence is determined by the environment.

The road is marked by safety flags, a chaos of colours bright against the varying shades of white, and fluttering manically in the wind. We reach the main junction, signposted by a crowd of flagpoles, tyre marks and ragged mounds of white and grey. This is where land meets ice, where pressure ridges form higher than buildings. One implacable force against another. In a few weeks it won't be safe to walk here, when the relative warmth of summer weakens the ice, and the island wins its battle for the time being. Ten minutes later, we're decanted from the Jeep into a long green building. Hot, cold, hot. Nev pulls open one of the doors.

'Boots off,' he says. 'And coats. Make sure you keep your water bottle full all the time. And keep drinking. Otherwise you'll dehydrate. You must drink. Even if it makes you piss all the time. Even if you don't feel like it. And in the cold, you won't. Thirst kills. This place is like the desert.'

We follow him through the unfamiliar, carpeted corridors, through a warren of homeliness and functionality. The air is dry, and there's the constant hum of air conditioning. The walls are cream, as if to offset the brilliant white light reflected in from the ice. And every section of the building is closed off by heavy fire doors we have to force open. As we walk, Nev points out what's what, what's where, and why it is where it is. We drop Birdie's bags in the room she'll be sharing with two other women. She throws me a hungry look as Nev drags us onwards to the room I'll be sharing with him.

'I know it's a pain,' Nev says, 'that there aren't shared quarters, not even for married couples. Problem is, there's just not enough space.'

The whole place is unreal to me, in my jet-lagged state. It has the touch and scent of being alive. It has a sense of history, and not just in the photos that line every wall, the age-worn noticeboards and the scuffed skirting boards. There have been adventures here. People have left from here and never returned. People have met here, and fallen in love or formed friendships for life. It breathes.

'Right,' Nev says. 'Almost time for our first briefing. And that'll be base safety and conduct.'

'Yippee,' Birdie says. 'That's the one I've really been looking forward to.'

Two hours later, we know we're not allowed to leave the base unless we tell someone. We're experts in when it's compulsory to take radios with us and when not. We're all too aware of the weather conditions and how quickly they can change. This is when Birdie almost throws something at the person leading the session. *As if we didn't bloody know already*, she whispers, red in the face, hair ablaze against the dark chairs. At least Nev doesn't desert us, sits through the talk with us, although he must know the presentation off by heart now.

'Come on,' he says when it's over. 'Time for some grub. And then I thought we'd go up Observation Hill.'

The canteen, drenched in sunlight, looks like a modern addition to the rest of the base. Sparkling stainless steel counters, long tables topped with hard-wearing Formica, elegantly curved chairs, and a row of windows opening out onto the pressure ridges and the blurred shadows of the huge seals on them. When the Antarctic night comes, the windows will be dark except for the moon and the stars. A darkness blacker and thicker than ink, a darkness I don't think I could survive.

Birdie's eager, and loads her plate as full as she can. Skips over to a table, starts talking with some folks who, it turns out, are here to do some weather research, and who'll be staying here through the winter. They have no doubt they'll find the sea ice being melted from below by the warm water that's coming further south every year.

Nev nods. 'I reckon we're not far off not being able to transport stuff to the huts across the Ice,' he says. 'It gets more and more dodgy every year. The worst thing is that soft sea ice doesn't look much different to the solid stuff. That's another thing we need to look out for.'

'Wasn't there a plaque out there for a guy who'd gone through the ice with his truck?' Birdie says.

'Unfortunately,' Nev says. 'Poor bastard. Didn't have a chance. And that was in the fifties when it was a lot colder here in the summers than it is now. It would have been minus fifteen in those days, and it's only minus five today. So you'll not need your long johns or anything like that to go up Obs Hill. But don't forget your sunnies, your hats and gloves.'

Les, one of the base managers, drives us. It takes fifteen minutes, up and down the curves of the island, along what looks like a real road. Birdie and I don't touch. It's the excitement and the nerves, and not knowing exactly what people will think, even though we're married. Are we going to tell Nev she's pregnant? Maybe we'll wait till we get away from the base.

We pull up at the foot of Observation Hill, climb out of the car into a gusting breeze. The hill looks like a slagheap, with different shades of grey, only lightly sprinkled with snow. I have to keep reminding myself it's summer here. It feels cold to me, and I'm glad of my gloves and heavy coat.

It's almost a thousand feet high, this hill. It crumbles as

we make our way up, its scoria, its lava, giving way under our boots and rustling off down the slope, which is steeper than it looks. I puff and pant. And Birdie, that tiny, fragile soul whose fainting is why I'm here, storms up ahead of me, full of the energy of new discovery, her feet making new tracks on the well-established paths. It takes me an age to catch my breath once we're up there, next to an enormous cross.

'So this is Cherry's cross,' Birdie says into the now biting wind.

'Not just his,' Nev says.

'But it was Cherry who suggested the inscription wasn't it?' she says.

'Yes,' Nev says.

The continent rolls away all around us. There is no horizon, because there is no end to this plain. Even the Transantarctic Mountains across the bay don't hinder the view. This landscape is eternity made physical.

'They used to climb up here to see if the ship was coming back,' Nev says. 'And to look south to see if the polar party was coming in.'

'But they never did,' Birdie says.

'They never did.'

The writing on the cross is faded by the constant wind. But we can make out the inscription. Birdie reads it out loud into the growing gale.

In memoriam Cap. R. F. Scott, Dr E. A. Wilson, Cap. L. E. G. Oates, Lt. H. R. Bowers, Petty Officer E. Evans R.N.

Who died on the return from the South Pole March 1912.

To strive, to seek, to find, and not to yield ...

When her voice breaks, I turn away to hide my tears and look into the unfathomable distance.

Chapter 29

The world had changed, and not only for Cherry. Everest had been conquered. The South Pole had been reached with tractors by the same man who climbed Everest. Exploration shifted from Earth to outer space. Yet, almost fifty years ago, he had waited at One Ton for Scott to return. That cold seemed so far away. Married now, Cherry was almost rid of his nightmares, but not of his secrets. Some things he would never share. Angela, his wife, did not question him. Thirty years younger than him, she kept him connected to the real world.

That May in 1959 was glorious. Cherry insisted they go for walks around Kenwood House on Hampstead Heath. It was his favourite place. On this day, though, he pushed himself too hard after all his illnesses and weaknesses and trials, and was dog-tired when they returned to their rooms.

'Angela,' he called. 'I seem to have slipped.'

'Hold on,' she called from the kitchen.

His arm was at a crooked angle. He thought of Scott's arm and Atkinson. 'It hurts,' he grimaced.

'I'll get the doctor,' she said.

He spent the next few days in bed, restless and impatient. And then increasingly tired. On 18 May, he could barely open his eyes.

'It's time, my dear,' he whispered to Angela as she held his hand.

'Not yet.' She cried as his head nodded towards the pillow.

Cherry was back at One Ton, waiting for the polar party. The cold ate away at him. He shivered. On a whim, he left the tent and walked a few yards southwards. He shielded his eyes against the lowering sun. There were moving specks on the horizon, he was sure of it. He began to walk towards them. The breeze carried a smattering of words to him across the vacuum of ice.

'Almost there now.'

'... safe ... respite ... food ...'

'... relief ... happy ... rest ...'

'Good old Cherry.'

He kept walking. There was no cold now. He was a young man again. He loved the sound of the snow under his boots. The sun exhilarated him. Only a few hundred yards separated him from his friends now.

'Is all well with you?' he called.

'All's well.'

Cherry began to run. Clouds of scattered ice flew up around him. He could see their faces now, all five of them. When he reached them, he embraced them, shook their hands. He had so many questions, and an eternity to ask them.

Chapter 30

Walking down off Observation Hill frightens me. I keep losing my footing. How did they ever get that cross up there? Birdie's off ahead again. When we get back to the car, I'm exhausted and sweating like a pig. I look back. To have had the will to walk up there, time and again, to wait, to hope against futile hope to see five men trudging in from the southern horizon, and then to be disappointed and take that disappointment to your grave. I shudder.

'Fancy a drink?' Nev says.

'I could murder a beer,' I say.

'An orange juice would be nice,' Birdie says.

'No booze?'

'Oh, maybe a glass of red wine then,' she says.

McMurdo Base sprawls like an ugly growth across the level ground at the end of the land towards the sea. This is where Scott and his men were moored in the *Discovery* in 1904, when they came up here for the first time, when they built the Discovery hut on the edge of the land, only to find it was too cold to live in. Just the thought freezes me.

We drive into McMurdo slowly. It's like a frontier town in a Western, ramshackle and deserted, with paths of dirt and scattered debris. We park up next to what looks like a bomb shelter, a semi-circle of corrugated iron.

Birdie grabs my hand. 'This is no place for Cherry's ghosts,' she says. 'It's a barren place.'

Nev grunts. 'It's the bar,' Nev says, 'but we're not going there yet.'

The frozen bay is straight ahead of us, and behind it the mountains scrape the clouds from the sky. Some are covered in snow, some not. And closer to us, growing from the dirt of the cliff top, higher than the mountains from this perspective, there's a steeple on top of a small wooden building.

'They call it the Chapel of the Snows,' Nev says.

'It doesn't look old enough to have such a lovely name,' Birdie says.

'The first one burned down over twenty years ago.'

'That's a shame.'

We crunch our way towards the chapel, on snowless ground, past more corrugated iron, along a line of telegraph poles, abandoned-looking provision piles, under a canopy of cables.

'Can we go in?' Birdie says.

'Yeah. There's so much soul searching goes on round here, specially in the winter, they think it's best to have it open all the time.'

The door leads into a small, dimly lit space. There is a kind of peace here, but there's nothing alive about it. I was expecting to find an echo here of the past, but there is none. It's too new, too surrounded by modern sheds and machines. Ironic that it should have such an evocative name, yet be marooned in what is essentially a desert of dry mud.

Birdie and I walk up to the altar, and the stained glass window behind it. A large cross makes up the central panel. And beyond that there is only the Ice. And the south. But McMurdo's just like an army barracks, over a thousand people in green steel boxes. I don't want to be among scientists who aren't interested in the beauty of this continent, who want only to exploit the richness of minerals that lie beneath the ice, minerals that nations will fight over when the greed for energy has eaten up the rest of the world's resources. I sigh and turn back towards the door. I want to be out there, on the Ice.

'Seen enough?' Nev asks.

Birdie nods. 'Let's go have that drink.'

My night is sleepless, and not because of the ever-present light. There are shutters to keep that out of the rooms and give the semblance of real night. I can't sleep because she isn't here with me, and the bed's too narrow. And Nev snores. I get up again, toy with the idea of finding Birdie's room and sneaking in there, but change my mind. So I wander around the base, along the corridors, and up some stairs to where the networked computers are. At least there's a satellite internet connection, but it's so slow. Better than nothing, though. I log in to send John a quick email. He's thirteen hours behind, so I don't expect an immediate answer. I log off again, head to the smokers' room to calm myself with some nicotine – not that it helps. I go back to bed, doze a little, can't settle. I just want to find the tent and the dead men inside it.

We have more safety briefings and group work. We read manuals, learn how to tell the difference between frostnip and frostbite, learn what medications we carry in our field kits once we're far off-base, and how to deal with injuries and sudden illnesses. The routine of the radio calls from the field is drummed into us again. Calls must be made at eight in the morning and eight in the evening, without fail. If calls are missed, the chopper's sent out. We have to learn the wind chill calculations off by heart, and get tested on them, again and again.

We're told how to dress quickly and well, how to set up a tent so it doesn't blow away, how quickly wind chill can give you frostbite. Damp kills. Cotton kills. Lots of layers of clothes so there's lots of warm air between the layers. We learn that snow blindness happens mainly on grey days when there's no difference between the ground and the horizon. That's why we should wear sunglasses all the time. There are different gloves for different types of work. Keep anything that might freeze in your sleeping bag with you. My head's full of the stuff. But I have to laugh out loud when they tell us not to confuse our pee bottle with our water bottle.

Tomorrow, if the weather holds, Nev, Birdie, a safety instructor and I will get dropped off about ten kilometres from here to live in the field for four days so we learn the ropes. If we manage that all right, they'll let us off the leash. Nev's already explained to Birdie that the two of us will be allowed to stay at the location of Scott's last camp on our own if we do well in this training, and if we sign a waiver which absolves the New Zealand government of any responsibility for us.

The field training's cut short after two days because we're quick learners – except for putting the tent up the wrong way round on our first attempt, with the door facing into the wind and snow. Once we get the hang of that, we do nothing wrong, and the trainer's happy to sign us off. Birdie's exuberant.

'No more waiting,' she says, as we jump out of the truck back at base that evening. 'Let's get some dinner.'

'Your GPR gear's been here since last year,' Nev says on the way to the canteen. 'We flew it out a week before you came over, so it would be ready.'

'No one's messed with it, then?' Birdie says. 'It'll still be OK?'

'We've not even taken it out of its box. All you've got to do is check the calibration when you put it all together. And then you'll be able to see through the ice. And the modded Skidoo's ready, too. We'll fly the lot out to the location Adam's worked out, so it's ready when you get out there. And I'll spend the first night out there with you. Just to do a recce.'

'You sure you've got the coordinates right?' I say.

'I've had the chopper pilot check, double-check, and triple-check, so yes.' He pushes his empty plate to one side. 'Now listen,' he says. 'This is the really serious bit. It was a hell of a job persuading the powers that be that we could shorten your field training, so don't let me down. Don't do anything stupid when you're up there without me. No running off because you've seen something you like the look of, no stomping off in a bad temper. The Antarctic's a dangerous place, so don't forget it.'

'Yes, boss,' Birdie says. 'Sorry, boss. Anything you say, boss.'

'It's important,' he says, and for once he's not smiling.

'Sorry, Nev,' she says. 'I am taking it seriously. Honestly.'

'I know,' he says. 'But regardless of that waiver you've signed, I still feel responsible.'

'Then don't. If anything goes wrong, it'll all be self-inflicted. I didn't have to choose to do this.'

'But I did,' he says. 'I did.'

She reaches out to him across the table, and takes his hand. 'I understand how much you've done,' she says. 'And I'll always be grateful to you. I won't let you down. I promise.'

He turns the touch into a handshake. 'Thank you.' He lets go of her hand. 'Right, I'm turning in. Don't you two go to bed too late. It'll be non-stop from tomorrow. Don't let the 24-hour light make you think you're not tired.'

'OK,' I say.

'See you in the morning.'

I sit down again when he's gone, turn to look at Birdie. Her face is as pale as the snow outside.

'You OK?' I say. She still hasn't told Nev about being pregnant, and I don't think she will.

'Fine.'

'You look dreadful. You're not gonna faint, are you?'

'No.' She laughs. 'Stop worrying. I'm eating like a pig. I feel stronger than ever.'

'They were just ruses, those fainting fits, weren't they? The first to snare me, and the others just to soften me up even more.'

'Oh, yeah. As soon as I saw you, I thought, I've got to faint to get that handsome bloke.'

'Thanks.'

223

'You asked for it.'

'Not for a while, I haven't.'

'I miss you,' she says. 'I wish we were sleeping in the same bed. And I'm sick to death of being told what to do and how to do it. All this shit, when all I want to do is find the grave.'

'You want to be safe, don't you?'

''Course I do. But all this stuff's just common sense. We don't need to be taught to be sensible. And, anyway, if something really does go wrong, they can just come and get us with the helicopter.'

'It's not that simple. They don't have that many helicopters out here. They're expensive to run. And what if there's a blizzard? It could take days to get to us.'

'We could last that long, couldn't we? It is summer.'

'Not exactly tropical, though, is it?'

'That's not the point.'

'What is, then?'

'Oh, everything. It's frustrating, that's what.'

'We're off tomorrow.'

'Yes,' she says. 'Finally. How long's it taken?'

'A year and a bit.'

'For you. It's been nearly all my life for me.'

'I hope you won't be disappointed.'

'Not much chance of that,' she says. 'I'm going to refuse to leave until we find them.'

We get up, rinse our plates, glasses and cutlery, walk out of the canteen, into the empty corridor. She takes my hand. We get to the corridor which leads off to the women's quarters.

'Hang on a minute,' she says. She disappears into the doorway of the women's toilets and showers. Reappears a moment later, a broad smile on her face.

'Change of plan,' she says, and grabs me.

'What?'

'No one in there. Come on.'

'I thought you said …'

'Forget what I said.' She drags me into the room, into a cubicle. 'I need you. Who knows what could happen tomorrow.' She drops her trousers, pulls her shirt off. Helps me with my clothes. 'Let's be clean for tomorrow.' She pulls me under the shower, turns on the water. Grabs my wet body, wraps her legs around me. 'Two minutes of hot water,' she gasps. 'Better be quick.'

She kisses me through the jets of water, scratches my back, bites my shoulder to stop herself calling out, pulls my hair, claws at me, makes me forget where I am, whispers into my ear, holds me tight when it's all over, when my muscles ache, when I start crying.

'Thank you,' she says. 'I love you.'

'I love you, too.' I look round the cubicle. 'Towels – there aren't any towels.'

'Doesn't matter.' She steps out of the shower. 'Use your shirt.'

She's still so skinny. God knows how I'll feel when she gets bigger. Will she ever be the same once she's had the baby, ever get back to that six-pack of a stomach that clenches and relaxes whenever I touch her? Does it matter? She bends over to pull on her pants.

'You cow.'

'Irresistible cow,' she says. 'You'd better take a good look while you can.'

Chapter 31

'Right,' Nev says after breakfast. 'We're all set to leave in an hour.'

'Finally,' Birdie says.

'We're flying out with field boxes with food for three months.'

'We're only going for six weeks,' I say.

'Better too much than too little,' he says. 'The only stuff you need to take are your extra-cold-weather gear and your radios. We'll take those to Evans with us.'

'I can feel a "but" coming on,' Birdie says.

'But we can never be sure of the weather,' he says. 'We could end up being stuck at Evans for some time if a storm blows up.'

'Better than being stuck here,' Birdie says. 'At least we'll be where they were.'

She's sitting in the lounge, under a lamp that's always on. It throws a yellow light over her face, colours her hair even brighter, even spikier, soaks into her cheekbones, her every tiny feature. The lounge, full of books and comfortable chairs, faces south, and the light is always on to guide Scott, Bowers, Wilson, Oates and Evans home. Birdie under the light is a guardian angel, the presence that could bring them back safely. What will we find of them when we get out to Cape Evans, where they left from, and never returned? Will there be anything tangible of them there, something to hold on to and carry with us until we, too, are lost?

Distances become incalculable, shapes indefinable, once we're up in the air. When we flew into Pegasus, the mountain ranges looked as if they'd been computer-generated, small ripples on a flat surface. Now they're massive and dangerous, too close for comfort. The chopper rears up into the wind, bounces up and down. My hands contract to fists.

'It's always like this,' the pilot says into our headsets through his mike. 'This is calm compared to most days.'

The headsets muffle the cacophony of the rotor blades slicing through the air. We can't hear the gusts that make this flying coffin shudder. Mount Terror and Mount Erebus, two of the four volcanoes that form this island, crouch in the distance. Patches of grey scoria are surrounded by accumulations of snow. And beyond them, far beyond, the cold blue of the sea, fighting its never-ending battle with the ice. We're diminished by the scale of this place, brought down to size by the immensity and power of this continent and the nature which created it, and harbours it.

We stop off at Cape Royds so we can see Shackleton's hut. There's hardly any snow. The wind has dropped when we land, and it feels almost like an English summer. The hut is much smaller than I expected, nestling shyly in a hollow between rising sea cliffs and the slope up towards the centre of Ross Island. Set deep into black soil, its pine has been stripped of colour by the elements.

It feels like a happy place, probably because I know all of the 1908 expedition survived, that they enjoyed being here, revelled in measuring themselves against nature. There's so much food left here: whole hams, untouched cans of an assortment of preserves. It's as if they had so much, they didn't know what to do with it. We even find Shackleton's signature, scrawled into the casing of one of the beds with a fountain pen. The wind ceaselessly batters the walls, the door, the roof.

Birdie disconnects while we're here, walks up the rises and down the falls as if she were the only one here. This is nothing but an interlude for her. Beyond her, the sea is black. And glowering, away in the other direction, the glittering cone of Mount Erebus crowned, not in clouds, but in volcanic smoke. A mountain breathing.

After lunch, we're in the air again for the short flight to Cape Evans, a two-day trudge for Scott and his men. We pass the Barne Glacier, split on its shore side into a hundred huge and monstrous crevasses. And then we see Scott's hut for the first time, set on a slight slope. It looks tiny from up here, as if it's about to slide from the land onto the ice. There are tide marks of snow and ice and churning soil around it.

We're put down on the edge of a small village of tents and containers. The chopper stays on the ground only for long enough to unpack the supplies we'll need while we're here, then takes off again from amidst the black scoria and seal carcasses that haven't moved for a hundred years. I feel a little deserted when it's gone, and search for Birdie's gloved hand. I've got butterflies in my stomach.

The light constantly changes. It's never still, never at rest. One moment it's bright enough to make razor edges from all the shadows, the next it's soft and almost tangible. Then a cloud flits across the sun and jars everything static into jagged motion. One moment is never the same as another.

A long, low iceberg is trapped in the sea ice. It looks close enough to touch, but is actually miles away. Beyond that, the Transantarctic Mountains rise out of the mist. It's minus 10C, and feels warm. Seals stretch out on the ice, less than twenty metres away. The only sound is that of our feet on the frozen ground, and the wind pushing its way around the metal containers further up the shore, behind the yellow A-frame tents of the conservation team.

By the time we've finished putting up our tents, it's late afternoon. Nev's embarrassed, because it took ages to put his tent up when Birdie's and mine went up in next to no time. I pretend to warm my hands on his face. He just shakes his head.

'It had to happen sometime,' he says. 'And that's the first time in ten years.'

'I hope it's not a bad omen,' Birdie says.

'Rubbish,' he says. 'No such thing.'

'So, when are we going to see the hut?' Birdie says.

'We'll get some grub first, and then we can wander over there,' he says.

'How far away is it?' I say.

'Four hundred metres,' he says. 'It'll take about five minutes to walk. Whatever you do, remember to stick to the flagged path. Things might look safe here, but nothing's ever really safe, specially at this time of year with the sea ice breaking up.'

'Understood,' I say.

'And where do we get this grub?' Birdie says. 'I'm starving.'

'In the kitchen wannigan,' he says.

'What the hell's a wannigan?' she says.

'It's one of those containers.'

'Why wannigan?' she asks.

'Couldn't tell ya, to be honest,' he says. 'It's just one of those words we've always used.'

'Fair enough,' she says.

'And tomorrow you'll be cooking,' he says. 'One of the others will do it tonight.'

The sun is still high in the sky, a pinhole of light through the threatening clouds. It doesn't feel like any time at all. I have the feeling that time doesn't exist here. The sun might change position, but it's always up there, never down behind the horizon. It dislocates me, this unremitting shining light, as constant as the wind. I wander round the camp, and find the only respite from the wind and the sun is behind one of the wannigans. When I finally find shade and calm, I get out my cigarettes and light one.

'Ah, another smoker,' a thick Australian accent says behind me. It's Ted, one of the carpenters. 'Mind if I join you?'

'Not at all,' I say. 'Want one of these?'

'That's what I was gonna ask you. I always leave mine on the mainland when I come down here.'

'Leading you into temptation then, am I?'

'Could say that,' he mutters. 'But who cares? I won't tell anyone if you don't.'

His skin is burnished by being outside all the time, and his fingers are dirty from his work. He's worked on historic wooden huts in Australia, and on another hut, Mawson's, on the other side of the continent. He's divorced, has one kid. He loves being out here.

'Don't you miss your kid?' I say.

'Oh yeah,' he says, 'but you can't beat this, can you? Who knows if we'll ever get the chance again?'

'Not easy to get out here, is it?'

'They're queuing to get this kind of work back home.'

'Why?'

'You know, that's the weird thing. It's not because of science, not even because of the restoration. It's because there's something about the human aspect of that age, something special and grand.'

'Grand?'

'Grand in the sense of wonderful, unique, unfathomable.'

'I don't understand. It's a building. Historic, fair enough, but just a building.'

'Just imagine the thought that went into putting it together, getting it ready. Where did they think they were going to put it? This wasn't their site of choice. And then they built it in two weeks when they did get here. Almost a hundred years later, it's still here. Think of the care that went into making those boards, the calculations to make sure all the bits fitted together as they should. You know, people nowadays think those days were so primitive, but they weren't. Those blokes were innovators and craftsmen. They relied on themselves, their eyes, their hands, not on machines, or on anything automatic. And then they lived here for two years. And others after them. Understand now?'

I nod while he grinds his cigarette out in my home-made aluminium ashtray.

'And that's why this is so important,' he goes on. 'Because otherwise the world will forget about it. I'm not interested in all that shit about the race to the Pole, or about why some people think Scott's a Pommie dickhead and some think he's a real hero. I'm just interested in saving a building that's got a soul, as far as I'm concerned, a place that speaks of human progress.' We get up. 'Sorry, mate,' he says. 'I get a bit excited about all this stuff.'

'I think I'm beginning to understand,' I say. 'Not just about you. About this.'

'You'll never wanna leave, mate,' he says. 'I don't.'

Dinner is a wonderful curry, concocted from rice, sausages, chickpeas, baked beans, peppers. I don't think I've ever eaten something more satisfying. We wash it down with beer and wine. In the background, the gas burner fizzes. Slow light floats in through the windows. It's an idyll in here, warm and comfortable, companionable. There's even some chocolate for dessert.

I look across the table at Birdie. She's animated, and her cheeks are flushed. She winks at me while she talks to the carpenters. I listen to the cacophony of conversations. It's fun to sit just outside these circles of words and absorb everyone else's words. It's something I've never really done before, to learn from others. I've been too busy trying to impose my narrow view of the world on others so I can move quickly and efficiently from one thing to another without being involved, or having to think too hard. I won't ever be able to do that again. Because I'm involved now. And not just because I'm in love. But because the passion these people have for this project, for this period in history, and this building I've not even seen yet, is contagious. Because, finally, I realise I have a heart.

Chapter 32

We've talked as much as we can talk. It's ten o'clock in the evening. There is some semblance of dusk outside the windows, more because of the cloud cover than a sinking sun. Inside, there's silence, an anticipation of what's coming next. Nev looks round the table.

'We done?' he says.

They all nod.

'The hut's all clear,' says John, the head conservator. 'Here's the key.'

'You keep it locked, even though no one's going to walk in there at this time of day?' I say.

'Touring ships,' Nev says. 'There's a lot of them around this time of year. They used to try to get in without letting us know. I didn't like that. So, the keys.' He turns to Birdie. 'Are you ready then?'

'Yes,' she says, her voice shaky. 'Lead on.'

We get up. Birdie has turned into that fragile, sullen little child she was when I first met her. She grunts when I help her into her jacket. No one says anything. We leave the wannigan and the door slams shut behind us. The cold is a relief after the oppressive warmth inside. My breath steams away up towards the clouds. I follow her, my feet uncertain, my heart in my mouth. I don't know what to expect – of the hut, of her, of myself.

The path across the ice seems to follow the curvature of the Earth. The yellow flags are spaced evenly, catch the sunbeams as they fall from the sky. The wind grabs at them, swirls them into flapping percussion, whistles around the hood of my coat. We push up the gentle slope. The sound of the snow and ice under our boots crackles away into the bay. The closer we get to the hut, the more the wind drops, and the slower we walk. It's as if we don't really want to get there, don't want to be disappointed, want to revel forever in the anticipation.

We cross from the snow onto the black scoria, heading downwards now. Nev, next to Birdie, points into the distance. I can't hear what he's saying to her. I follow their footprints through the dirt. Behind the pale wood of the hut, a range of hills reaches out towards Erebus. They're only partly covered by the ice. In the winter, the hut is almost fully immersed in snow, and at the beginning of each summer the teams have to manually shift almost a hundred tons of snow from around and on top of it in order to get in.

The last few metres of the path are melting ice. Nev fiddles with his coat pockets, pulls off his gloves so he can reach the key. We're there now. A ramp leads up to the door. I shiver. The wind blasts one more time, and flees. We're left in the silence of this nothingness with only our fears and memories and anticipations. Nev turns the key, and pulls open the door.

'You go first,' he says to Birdie.

She wipes her feet before she steps into the gloomy annexe. Nev and I follow her into it, an airlock built almost a century ago, so the wind and snow would not penetrate into their living quarters whenever the front door was opened. Our footsteps become muffled as soon as we're inside. There are no floorboards, just the bare earth, and a stockpile of rancid seal blubber that drips its grease out onto the ground. We follow the annexe round into what were the stables. Old shovels hang from the wall, rusty with age and lack of use. The stables have no windows, except for one at the far end, one bright tiny light at the end of a long tunnel, remnants of straw, and a clinging scent. I feel like I'm being watched.

We pad our way back round to the inner front door. Birdie pulls up its rope latch, looks back at me and hesitates, tries to smile. But it doesn't quite work, and she looks fearful and despairing. I try to reach out to her through the bleakness. Is it because we know what happened to the men who lived here, because of the sadness that must have pervaded when five of them didn't return? The door springs open with a small creaking sigh. The wood is dark from age and the handprints of now-dead men.

Time has created its own scent here, in the still air, heavy with an indefinable odour. Pipes from what looks like an old boiler disappear into a room on our right. The old lino which covers some of the floor is pockmarked and ripped in places, scarred by the comings and goings of feet that have long stopped moving, become bones filling unnamed graves.

The room the men shared stretches away from the door. It's immense, much larger than Shackleton's hut, much longer and higher and wider than I'd imagined. The light passes weakly in through the larger windows, and casts a pale reflection onto the floor. Shadows and shards of light mingle. In the aisle sits the long, heavy, broad wardroom table, a natural focus for the entire space, around which all else gathers. Scott celebrated his last birthday here, in June 1911, when he had only nine months left to live. I can see him sitting there, at the head of the table, longing to reach the Pole before Amundsen, and to get home to his own beloved artist, as I would have longed to get home to mine.

We're in a different world, moving in slow motion, in a separate time. We see nothing modern, have lost touch with our own era. We wander off in different directions. We don't speak, don't look at each other, try to make as little noise as possible. We tread as lightly as possible, each of us in separate parts of what is so much more than just a wooden hut. Even Nev acts as if it were the first time here for him. Yet he must know it better than anyone else.

I imagine the door opening and some windswept,

frosty-bearded explorer walking in as if he'd just returned from the south. I can hear them tramping to the front door on that first day in November 1911, ready to start out on their trek. I see them looking back into the long room, marking down all they wanted to remember, a final picture of home before the desolation and the cold of the march. I sense the hope with which they left here. Their story is imprinted on these wooden walls, on these shelves, bunk beds and floors. It speaks of unfulfilled hope and tragic destinies, not of human vanity. These were honest men, men of endeavour, regardless of their skills, capabilities and brittle personalities.

The hut's geography is familiar to me. I've read of it over and over again. Above me, sledges are suspended from the roof rafters. Straight ahead of me is Ponting's darkroom, where he developed all his Antarctic photographs. I know what's to the left of that room, yet I won't move towards it. I turn back. I need Birdie there, to know what she's feeling. I'm suffocated by grief.

Nev and Birdie are standing in front of the bunk beds nicknamed The Tenements, by the bunk nearest to the main door. Birdie turns to me. In the darkness of this windowless tunnel, I can't see her clearly. She reaches for me, breathes a sigh only I hear.

'This is where he slept,' she says. 'This is Henry's bed. The last real bed he slept in before he died. It's sad, isn't it?'

I embrace her. I say nothing, nod.

'Is there anything left of his?' she says to Nev.

'Not that we know of,' he says. 'All the really personal effects went back on the *Terra Nova* when they moved out in 1913. And then the hut was used by Shackleton's men in 1914 and 1915, so clothes got reused and muddled.'

'But it's not impossible?' she says.

'No, it's not impossible. There's so much stuff here, we're discovering new material all the time.'

'Cherry was on the bottom bunk, wasn't he?' she says.

'Yes.'

'Weird, seeing all this,' she says. 'I never really could visualise how closely they lived together. I'm surprised they didn't lose their rags with each other.'

'They had a common purpose, though, didn't they?' I say. 'A common purpose. That would've meant a lot, wouldn't it? And then Bowers and Cherry and Wilson became inseparable after the winter journey to Cape Crozier.'

'You're right,' she says. She turns towards the door, points at the food crates dividing the hut. 'Did they really have to separate the men from the officers with this?'

'They all thought it was perfectly normal,' Nev says. 'Just like on a navy ship. They all accepted it, because that's the way it had always been.'

'But lots of people say that's why the expedition failed,' Birdie says. 'Because it was so rigid and based on Empire and class.'

'That's a load of old bollocks,' Nev says. 'They might have been separated in here, but everything else they did together. They sledged together, for heaven's sake, and I don't think class came into it then. It's fair enough now to say that it was an odd way of doing things, but it wasn't then. It's easy for people to say that they were in an age when the Empire was weakening and all sorts of questions were being asked of the status quo, but to say that's why they failed is just not to accept the facts.'

'So why did they fail?' I say.

'Lots of reasons. Scott made some errors of judgment. Some of his orders, especially about how the dogs were meant to be used, were ambiguous. He cut it too fine with his timings and his food rations. And the weather was unusually cold that March. All these things add up. And ...'

'And?' Birdie asks.

'And I guess the approach they took was, for that time, and I suppose now, typically British. You know, we'll muddle through, we'll be OK, we're not professionals, but we'll do our best. Amundsen was a professional. He knew what the weather could be like. He loaded his bases, made sure he had enough food and fuel to get to the Pole and back twice. And that's because the Pole was his only goal, because he wasn't interested in science, because he was single-minded. It doesn't make him bad or Scott useless. It just makes them different. I think Scott was unlucky to die, but I also think he never had a chance of getting to the Pole first once Amundsen had decided he was going for it.'

'Both of them should be remembered as strong, brave men,' Birdie says. 'And all those who were with them.' She rubs her face.

'The thing is that Amundsen had one stroke of luck,' Nev says. 'He built his base onto the sea ice without knowing it. That's why it's gone. He assumed it was land-based ice. If things had gone against him, he and his men could have been lost as soon as they got there. He just didn't get punished for his error of judgment.'

Birdie squeezes my arm. We haven't told Nev about the Amundsen note we found. I guess we never will.

Nev coughs. 'I think we should celebrate being here. Give me ten minutes. I'm just going to nip back to the camp to get a coupla things. Make yourselves at home.' He bounces out through the door.

'Was he about to cry?' Birdie says.

'Why would he?'

'Because the hut's safe now. He's put the best part of his life into this.'

'Like you have. Just in a different way.'

'It's the same obsession. Despite what Nev says, no one knows why they died. OK, we know they starved. We know Evans must have had a brain haemorrhage or cerebral oedema, and that Oates died in a blizzard after his feet went. But we still don't know why the last three just stayed in the same place for almost two weeks.'

She walks up to Birdie's and Cherry's bunk.

'He won't mind me climbing up here, will he?'

'Don't ask me.'

She takes off her boots and coat, climbs gently and swiftly up onto the top bunk. She lies down on top of the sleeping bag up there, on her back, arms behind her head.

'It's really comfortable,' she says. 'I hadn't expected that. And it smells quite nice, you know. Although it's been here for so long.'

Then she's quiet for an age. I can hear her breath, regularly and slowly, like she's asleep. I don't disturb her, keep looking at my watch. Eight minutes since Nev went. That'll do.

'Nev'll be back any minute,' I say.

'I know. Time I came down.'

I take her into my arms before she's down the steps. Hold her tight. 'You OK?' I ask.

'Fine,' she says. 'I thought it would upset me, but it hasn't. If anything, I feel better now. Now that I've been here, with them all, I'm ready to follow them, ready to find them.'

'You sure?'

'More than ever.'

'I'm glad.'

'So am I,' she says.

Nev bursts in through the door with a bottle of whisky in his hand.

'A small tot won't do us any harm,' he says. 'And we haven't got any champagne.' He puts the bottle down on the floor. 'And now the celebration,' he says and pulls three glasses out of his jacket. He picks up the bottle and pours three large measures.

We say cheers and drink. I look at him and see Birdie was right. He's very moved. The three of us link arms, all of us in tears now, clinking glasses in the footsteps of our ghosts.

Chapter 33

When I bought that handful of Antarctic books the day after I'd met Birdie, I leafed through them all to find the pictures, a typical thing to do with new books, I suppose. The one that made the biggest impression on me then was the one of Scott in his cubicle writing his journals, pipe in hand, legs crossed, his greatcoat on his bed, rows and rows of shelves of books around him, and photographs pinned to the wooden walls. Now my heart is thumping, my hands shaking.

We walk towards the darkroom and turn left, the light harsh after the gloom of The Tenements. Birdie steps across me, sighs. I turn the corner, too, and gasp. It's different from the picture. The table's been changed, and the books have gone. There's no blanket over the sleeping bag, no greatcoat, no photos, no suitcase under the bed, and the bedside shelves have gone, too. But it's essentially the same. And opposite it are the beds that Wilson and Teddy Evans slept in.

'So why did Scott have an open cubicle, but Shackleton a room totally separate from his men?' Birdie breaks the silence.

'I don't know,' Nev shrugs. 'Some reckon Shackleton lent his room out to his men for some privacy, if you know what I mean. Others think that underneath that varnish of being everyone's friend, Shackleton was a bit of a self-centred bastard.'

'And Scott not as rigid as many people thought?' she says.

'Possibly,' he says. 'It could be that he wanted to hear what was going on around him, or that money dictated the design of the hut. No one really knows.'

'But everyone assumes that everything's understood about what happened here all those years ago,' she says.

'I think you'd only be able to understand it if you'd actually been here at the time,' Nev says. 'Anything else is guesswork.'

'D'you want me to take a picture?' I say to Birdie.

'Not really. It'd be a bit like being photographed in a coffin. Makes me feel a bit uncomfortable.'

'You being superstitious?' I say.

'No, no,' she says. 'It just doesn't feel right. But take one of it just as it is. It'll be interesting to compare it with Ponting's photo of him in here smoking.'

I grab a couple of frames before Birdie's curiosity carries her over to Ponting's darkroom.

'Have you catalogued everything in here?' she says.

'No, not yet,' he says. 'It's probably the room with the most artefacts in it, and the most fiddly because there are so many small ones.'

'Can we have a look?' she asks. 'And move things round a bit?'

'Just remember where you found it,' he says. 'Put things back exactly where you found them.'

'Thank you.'

We need a halogen lamp to be able to see what's in the room. Nev rigs one up for us. He points out the reels on which Ponting dried the prints for *90 Degrees South*, his documentary of the expedition. There are chemicals still here which Ponting used to develop his photos, and plates and all sorts of detritus and unrecognised artefacts. Birdie walks into the room and starts to move piles of these things around, carefully and slowly. She puts her hand into a narrow shelf, feels around, pulls a face, pushes her hand even further into the narrow gap.

'How thoroughly have you looked at the stuff in here?' she asks.

'Not at all,' Nev says. 'We'll be doing this room last. We

wanted to get all the dangerous stuff from the chemistry lab next door catalogued first so we could make it safe. Why?'

'Because I'm touching something that feels like artist's paper, not photographic paper.'

'Can you reach in far enough to get it out?' I say.

'Yes,' she winces. 'I just don't want to break anything.' She bends down and works her hand painstakingly back out of the gap. Finally, she stands up again. She has an A3 piece of paper in her hand. It's grimy. Time has not been kind to it, after over ninety icy winters and freeze-and-thaw cycles. She brings it out to the table in Scott's cubicle.

'I need natural light for this,' she says.

'What is it?' Nev asks.

'I think it's a Wilson watercolour,' she says. 'Look, here.' She points at the middle of the painting. '*Ross Island from Cape Roberts, Granite Harbour.* It's not signed or dated, though.'

'What makes you think it's Wilson's?' I ask.

'It looks like his work,' she says. 'I'd be very surprised if anyone else had done it.'

'D'you think it's significant?' Nev asks.

'Not in the greater scheme of things, no,' she says. 'But for anyone wanting to get a full record of his work it is. It would be a shame for it to be lost to the weather.' She touches it with her finger tips, runs them round its edges, shudders.

'I'll get it looked at tomorrow.'

'Thanks.'

She moves to replace the painting where we found it when there's a sound like a striking clock from the chemistry lab beside the darkroom.

'What the hell was that?' I say.

'No idea,' Nev says. 'Never heard anything like it before.'

There it is again. Birdie quickly slots the painting back onto its shelf. We walk across to the wall the sound comes from. There's nothing there.

'Did there used to be a clock here?' Birdie asks.

'I can't remember seeing any on any of the photos,' Nev says. 'And we certainly haven't found one.'

'Weird,' she says.

The sound again.

'There used to be a wind meter outside,' Nev says. 'Only the pipes are left now. I guess they used to lead into this part of the hut.'

'Doesn't explain why it sounded like a clock,' she says. 'I'd have expected to hear a whoosh, not a chime.'

Nev shrugs. He's at a loss. The light fades.

'D'you believe in ghosts?' Birdie says.

'Not as such,' he says. 'But people have talked about strange things happening in here.'

'Hauntings?' she says.

'I guess that depends on how you interpret it. Some say they've felt a presence so oppressive they had to get out. Others reckon they've seen shadows or bright figures. Some people are totally untouched by it.'

'And you?' she presses him.

'I've always thought there's a presence,' he says. 'But I've never been able to decide if it's just because there's a unique atmosphere here, or because there really is something here.'

'Sir David Attenborough's been on telly back home saying he felt something here when he was filming years ago,' I say.

'Has anyone ever spent a night in here on their own? Even if the night's been light?' Birdie says.

'Not that I know of,' Nev says. 'I reckon it'd be too spooky. And we don't want people staying in here on their own, anyway.'

'It'd be interesting to get together people's accounts of what they'd seen or heard,' I say.

'But it's all second-hand again, isn't it?' Birdie says. 'Nothing that can be proved or disproved.' She folds her arms over her chest. Looks round. 'Mind you, I believe there's something here, and I'm not that suggestible.'

The light dims even further.

'Have you seen enough for today?' Nev says. 'We've all got an early start tomorrow.'

'I think I have … Adam?'

'Ditto. Thanks very much.'

As we make our way out of the hut, we hear the clock again. There is no wind outside. It is now perfectly calm. After he's locked the door, Nev takes us round the hut to the wall where the wind meter was. The pipes are still there, but there is nothing loose there that might have caused a noise inside. The clouds race away above us, on a collision course with Erebus.

Back at camp, only Ted is still up. He's melting snow for the next morning. I share a tot of whisky and a cigarette with him before he turns in. Birdie and Nev sit outside the wannigan. They both look exhausted. For some reason I feel wide awake. Must be the nicotine.

'Right, I'm bushed,' Nev says. 'Time to sleep.' He smiles at us. 'Make sure you get some kip, too. Sorry about the single tents, but that's just the way it is out here. Don't want to cause discontent amongst the troops.'

'I'm too tired for anything but sleep,' Birdie says. 'Not that you needed to know.'

'Correct,' Nev says. 'Too much information. G'night.'

'Night,' we both say and watch Nev trudge to his tent. When he's disappeared, we move back into the warmth of the wannigan. The gas heater stays on all the time. It's a refuge for the conservators and carpenters who work in the cold all the time. The hut can't be heated. It would destroy the artefacts.

'And now?' I say.

'We've got one more night here after tonight,' she says. 'We'll be able to have a less emotional look round the hut tomorrow. And then we'll finally be off.'

'You excited?'

'Scared we won't find anything. But less scared than I was

243

about being out there. And I'm really chuffed we found that Wilson painting.'

'You found it.'

'Whatever. I'm excited about getting a copy of it and painting it my way. But that's some time off. D'you mind if I go to bed now?'

'No. Why should I? S'pose I ought to go, too. But I'm so hyped I think I need another drink and another smoke.'

'Don't overdo it,' she says. 'And remember to drink lots of water.'

She kisses me, hugs me, puts her head against my chest. 'I'll miss you tonight,' she says.

'And I'll miss you.'

'A couple more nights, and we'll be sharing a tent again.'

'Maybe a sleeping bag, too, if we can work out how to put one together.'

'That'd be good.'

She kisses me again, pushes open the door to let herself out and a cold fist of air in, closes the door gently from the outside. I drink a big glass of water, then wander slowly to where the ice meets the land, the quiet scrunch of scoria under my feet, a small glass of red wine in my hand. I worry about waking people up. I sit on the ground, light a cigarette, sip my wine and inhale the smoke. There are no sounds at all. Everything has stopped. I love being in this vacuum of time with no concerns or pressures. I could sit here forever.

Back in the wannigan to get another glass of water, I notice that Nev's left the key to the hut on the table. I pick it up, weigh it in my hand, wrap my fingers round it, put it in the pocket of my coat, steal outside, and close the door behind me as quietly as I can. I tiptoe out of the camp in the direction of the hut, then speed up when I think I'm out of earshot. The gloom is complete, not a single gap in the clouds.

The key turns easily, and I step into the hut, into the smell of rope and tar, so familiar I'll have it in my nose every time I think of this place. I lift the rope latch on the internal door, push my way in, walk straight down the hut towards the wardroom table. Then it starts, a quiet hum from where Scott slept, and the temperature drops, and I get the feeling again that I'm being watched, but much stronger this time, like there's someone living and hiding in here, like there's someone trying to speak with me, trying to keep me here. I'm covered in goosebumps, daren't advance any further down the hut, turn and walk as quickly as I can without running to the door, try to pull it shut. It won't close. It's like someone's fighting me on the other side of it, trying to keep it open. Then it shuts with a dull thud.

I slam the outside door shut, run back across the sloping ice, keep looking over my shoulder. I'm out of breath when I skid into camp, and up to Birdie's tent. I open it, don't care how much noise I make. I shake her. 'You've got to come,' I say.

She's out of her bag without asking questions, throwing her coat and boots on.

'There is something there,' I say. 'I've just felt it.'

'Calm down,' she says. 'Let's get there.'

As we run to the hut I tell her what happened.

'You should've taken me with you in the first place.'

'Didn't want to wake you.'

'Doesn't matter.' She takes the key from me.

I'm shivering again.

We walk in together. She tries to lift the latch, but can't. 'What the hell? It's like someone's holding it down from the inside.' Her eyes are wide open, whites prominent. She keeps rattling at the latch, pushing against the door with her shoulder. 'Come on, let us in.'

I try to help, and finally, with all our hands pulling at the latch, it lifts and the door crashes open. The place is even darker than before, and colder. She takes my hand as we walk in. Nothing's changed in here, nothing's out of place.

There's just the subdued echo of our breathing, the steam not rising, but falling down onto the old floor.

'Did you hear any singing?' she says.

'I don't know.'

'They're here,' she says. 'I knew they'd be. They want to be at home. Let's leave them in peace.'

The latch drops easily this time, and the outside door closes soundlessly. We walk slowly back to camp. Outside her tent she puts her arms round me as far as she can.

'I don't think there's any evil here,' she says. 'Just loneliness and grief.' She kisses me. 'Now sleep.'

'Sorry,' I say.

'Don't be sorry. I'm glad you woke me.' She opens her tent and disappears into it. 'I love you.'

'I love you, too,' I say through the tent wall.

It's almost two o'clock in the morning. I climb into my tent, rip off my outer layer of clothes and wrap myself into my sleeping bag, pull the gaiter over my eyes, fall asleep quickly.

I wake to the sound of footsteps. Slow footsteps, carefully placed, one after the other. My skin crawls. In the darkness, I daren't open the tent, daren't unzip the flap to look out. I feel cold and exposed and alone. I have a vision of Scott, dressed like his statue back in Christchurch, walking along the shore. I try not to listen, try to get back to sleep. I'm afraid, too afraid this time to find Birdie and her comfort. I shiver in my bag, shiver in my sweat.

The next morning I feel worse than the day before. It takes three cups of tea to make me feel normal. Perhaps it was the whisky.

'Did you drink enough water yesterday?' Birdie asks me.

''Course I did,' I say. 'I'm not stupid.'

I stay in the wannigan after they've all gone off to work on the hut. Nev leaves too, probably to use the bucket in the portaloo that's so small the door doesn't close properly when you try to take a dump with your ECW gear on.

'I didn't dream what happened last night, did I?' I say.

She shakes her head. 'Could you sleep?'

'Sort of. You didn't start walking round the camp, did you?'

'No. I was going to ask you the same.'

'Why?'

'I got woken up by footsteps,' she says. 'It scared me.'

'Me, too. Could it have been one of the others?'

She shakes her head again. 'I've already asked them all. It wasn't any of them. And they didn't hear anything either.'

'Then what?'

'I don't know,' she says. 'But I'm going to find out.'

Chapter 34

The Barne Glacier creaks and rattles. Above, the sun and clouds combine into a chaos of shifting light and colour. We've walked for two hours when the shining expanse of ice gives us our first unimpeded view of Erebus.

'That can't be forty miles away,' Birdie says. 'Looks more like two.'

'Foreshortening,' Nev says. 'The human eye can't comprehend the scale of things out here.'

'Can't we just walk across and see how far we get in another couple of hours?' Birdie asks.

'No way,' Nev says. 'The glacier's not safe. It looks all nice and flat and solid from here, but remember those huge cracks you saw at the edge of it yesterday from the chopper? Well, they're there, too, under all that lovely blue ice.'

'Every part of this continent's dangerous, isn't it?' I say. 'We can't trust anything.'

'No, you can't. When I check the site you're gonna be working on, and it seems dodgy to me, I'm gonna pull you straight out,' Nev says.

'You can't do that,' Birdie says. 'We signed a waiver. It doesn't matter what happens to us. It won't be your responsibility.'

'You may not like this, but I'm human, you know. I can't just let you off the leash if I think it's a risk.'

'Yes, you bloody well can,' she shouts. 'Don't be so bloody emotional. We're just people. The mystery's more important.'

'Look, let's talk about this when we get there, why don't we?' I say. 'No point wasting time over it now.'

'You're right.'

We take lots of photos of Erebus, of Birdie and Nev in front of Erebus, of Birdie and me in front of Erebus, of Nev and me in front of Erebus. Lots of recorded memories. The wind picks up, sends snow and ice crystals scurrying along the glacier. They etch fine lines into the ice I thought impregnable. Such fragile and abrupt beauty. Such treachery.

We turn. The hut is a tiny wooden glimmer at the foot of this slope of solid land, down by Skua Lake. And the islands beyond, the islands it took them days to sledge out to, look within reach. Another optical illusion. We begin to walk back. Everything's steeper, further, more jagged than it looks. Half an hour on, we see the glacier butting out into the bay. The sun sharpens the cruel edges of its crevasses, at least twenty metres from top to bottom. It doesn't bear thinking about.

Birdie and Nev carry on walking as I sit down on the shoreline to change the film in my old camera, and the storage card in the new one. I decide to have a smoke. Their voices carry back to me on the wind, through the frozen air. When I've finished, I gaze across the sea ice before I get up, pack everything back into my bag and follow them. The clouds race me across the static blue sky.

When I catch up with them, they're waiting outside the hut. The sun is brilliant against the whitened pine. I'm drenched in sweat. It congeals almost as soon as it comes off me. It is still below freezing.

'Hard to understand, on a day like this, how they could die, so ... almost ... easily,' Birdie says.

'Their clothes were different. They didn't have a limitless supply of fuel. We've got six months of meat in that food wannigan,' Nev says. 'Totally different. And they didn't have choppers to lift them off if they got into trouble. Or radios. They were totally on their own. We're only fifteen miles from civilisation. We're just tourists, visitors. They were real explorers.'

We spend the afternoon rummaging around the hut. It's lost that initial magic we felt when we walked in for the first time last night, with the conservators' gear now littering the floors again. There's nothing oppressive here, but there's still a presence. They all say they feel it, even when they're working together, under artificial light, and in sunlight. It never leaves, they say. And it's not their imagination. There's a hundred years of history looking over their shoulders, experiences modern people could never comprehend.

The team leader, Alf, asks if I want to help him dig a trench at the back wall, so they can put in a membrane to keep out the melt water next spring.

'Sure,' I say. 'I've used a jackhammer before.'

I give up after ten minutes. Digging into concrete is child's play compared with hacking down into permafrost. The hammer keeps slipping out of my control. So I shovel away all the frozen earth and ice Alf digs up with the hammer once I've handed it back to him. More sweat. Lots more. Three hours of work in the cold, and I'm soaked and tired and befuddled. But it feels good, like I've done a little bit to pay my way, like I've made my mark in the history of this small but epic hut, something that'll be here long after I've gone.

Back at the camp, I head straight for the food wannigan and get myself a can of beer. It's past seven in the evening, and there's a chill in my bones. I sit down on the scoria in the lee of the wind with my bushman smoker friend and his can of beer.

'Enjoyin' it?' he asks.

'Amazing,' I say.

'D'you think you'll ever come back?'

'Dunno. Hard to say.'

'You will,' he says. 'We all will. This place won't let us go. Not just on account of the hut and the work we've done on it. Because of the peace, the stillness, the beauty. There's no place like this anywhere else on Earth, and that's a fact.'

'I'll drink to that,' I say.

'Cheers,' he says. 'Good on yer.'

Birdie and Nev have been cooking. Rice, veg, pork.

'That's a turn up for the books,' I say when I walk into the kitchen.

'What?' she says, lithe and sexy, and without her fat clothes on.

'You cooking a decent meal.'

'Nev did the cooking,' she smiles. 'I just did the chopping and assisting.'

'It's a start,' I say.

'Sure thing,' Nev says.

After dinner, Alf makes the radio call to base. There's snow forecast for tomorrow morning.

'If it closes in, we'll be stuck here,' Nev says.

'I know,' Birdie says. 'But not for long. It doesn't worry me anymore. This is a good place to be.' She smiles, puts her hands on the table. 'D'you mind if I take my husband for a walk?'

'Just don't go too far,' he says. 'And if there's any sign of the wind picking up, or the clouds coming in low, head straight back.'

'I only want to sit up there on the bluff with him, the other side of the helipad.'

'No worries,' he says and takes another sip of his coffee. 'See you later.'

Outside, she hooks her arm into mine. We walk into the wind, past the dead seals and stones marking the helipad, up the incline to the rock tower that oversees this tip of Ross Island. We walk with our heads down, say nothing. It's so good to feel the pressure of her arm in mine, to feel connected with her again. There's been so much to take in, so much to do and remember, that we've not really had time to think of each other.

At the top, we turn a slow circle to take in the roof of the hut dwarfed below Erebus in one direction, gaze across to the Transantarctics in another, and try to make out features on Inaccessible Island we've read about. We train our eyes on the south, up over the high centre of the island from here. She grunts.

'Let's sit down and watch the seals. Maybe we'll see some orcas, too. Eating penguins.'

'I doubt it,' I say.

'We can always hope.'

'Are you OK?' I ask when we're sitting on a couple of flat rocks.

'Yes, I am,' she says. She takes her right hand out of its glove, pulls my left hand out of mine, and kisses it. Takes my bare hand into hers. It's warm. She squeezes my hand, leans forward to look into my eyes.

'Are you all right?' she asks.

'Never better.'

'I'm glad.'

'Any reason for coming up here?' I ask.

'Just to be alone with you. We've had so little time lately. One thing and another. All this new stuff. All this excitement. I wanted to have you to myself for a while. And not share you with Nev or with all this wonderful landscape and history.'

'You've always got me. All of me.'

'I know that. That's what I wanted to say, too. I've never felt so safe, so replete. There's always been one worry or another. And sometimes grass on the other side that's greener. And sometimes boredom and fear. But with you, there's nothing like that. And I want you to understand that I've never felt like this. I've never hoped to be like this before. When people spoke of true love it always seemed like something predictable, nothing to do with passion, nothing to do with wanting to make something of life. It was always a cop-out, something weak people did because they weren't happy with their own company, because they couldn't hack being alone. But it's not like that, is it?'

I smile. 'No, it's not like that. I've never been brave enough to move out of my comfort zone before. Not since someone left me. And then depending on anyone started to scare me, made me feel like I was giving part of myself away, like I was a hostage to them. I was happier with my machines and darkrooms. And then came you.'

She leans even closer into me, brings her face so close to mine I can feel her warm breath on me. 'Adam, dear Adam, will you ... if anything ever happens ... will you look after our child?'

'Nothing's going to happen, Birdie, nothing's going to happen. Why would something happen? Is there something you're not telling me about?'

'No,' she sniffs. 'I just need to know. I feel very mortal all of a sudden. Before this trip out to the grave. Dad. Amundsen's words. What we felt in the hut.'

'I shouldn't have woken you.'

'Yes, you should. It's important. I just don't want the mystery to get lost if ... You know.'

'I'm always going to be with you, no matter. You don't need to ask. And it's me who should be asking you about looking after our child.'

'No, no, not really. I feel connected to it already, somehow, although it's still only this teeny thing without consciousness. Although my body hasn't really started to change yet. There are two lives in this one body now, and that's weird and comforting and frightening.'

She leans back against the rocks behind us and doesn't let go of my hand. She looks out into the distance. Her eyes always return to the south.

'D'you think we'll make it? D'you think we'll find something? Will we change the world with what we find?'

'That's up to us, that last bit,' I say. 'But even if we find nothing, we can achieve things in the world. You and me and the child.'

'Do you really think so?'

'I believe so,' I say, lean over and kiss her until the cold rips into my lips.

I wake at six in the morning. The sky looks clear. I sit in the kitchen for half an hour with my breakfast. I've come to love tea in the last few days. At seven it starts snowing, horizontal snow. Base radios to us. Unless the weather gets much worse, the chopper will still be coming to pick us up. It only takes five minutes from base to get here.

'Leave your tents up,' Nev says. 'Just in case. Pack all your bags and put them at the front. If we leave today, the guys are quite happy to take the tents down or leave them for the next visitors. And if we don't go, you won't have to build them again.'

'Win-win.' Birdie laughs.

The snow's getting worse. Big flakes now. And the wind stronger.

'That a blizzard yet?' Birdie says.

'Nowhere near it, mate,' he says. 'Hope you never get caught in one. Bad things, they are.'

The radio crackles. 'Chopper on way.'

'Right,' Nev says. 'Let's go.'

We can hear the chopper now, and look up over to the bluff, from behind which it should appear. There it is, red and white, noisy. It touches down much too soon. We throw our gear in, jump in, slam the doors. Seatbelts on. Headsets on. And we're up into the air again. I'm crying. It felt like home down there. The camp and the hut are obscured by the driving snow. Gone.

Back at base, the snow stops almost as soon as we've landed. We drag our bags out of the chopper and into the warmth. I feel claustrophobic in here after half an hour. I thought I'd be really excited to be back, would enjoy the squareness of man-made buildings, and not having to drag myself from a cold tent out into an even colder wind. But no, I feel hemmed in now; too many people, too much noise.

So I keep myself to myself. I skulk in the smoking room. I fiddle with kit in my room. I stand outside the smoking room in my shirt sleeves in the sun. But I can only manage ten minutes before I feel really very cold. Birdie watches all this with great amusement.

'So you're turning into a wild man, are you?' she laughs.

'Not really, but this is all just a bit too much.'

'But it's a quiet place. Not very many people here, really. And it's not like we've been gone from here for ages.'

'Well, it feels wrong.'

'That's fair enough,' she says. 'We're out of here tomorrow, anyway. Nev said the weather looks well set.'

'Good,' I say as my stomach lurches with excitement. 'Should we try the sleeping bags now?'

'Good idea,' she says. 'I thought you'd forgotten.'

I carry my bag down to her room. As soon as I close the door behind me, she rushes up to me and locks it behind me.

'What you doing?' I say.

'My old room-mate's gone, and the new one doesn't arrive till this evening.'

She starts undoing my shirt, almost rips it off me, pulls off her T-shirt before I can even get my hands on her. And then she presses her nakedness against mine, kisses me, and carries me to bed with her words.

Later, much later than I think, I watch her get out of bed. Her body is starting to change. Her pigmentation is darker. Her thinness now looks more solid, and she looks more grounded. It's almost imperceptible, but I like it. And I can imagine liking it an awful lot more when she's really hugely pregnant.

After some fiddling, our two separate sleeping bags have become one.

'Let's leave them like that,' she says. 'They'll still fit into one kitbag.'

'What about Nev?'

'I don't think he'll want to share it with us.'

'I meant, what will he say?'

'He'll be fine.'

It's a restless night, despite the interlude of lust. I do the rounds of the base again, like I did when we first got here. I check my emails, but there are too many to answer. There's one from John that I do read.

Hope all's going well. Take care, and bring me good news when you get back. Much love from us both.

He's getting soft in his old age. I feel guilty I've not been thinking about him while we've been away. But then I don't think he'd really expect me to. I email back.

All's well. Leaving for the site tomorrow. Will bring lots of news, I'm sure. Take care. See you in a couple of months.

It's past midnight. The sun streams in through the canteen windows. But the lamp in there glows on, still waiting for Scott and Bowers and Wilson, and Oates and Evans, to find their way home. There can be no end to their days of striving.

Chapter 35

Wide awake from lack of sleep, I'm hyper by the time we congregate in the canteen for our last breakfast before our flight into the unknown. Birdie and Nev look exhausted. She has black rings under her eyes, and he can hardly keep his open.

'Hey, Nev, you were snoring all bloody night. How come you're so tired?' I say.

'Catching up, mate, catching up.'

'Bloody kids. No stamina,' I say, filling up my plate with as much food as it'll take.

Birdie just shakes her head, stares into her cup of tea, and smiles to herself.

'It's not a competition,' she says when I come back to the table. 'We've got an hour before we go. Are you both all set?'

'Yup,' we two blokes say. 'No worries.'

I sit opposite her. 'You OK?' I ask.

'Yes,' she says. 'I just didn't sleep very well, but unlike you, I don't go prowling round when I can't sleep. I just lie there and wait for sleep to take me. You should try it.'

'But I feel fine.'

'Bastard,' they both say.

'What a team,' I mutter.

Nev sits up straight and puts his serious face on. 'You do realise this is like looking for a tiny needle in a huge haystack, don't you?' he says to Birdie.

'Yes, Neville, I do realise,' she says. 'We both do.'

'I just don't want you to get too disappointed if you don't find anything,' he says.

'We will be disappointed if we find nothing,' she says. 'But then I'll come back next year, and the year after, until I do find something. This is only the beginning.'

'You're mad,' he says.

'Not really,' she says. 'I just need to know. I'm the sort of person who deals in certainties.'

'But you're an artist,' he says.

'We need certainties in our lives more than anyone else,' she says. 'We wouldn't be able to deal with the chaos in our minds otherwise.'

He shakes his head, grumbles into his growing beard. 'Bloody weirdoes.'

We walk through the base to pick up our gear from Hillary Field Centre, drag our bags out through the hangar's high double doors. It's the same chopper as the day before, the same pilot, the guy who doesn't say much, and when he does talk, it's to the point.

'It'll take us about an hour,' he says when we're all strapped in. 'I'll drop you, and then you're on your own.'

'How's the weather looking up there?' I say.

'Good,' he says. 'Not so good at Evans.'

And so we fly south, up over the edge of the Barrier, that huge wall of ice, across territory where Scott and his men relied only on their own efforts to carry them forward. I stare at the surface below, see them struggling in their home-made boots and clothes. The undulations in the ice, invisible from here, made even the beginning difficult and fraught for them. Some days they could manage only four or five miles.

The white highway below us stretches out ahead further than we can see. The chopper rocks and sways in the wind. Not long now, and we'll have our answers. I can't stop looking out and down, as if I'm searching for black specks moving north in front of the wind. Five small black dots finally awoken from their century of sleep and coming home.

And then we're there. The age of waiting is over. We touch down, jump out onto the crisp ice, so different to Cape Evans. There, the white was offset by black and grey. Dark mountains sprouted from the snow, black ground uncovered by the melt of the Antarctic summer. Here, there is nothing but whiteness. It's all around us, beneath our feet, whipped up into the air by the spinning blades. The artificial blizzard covers us and the gear we drag out of the freight bay. The helicopter takes off towards the north, and there's nothing left but the whining of the wind, the thud of our boots on the frozen snow, and the crumpling of our clothes.

'This is it,' Nev says, his breath steaming. 'The centre of your search square. Most people would've made a circle, you know.'

'That's what I thought of first,' I say. 'But then I reckoned if we had a square, it would be easier to move the radar in straight lines, and to block off small areas. A bit like Minesweeper on the computer. It gives us the option of extending in straight lines, too. It just made more sense.'

'Well, I hope it works,' he says. 'What I want to do today is to use the Skidoo to make diagonal traverses of the area so I can check the safety angle. You two can take it in turns to stay here and keep the brew going. Should only take about four hours to assess the whole square.'

'And then?' asks Birdie.

'Then I'll help you fix the GPR gear to the Skidoo, make sure you know exactly how everything works here, like refuelling, cooking, and all that stuff. And then we sleep, and tomorrow, I desert you two lovebirds, and you can get on with it.'

Nev doesn't zoom off on the Skidoo as I expected him to. He makes sure he keeps it at a slow, even pace. He looks carefully ahead of him along the ground, keeps the speed level. No quick starts, no quick stops. The wind beats at our faces, even at this pace. After about forty-five minutes, he stops.

'This is one corner,' he says. 'Now let's go halfway along one side of your square.'

We come across nothing untoward, and another ninety minutes later, we're back at our camp. Birdie's in the tent, now warmer than before. She's even made some lunch.

'What should I do while you two are gone?' I ask.

'Look at your calculations and decide where we're going to start tomorrow,' she says. 'See if your gut instinct tells you anything above and beyond what the machine's given you. It would be great to find them quickly.'

'If we find them at all.'

'Maybe we'll be lucky.'

'Maybe.'

When she and Nev disappear into the distance, I'm suddenly uncomfortably aware of my insignificance out here, on this forever plain. When you're with others in such a wilderness, you can measure yourself against them. You have their company as a yardstick for your own stature as a human being. When you're alone, you're unguided. Humanity can't measure itself against nature. Nature will always be the greater of the two. And one man alone in a vast expanse of snow and ice and air is nothing, an insignificance, lost.

The minutes stretch into eras, although I'm looking at my calculations wrapped in our sleeping bag, although I'm warm and safe, there's no wind to speak of, and I don't feel threatened inside this tent. What if they don't come back, those two? What if something did happen? I jump out of the bag, pull on my ECW, and get my smokes. I wander across to the store and find the lee of the wind to light my cigarette by. I hear the growl of the Skidoo before I can see it. Although the eye can see for huge distances out here, and there are mountains at the edges of my vision, it's difficult to pick out small things. Birdie jumps off the machine and pulls back her hood. Her face is red from excitement and the cold.

'That's bloody fantastic, that thing,' she says. 'Even when you're just pootling along, it feels like you're going really fast.'

'Scott's tractors were the precursors of these things, you know,' Nev says. 'His detractors forget even that.'

'Find anything to concern you this time?' I say.

'No,' he says. 'I'm really pleased with the way it's panned out. Looks safe and solid all round.'

'But?' Birdie says.

'It would suggest you'll have problems getting readings,' he says. 'Most of it'll be ice, and there'll be nearly thirty metres of it.'

'We'll see,' she says. 'We'll see.'

We make one more trip each. Nev's right. The terrain looks remarkably reliable. Good. One less thing to worry about.

We work on fixing the radar gear to the Skidoo. It takes us a couple of hours. We make a few trial runs to make sure it works. It does, although the readings are negative. It would have been great to find something straightaway, but that's dreamland.

'If a blizzard sets in,' Nev says at dinner, 'don't panic. But don't leave the tent either, even if it means you have to take a crap in here. You'll get forecasts from base every day. If there's a bad forecast, make sure you rope the tent to the store. Or even get a load of stuff into the tent as a precaution.'

'Is the weather what you're most worried about now?' she asks.

'Yes,' he says. 'Because it's the most unpredictable thing out here. There's no long-range forecasting out here. It's impossible.'

'It'll be fine,' she says.

Birdie calls base after we've washed up. No adverse weather expected tomorrow. Nev will get picked up at ten o'clock.

'You've got all the gear to mark the site with if you find it, have you?' Nev asks.

'Yup,' she says. 'Everything we need is here.'

'And you know how to read the GPS so we can get a fix on it?'

'Yes,' I say. 'And the poles are long enough to still stick out of the snow if there's two metres in between now and next year.'

'Good,' he says. 'Here's hoping.'

'I'm still not convinced about the radar,' I say. 'Won't it all be really compressed down there, the bodies flattened by the weight of the snow and more difficult to find?'

'That's the most interesting bit,' she says. 'Some of the research I've read says that because it's been a slow accretion of snow, the compression will be something like diving at twelve metres down, about one more atmosphere than on the surface, And not just that, but the initial layers which turned to ice may have acted as protection rather than compression.'

'What's that mean in plain English?' Nev says.

'It means they may well be totally undamaged. There may even be a hollow down there, rather than ice and snow covering everything. The only chance of damage would be if a tent pole's pressed across one of them.'

'You reckon you've got a really good chance of finding them, don't you?' he says.

'Yes, I do,' she says. 'I wouldn't be here otherwise.'

'Well, I wish you luck,' he says. 'Time for some shut-eye now, I reckon.' He turns to me 'Not too much noise, please, Mr Caird.'

'No chance of that,' I say. 'Wouldn't want to scare you.'

To have Birdie in my sleeping bag with me is a wonderful thing. I can feel the smoothened contours of her body folding into mine. I can feel her warmth against my back when I turn. When I wake, our arms are draped around each other inside the bag. It's a blessing to have her so near to me, not estranged in another bag across the ice floor. How long will it be before I can feel the new life beating inside her?

There's no change in plans for Nev's pickup. The weather is glorious. No wind. No clouds. The sun gusts down from the blue. Even the air feels warm. Until you're in the shade.

'I'll see you in six weeks, then,' he says when we hear the chopper.

'All being well,' Birdie says. 'Have a good time at Evans. And say hello to Welland if you talk to him.'

'Sure thing,' he says.

'Thanks for everything,' Birdie says. She kisses him on both cheeks. 'We won't let you down.'

Nev smiles. He can't speak, and mutely shakes my hand. Manly hug. And then he's gone. The noise of the helicopter fades, then the helicopter itself. We're all alone now. It's an idyll.

'You reckon we can go back to bed for an hour or so?' she asks me.

'I'm certain it can be arranged,' I say. 'You sure?'

'Positive,' she says. 'I want you. Here. Now. And let the dead watch us.'

'Pervert.'

'No. I don't know what made me say that.'

We crawl into the tent. Into the bag. It's retained some of its warmth. We dare to undress totally, and make love in silence. I bury my face in her shoulder, drink in that unique scent of hers.

'Thank you,' I whisper.

'Thank *you*,' she whispers back.

'We should get dressed again.'

'Five minutes,' she says. 'Let's just wait five minutes. This is the cleanest we'll be for weeks, and I want to savour it.'

That day, we do nothing.

Chapter 36

The ice floats on shifting water, kept in place only by its connection to the land ice. Sooner or later, it will push closer to open water, thin and break out. But not yet, not now. Over a hundred miles from the edge, we're living on a slab of ice over two miles thick.

For a week we drive the grid I plotted almost a year ago, look at the readings, day after day. The lack of any positive readings on the tiny screen is not unexpected, but every empty day bears down on us. Little by little, it shaves another ounce of hope from our souls. The void of silence after we've turned off the growling Skidoo for the day is a shriek into the blue. We are alone.

The weather doesn't change. Hardly any wind, bright sun, hundreds of miles of visibility, a bearable temperature. All good portents. And every night, every gloaming night, when the sun fades minimally, we bury ourselves in each other, and get dressed again for sleep. We work at least twelve hours a day, some days eighteen, plodding along those predetermined plot lines. We call base twice a day. *All's well.* We even get patched through to Nev at Evans once. The work there is going faster than planned. He tries to cheer us up. 'Long way to go yet,' he says. 'Plenty of time.' But we know time is running out.

By the third week, we've lost track of the days, though not of time, because the nightmare of finding nothing haunts us. We lose our bearings on the day of the week, don't know if it's Sunday or Friday or Wednesday. But it doesn't really matter. What matters is the ground we cover. It's hot in the sun, cold in the shade. We try to keep sweat to the minimum, and drink as much water as we can, melting snow almost continuously. The daily tasks become increasingly difficult to maintain. A layer of dullness descends on us, a cloak of hopelessness. The beauty of the landscape dissipates. We become a malodorous couple ploughing a field of snow with no promise of harvest.

One night, after putting the Skidoo away, I crawl into the tent and find her crying.

'What is it?' I say and put my arms round her.

'I feel like giving up,' she says. 'There's nothing here, is there?'

'We're nearly halfway through. We can't stop now. We might find something tomorrow.'

'Or not.'

'Or the day after.'

'So little time.'

'Then we'll come back,' I say.

'Would we have the will to come back? I mean, really?'

'Of course we would,' I say. 'It's not like you to give in.'

'I'm starting to feel slow,' she says. 'It's growing quickly, this child of ours. How can we come back once it's born?'

'We'll just have to wait a couple of years till it's old enough to come with us.'

'Or just never leave and have it here.' She laughs.

'That's more like it,' I say. 'You'd do it as well, wouldn't you?'

'They'd never let us, those bureaucrats, though, would they?'

'You'd find a way, I'm sure.'

'Like hide in a snow cave and hope no one finds me?' she says. 'I'm not sure I'd last until the last plane had gone. And the thought of half a year without sunlight.' She shudders.

'So the only option is to find them,' I say. 'Simple.'

'Can't we rest for a day?'

'No. There'll be enough time to rest when it's done.'

'Can we get up an hour later tomorrow, at least?'

'I think we might just manage that.'

She smiles. 'Thanks.' She frowns.

'What?'

'How about driving out to the furthest edge of the square and doing a couple of days there instead of following your plan?'

'It's doable. If that's what you want.'

'It is.'

'Then that's what we'll do.'

'Thank you.' She leans against me. I can feel her weariness seep into me. I try to fend it off, try to share some of my new energy with her.

That night we sleep like the dead. We wake two hours later than normal, into a grey day. We spear flags into the ice every five metres on our way to the southernmost edge of the search area. And then we start again, line after line after line, slowly.

She stops the machine without warning. For a moment, I'm distracted by her pale beauty.

'Look at this.' She points at the screen. 'I've got an odd reading.'

I stare at the screen. There are bright, yellowish markings in between the dark blues of the empty ice. 'Something metal?' I say.

'You tell me.'

'Difficult to say. We need to do another couple of passes over this bit to make sure.'

'Could it be something modern?' she says.

'That's why we need to check again. If it's just a ski pole from some mad Norwegian who's done this trek, it won't show up over three narrow passes. If it's something bigger, it will.'

I tremble as we turn the Skidoo round and make five tightly parallel runs, either side of where we took that initial reading. I steer the runners of the Skidoo in the tracks of the previous run. An hour later, we're done. I line the images up on the screen, shake my head. My heart's pounding.

'It's them, isn't it?' she gasps. 'Tell me it's them.' She grabs my shoulder.

'Gently,' I say. 'Gently.' I rub her back. 'Whatever it is, it's bigger than a ski stick. And the colours suggest that it's about twenty-five metres down.'

'It couldn't be One Ton, could it?' she says, her voice heavy with doubt.

'Not unless my calculations are really way out.'

'Impossible, then?' She laughs. Nervously.

'I'd say so.'

'We're only six hours into our day,' she says. 'We could just stay here and take some more readings, get more definition on the picture we're getting.'

'Hang on,' I say. 'We need to bring another tent and supplies. It'll take more than another six hours to do all that.'

'Do we really need to be so bloody organised?'

'Yes, we do. This way we can have a whole day tomorrow, make sure we use the technology properly. And I'm not being anal. We need to do this properly and safely. And to do that we need at least a week of supplies with us. Agreed?'

'S'pose.'

'Stop being a sulky kid.'

'Not.'

I silence her with a kiss. 'I do so love you,' I say, my mouth still warm from hers.

She doesn't let me go, kisses me back, just longer, this time. 'Mm, I could get used to you,' she says. 'Later.' She pushes me away. 'Right. Let's mark this place properly and go get the necessaries.'

It takes ages for us to ferry everything we need back to the new site. We build the tent quickly, though, and the way it should be, first time round. Nev would be proud of us.

'Should we call Nev and tell him we've found something?' I say.

'No. God knows who's listening in. We'll have the world and his wife here before we know it. And it could be nothing. Technology's not always reliable, you know.'

'It is if it's used the right way. Respected. Machines have souls, too.'

'If you say so, dear.'

We secure everything for the night. Make sure we keep any excitement out of our voices when we call base. We cook dinner and crawl into our bag, dog-tired, too tired even for *that*. She just strokes my back, through my thermal vest. That's the last thing I feel.

It's a dead day. Grey. Cold. No wind. No horizon. A perfect day for snow blindness. We repeat the radar scans and get the same anomaly. Change calibration and go again. The image is much clearer now, burns itself into my mind. Three shapes, foetal, unmoving, straight black lines around them.

'Oh God,' she says. 'Bodies and bamboo poles.'

'It can't be anything else.'

We don't jump up and down celebrating. We get on with what we came to do. Our mood is sombre, not elated.

She sets the video scope and drill down in the snow, adds a two-metre length of tubing, sets it in motion. It makes hardly any sound at all.

'You sure this won't overheat?' I ask her.

'Yes. The heat from the drill melts the ice. The water cools the drill.'

'Doesn't it freeze again and block the mechanism?'

'No. I got it tested down to minus fifty degrees, and it still worked. It's like the opposite of a vicious circle.'

'Smart arse.'

'No. Just obsessed.'

'One metre,' she says half an hour later.

'Only twenty-four to go.'

'Patience.'

'Bit rich coming from you.'

'How evenly matched we are, dear husband,' she smiles. Looks into the eyepiece. Stops the drill. Adds another two metres of tubing. 'If we keep going at this rate, we'll be down there in less than eleven hours.'

And the drill keeps going. Through blue ice. Through white ice. Through softness. That confuses us. We thought it would be solid all the way down. Then hard ice again. Nothing is simple out here. Nothing conforms exactly to the science we learn and believe. Probably because it's more than science that governs our planet and universe.

The wind picks up. Shards of white burn into our faces. Hoods up. I rope her to the Skidoo.

'Should've done this from inside the tent,' I say.

'There wouldn't have been room to sleep.'

'What if it turns into a blizzard?'

'Base said nothing about that. And if it does, it does. Nothing I can do about it. We can't just stop.' She's covered her face with her neck gaiter, goggles on, yellow gloves bright.

I have an idea. Scott and Amundsen built walls to protect their camps. So I do the same. I grab a shovel and start making blocks of snow. Build them into gently sloping walls all the way round her and the gear. It takes me four hours, but by then she's sheltered in a pyramid igloo. I crawl in through the small opening I've left.

'Thank you,' she says. 'It improves the visibility through the eyepiece, too.'

'When are you going to connect it up to the monitor?' I say.

'Once we get to twenty-three metres. We're only at thirteen.'

Despite my hopes to the contrary, there is a storm building outside. I rush to the tent and weigh it down with more blocks of snow. Back in the igloo, the sweat drips from my nose onto the ground. I feel cold. Almost fevered. The wind shrieks through the hole in the wall. I look out and can barely see the tent now, although it's less than ten steps away. I make a rope gangway between the two. It's too windy now to try to build a tunnel.

'Shit,' I say to Birdie. 'Didn't see this coming.'

'Maybe it's localised,' she says.

'What if it's a ten-day blizzard like Scott's?'

'It won't happen. It doesn't happen. It's impossible.'

I've cooled too much. I start to shake. Stamping my feet doesn't help. So I walk round in circles in the cramped igloo. The storm howls louder. The ground shakes. I block the igloo opening with whatever I can find to stop the wind and snow.

'We're going to have to stop and get to the tent,' I say.

'No,' she shouts against the storm. 'We can't stop now. Ten metres to go.'

'It might have stopped in a couple of hours.'

'I can't stop it for a long time in case it freezes fast,' she says. 'The drilling, cooling and melting cycle only works when it keeps going.'

'But I'm cold.'

'Then you go to the tent. If you've roped it, it must be safe. Go make some soup.'

'But I don't want to leave you on your own.'

'I'll be fine.'

Half an hour later, I'm back by her side. Hot soup for both of us. And our pee bottles.

'Can't it drill on its own?' I ask. 'You need to rest.'

'You're being overprotective.' she says. 'You feeling warmer now? You were probably so cold because of all that sweat. You shouldn't have worked so quickly and hard. Plod, plod – that's the name of the game out here.'

'I worry about you,' I say. 'And the baby.'

'Everything will be all right.'

She's so much stronger than I am.

'Twenty-three metres!' she shouts.

'Can you see anything?' I say.

'No,' she says. 'But it's time to get this connected to the screen.'

I fiddle my hands out of my gloves. Pull the necessary cables out from under my shirts. The only place to keep them warm. It takes a couple of minutes to connect the two machines. A couple more minutes and heart-stopping seconds to get a picture on the screen. Still just the whiteness of the Barrier ice.

Minute by minute the drill sinks deeper into the ground. Nothing changes. An hour passes. Only fifty centimetres cleared. It's getting harder to get there. Another hour. Twenty-four metres. I close my eyes and turn away.

'Adam. Look. Look!' she shrieks.

I turn back. The screen shows nothing but green. Green canvas. It's the tent. We've found them.

Chapter 37

'What now?' I say. 'We're stuck.'

'No, we're not,' she says. 'There are all sorts of tools at the end of that thing. Like cutters.'

'You're going to cut into the tent?'

'No other way.'

'We agreed with Nev we wouldn't touch anything.'

'I s'pose I could spend days trying to find a way in, but there's no time for that. I just need to make a small hole.'

'Just be careful then'

'I will.' She's shaking. Sweating. Dark rings under her eyes. Hood up over her now messy hair. 'Here we go.'

I watch on the screen. The lights pick out two small blades. They taper to a point. Move slowly in a circle. Move backwards and forward at the same time. It takes half an hour to see if they've had any effect at all. And the canvas falls away.

'It's a void,' she shouts. 'Adam, it's a bloody void. A hollow. The ice hasn't compressed it all.' She jumps up and down. 'The way they built the cairn must have protected the tent and what's in it. And the first winter's snow.'

'How big is the void?'

'We'll have to see,' she says. 'Not very big, I shouldn't think.'

The camera advances slowly. Two pale rods swing into view.

'Bamboos,' I say.

'Yup. But where are the bodies?'

'I don't want to see their faces,' I say.

'You won't. Wilson and Bowers were in their bags already

272

when the search party found them. And I'm sure they covered Scott before they collapsed the tent.'

'I thought Cherry said they buried them as they were.'

'He did, but I assumed he meant they'd covered his face first,' she says. He adds two more one-metre lengths to the video scope. 'Let's keep going.'

It's like being under water. The lights don't penetrate far into the darkness far below us. The wind outside howls even louder. We have to shout to hear each other. I move closer to the screen. At last something comes into view. Another familiar fabric.

'That looks like the sleeping bag Nev showed us in Christchurch,' she says.

'Yes.'

The camera creeps along the length of the leather bag. The top is tied closed.

'Who is it?' I ask.

'I don't know. I need to get my bearings.'

'Could it be Wilson?'

'If we explore a bit more round it, we might find out.'

She veers the camera to the right. Adds another metre. Nothing there. A green expanse of ground cloth, joined to the wall of the tent. The head end of the bag seems to be facing north.

'It must be Wilson,' she says. 'He was on Scott's left with his head towards the door when they were found.'

'And the prevailing wind was from the south, so the door would be on the north side.'

'So we go left again,' she says.

She moves the camera carefully. Tries not to touch anything. Controls it with such a light touch she must've been practising.

'How– ?' I start.

'I've been planning this for years, Adam. I had to wait for the technology. And had to wait to get good at handling this thing. And had to wait for lots of things. Then Dad died.' She looks at me briefly. 'Had to wait for you.'

'What … ?'

'Shush,' she whispers. 'I wouldn't be here without you.'

In the void of death, the camera finds another bag. Works its way along it.

'Oh God,' I shout. Take a sharp intake of air. 'They didn't cover him.'

Scott stares at us. Fierce. Proud. Full of loss, and pain. The cold has rotted nothing, and nothing lives here to consume the dead. His teeth are bared. Skin yellow in the lights.

'Shit,' she says. 'Shit, shit, shit. I didn't expect that.' She closes her eyes. Moves the controls by memory and instinct. Gasps. Retches. Breathes deeply to stop herself shaking. 'He must have gone by now.'

He has.

'The next one's Henry,' she whispers.

The camera hovers by the bag for a long time without moving.

'I want to spend some time on him now,' she says. 'We can always go back to the others. But Henry now. Just in case everything goes wrong.'

'D'you reckon they missed some of his things in 1912?'

'I don't know,' she says. 'But I've always had this feeling they must have. Don't know why. Just my gut. They all admired him, yeah, but they didn't think of him as a great intellectual, and he was a different class. So they may not have looked that carefully. It was Scott's words they wanted, really. He was the leader and the writer.'

'You're saying they got all Scott's and Wilson's stuff out because they were the de facto leaders, and didn't bother searching for Bowers' stuff?'

'I'm saying they might have overlooked something,' she says. 'Not deliberately. They all loved him. But they wouldn't have expected anything other than his diary and his beloved instruments.'

'What if what you're looking for is in his sleeping bag?'

'Then we won't be able to find it. I can't cut open his bag. That really would be desecration.'

The camera inches forward. Birdie flicks a switch on the controls.

'Scanner,' she says.

'So you're looking into their graves.'

'Sort of,' she says. 'It's calibrated for metal, not bones. This way I can see if there's anything under his bag.'

'Have you thought of everything?'

'I won't know till I come across something the machine can't deal with.'

She leads the camera back and forth along the sleeping bag. A faint bleep and flash of something on the screen. But it's gone before she can stop. So she just carries on. Long, slow sweeps. Seamless. Nothing jerky or sudden. She starts again, even more slowly. About halfway along, there's the bleep again. She's ready for it this time. Stops. Hovers over the area. On the screen, we see a black shape inside the bag. And beyond that, beneath it, there's a shadow of light. Something bright and ornate. Tiny. Oval.

'What d'you think that is?' she asks.

'A pendant?' I say. 'Signet ring? Dunno. Anyway, it's irrelevant. We can't get it out.'

'Wrong.'

'But the drill hole's tiny.'

'It's an inch across,' she says. 'And I reckon whatever it is will fit up through it.'

'How long?'

'I don't know exactly. That's one thing I haven't practised.'

She guides the drill to the side of the bag. Starts to excavate a tunnel under Bowers without moving him. It takes over an hour to get there.

'Right,' she grimaces. 'Let's see what we've got.'

The drill burrows upwards. Millimetre by millimetre, the ice gives way. Then stops. The screen is filled with gold.

'It must be a pendant,' she says. 'Let's find the edges.'

The drill scrapes against the ice. Back and forth. Until the gold gives way to white. Around all its sides. It's tiny, this pendant. And there's a chain attached to it. She loosens the ice around it. It plops noiselessly down into the tunnel.

'We can only find out what exactly it is by bringing it up here.'

'And how are you going to do that without damaging it any more?'

'Patience.' She scratches her nose.

The storm increases its intensity. There's no sign of it easing. I look out of the igloo and still can't see the tent.

'I've got an idea,' I say. 'If I'm not back in fifteen minutes, I'm lost.'

Instead of dying down, the howl of the wind increases. The dark makes it seem even louder. There's no point trying to talk. The tent creaks and groans and flutters. The material slaps against the poles with cracks that sound like shots. They make me jump every time.

I must have wanted to rest, must have nodded off, despite the wind. Something wakes me that's not a screeching wind, that's not a scream. A song? Then I wake up properly. It can't be a song. There are no living creatures this far away from the coast except for us. What is it? I keep my eyes closed. There it is again, a swell of notes, a sweet sound, instead of the howl of the wind, a constant hum. I want to open my eyes and get up to find out where it's coming from. When I open my eyes, everything changes. The wind rattles the tent again.

'Shit,' I shout. 'Oh God.' I crash out of the tent.

It's difficult to breathe outside. Visibility zero. The wind snatches the air away from my face. Its screech sounds even wilder than before, a shriek from nowhere, a scream from a million throats. It drives goosebumps all across me. My cheeks are frozen solid, and my hands have trouble moving.

I sway, almost fall over, fight my way back into the igloo to Birdie. Except she's gone.

'Birdie!' I howl. Nothing. I grab a length of rope, crawl out of the tent. It seems more sensible than trying to walk into the wind. I've covered all of my face with my neck gaiter, and my hood's down across my goggles. The hood muffles the sound of the wind, but not much. I see no footsteps, even with my nose so close to the ground. It takes what seems an age to find the Skidoo. I'm covered in sweat. I tie one end of the rope to it, try to get my breath back. The noise is unbelievable. It's unreal.

The Skidoo should start. I climb onto it, look for the starter with my hands. If I get it to start, the sound will guide me through the white darkness. It takes ages to get it started. I leave it sitting there, idling in neutral. Its calming thrum cancels out some of the wind's noise. I climb off again, feel my way round the snow, come across some of the spare tubes for the scope. I can use them to lay a track through the snow. I fasten the rope to the skid and then the first section of tube to the rope.

I start crawling in as straight a line as I can manage away from the igloo. The rope pulls taut. That's the first five metres. I drop the rope and crawl on with the section that's tied to the rope. Is this still a straight line? I get to the end. Ten metres from the skid now. Still nothing. How far can she have gone? I lie down in the snow, try to slow my breathing. Maybe the wind will drop, and I'll be able to hear something. I count to a hundred, and hear nothing but the wind. Dammit!

I screw the next section to the tube, and keep crawling, scrunching myself into as small an obstacle to the wind as I can. I'm still sweating, and that's bad. I try to slow down, try to work less hard. I close my eyes, thinking it'll be easier to stop myself from going in a circle that way. I stretch my arms out in front of me, like antennae. Then suddenly, I feel my hand bump into something. I grab hold of whatever it is. It feels solid. I pull myself towards it, my head nearly on the ground. It's a boot, one of Birdie's boots.

'Birdie,' I yell. 'Where are you?'

Nothing.

I fix on the next section of tube, keep crawling and shouting. The wind doesn't stop. I'm starting to feel cold again, desperately cold. My hands are wet, and I don't know if it's the sweat or the wetness of the snow through the gloves. I don't care anymore. I sit on my haunches. Where is she? I've only got fifteen metres of tube left, and God knows how long I've been out here.

'Adam?' Is that her voice, or a trick of the wind? 'Adam?'

I lie down again, somehow convinced I'll be able to tell the direction of her voice better like this. I scurry towards where I think she is. I run out of tube, add another bit. Only ten metres left. I'll have to untie if I don't find her soon.

'Birdie!' I scream. The wind grabs her name and carries it south. God, I'm so cold, and so tired. I just want to lie down and sleep. Don't, don't – that's the way to die easily. 'Birdie!' I'm sure I can hear her, sure. I keep scrabbling through the snow. Last section of tube. I crawl along it. I'm almost at its end.

'Adam!' Her voice is right in my ear.

'Birdie,' I shout. 'Keep calling.' I reach out in her direction, find something that grabs hold of my hand.

'What the hell were you thinking of?' I shout when I see her hand in mine. She's sitting in the blizzard, her feet bare, the pendant in her hand.

'The song,' she says. 'It wasn't threatening at all. It was just warm and inviting and friendly. It wants me to go to it.'

'It's your imagination,' I say. 'Come back with me now.'

'But they're calling for me; they want me to be with them.'

'We'll come back, Birdie, I promise. We'll come back.'

'But they're here,' she says. 'Henry and Scott and Wilson, Cherry and Oates, and Evans, too. They're all here. We can be with them forever.'

'We'll come back,' I say. 'When we're old and tired, and our children ...' I bend forward and kiss her on her mouth, a desperate kiss.

She grabs hold of me, kisses me back, and I put my arms all the way round her, and start dragging her back along the tube to where I found her boot. By the time we reach it, I can hear the skid's engine. I keep dragging her, keep pulling at the rope, keep fighting the wind.

What happens next is a confusion in my memory. All I remember is stumbling back into the tent with her. My lips are cracked and bleeding, my hands and feet frozen. I try to walk around in the tent to get warm, but keep falling over. She's untouched by the weather, has the radio in her hand, keeps calling into it, but I can't hear a word she's saying.

And then the wind stops, there's the noise of helicopters overhead, and the sun comes out. The tent's warm again. I'm exhausted. I can't move. The last thing I remember is Birdie's face coming towards mine.

'I love you Adam Caird, and I always will.'

Chapter 38

There's a bright light in my face, and an American voice behind it. It's difficult to keep my eyes open. I feel tired, deadly tired. I just want to sleep. The screaming's still in my ears, and the beat of the helicopter blades. I've got nothing left with which to fight. I just want to give up and stop, stop breathing, stop thinking, run away to silence.

'Adam.' It's Birdie. She puts her hand on my face. 'Tomorrow,' she says. 'Tomorrow'll be fine.'

'Where are we?'

'The American base.'

'How long have we been here?'

'A couple of days.'

'I can't remember getting here.'

'You don't need to remember. Go back to sleep. I'm here, I'll always be here.'

Dreamless sleep takes me. A blank. More lost days.

The next time I wake, I manage to sit up. 'Birdie?'

'Yes?'

'Are you really OK?'

She nods. She's in jeans and a baggy jumper. 'They brought our clothes over from the other base.'

'Why aren't you hurt?'

She shrugs. 'I don't know. The cold didn't touch me.'

'Why?'

'Because they didn't want to hurt me?'

'Who?'

'All of them. They're all there, you know. Kathleen, too, and Amundsen, and Johansen.'

'That's mad.'

'Is it?' she says.

'Ghosts? No one'll believe you.'

'No, not ghosts, just echoes. And who says I'm going to tell anyone? It's our secret.'

'But they tried to take you away.'

She shakes her head. 'No, they didn't. They just sang their song, and I followed it.' She kisses me on the cheek.

The days don't have a chance to drag, because I doze through them. I feel my strength coming back every time I wake, every time Birdie talks to me, every time she puts her hand in mine, every time she looks at me and smiles. A week after the blizzard, I'm strong enough to get up.

The next day, I'm allowed to leave. We walk out of the hospital into the bright sun, climb into the warm car, and twenty minutes later we're back, back where this all started.

We meet in the lounge at base. Nev sits down under Scott's lamp.

'Ah,' he says. 'Good to have you back.'

None of us says anything, just stare out of the window to the south. The canteen's deserted. You could hear a pin drop.

'What about the grave?' I say when the silence becomes uncomfortable.

'We know where it is,' Nev says.

'Are you going to tell anyone?' Birdie says.

'D'you think we should?' Nev says.

Birdie turns to look out of the window again, and shakes her head. 'It seemed like a good idea back in England,' she says. 'To find them and to let the world know where they are. But not now. It would be sacrilege to let people know exactly where they are, to have tourists stomping around above them. Let them be in peace.'

'So we're no closer to finding out what happened in those last ten days,' I say.

'I think I've got a good idea now,' Birdie says.

'Really?' Nev says.

'I don't think there was a real blizzard,' she says. 'Just like ours wasn't real, not to me anyway. I mean, I didn't get hurt like Adam did. I think they died because they wanted to. They chose to stay. There's no mystery. I'd have stayed if Adam hadn't come to find me.'

'Then why didn't Amundsen die?' Nev says.

'Because he saw nature as a threat, something to be vanquished, not embraced?' she says. 'He saw the unexpected as evil. Maybe they saw death as benign and gentle, come to save them.'

'Is that what you think?' I say. 'That death would be benign? Is that what Scott's face said to you?'

'I ask myself every day what death would be like, and try not to be afraid. Does pain matter if it's only temporary, if it's the only way to cross the threshold into the next life?'

'Do you wish you'd stayed?' I say. I'm shaking. I don't want to lose her.

'No,' Birdie says. 'There's too much for me to do before I come back here.'

'What about the pendant?' I say.

Birdie rummages in her pocket, pulls the pendant out, dangles it from her hand.

'Have you opened it?' Nev says.

She shakes her head.

'Do you want to open it now?' he says.

'I'm not sure. I'm not sure I should ever open it.'

'Why?' I say.

'It might disappoint me, might make everything I've experienced here seem less real.'

'What are you going to do with it?' Nev says.

'I was going to ask you a favour,' she says, smiling her sweetest smile.

'Which is?'

'To get us back to the grave, so I can bury this again.'

'Bury history?'

'I shouldn't have taken it in the first place,' she says. 'I realise that now. But I was just crazy for it, wanted to see what was down there with them.'

'You're impossible,' he says.

'But loveable,' she says.

'He can't go yet,' Nev says, looking at me.

'I'll be fine.'

He shrugs. 'But there's a price.'

'Another painting?' she says.

'No. Open the pendant. I'm sure Henry wouldn't mind. If you're going to bury it again, let's at least know if he kept something in there.'

She takes a deep breath. 'OK.' Her fingers envelope the ornate gold, push into one side. It opens with a click. There is a photo in either half of it. 'His mother and sister,' she says. 'That's it.'

'Anything behind the photos?' Nev says. He hands her a handkerchief.

'I'm not sure I dare.'

'It'll be fine,' he says.

There's nothing behind his sister's picture. When she takes out his mother's, a piece of paper, white, falls onto the table. She picks it up and soundlessly unfolds it. 'God, it's his writing. Exactly like in his diary.' She shows us.

'Can you read it?' I say.

She squints at the tiny piece of paper. *'This is the end. We have done all we can, and we will find no earthly path forwards from here. There are three of us left. We have been soothed by the songs of the wind, playing outside our tent, keeping us company on our march. The days are dark and cold, and even the gods can no longer keep us warm. There is a beauty in this place beyond our wildest imagining. May it preserve us for all time. HRB 27th March 1912.'* She folds the paper back together, puts it in the pendant, clicks it closed. 'I think I was right.'

Nev nods into the silence. We stay like that until clouds cover the sun and make a new evening.

We scrunch our way into the igloo under a blue sky. It takes Birdie a couple of hours to put the pendant back where she found it. We drag out the gear, take down the tent, dump everything in the helicopter. Finally, we collapse the igloo over the drill hole, stand around the mound of snow, our heads bowed. Nev says a short prayer, a brief eulogy. In the distance ahead, a plume of snow drifts from the highest peak. Behind us, the weak sun struggles against the advancing season. Birdie takes my hand, puts it on her belly, under her coat.

I understand now. We are always surrounded by the souls of all those who have ever lived. Nothing we do is done without them. But theirs is a different world, a different place, a different life. They are not us.